SHORTS

A BUNNY MCGARRY SHORT FICTION COLLECTION

CAIMH MCDONNELL

Caimh McDonnell

Visit my website at www.WhiteHairedirishman.com

ISBN: 978-1-912897-60-5

INTRODUCTION

How Not to Plan a Career

Hello and welcome to *Shorts,* or what I like to think of as volume one of the collected shorter fiction, featuring Bunny McGarry. I'm not saying there'll be a second volume but given my haphazard approach to the writing process, let's not rule it out. For the moment at least, these are all the short stories and novellas the big fella makes some form of appearance in[*].

Short fiction plays a big role in the tale of how Bunny and I came to be inextricably linked. It all started when I began writing a short story called 'A Man With One of Those Faces'. I had the title in the notes app on my phone and not much else. I'd never written a novel, so I was trying my hand at stories to get a feel for this whole prose-writing malarky, to essentially see if I could string more than two coherent sentences together[†].

---

[*] Appeared in as of 2024. If you're reading this in the future, which come to think of it you definitely are, as you're not reading it over my shoulder so that excludes the present, and the past implies time travel has been invented and you're using it to read books. Actually, that last bit is a brilliant idea – forget killing baby Hitler, going back in time to read books sounds like it'd be humankind's greatest achievement. C'mon science, get your act together and sort that out.

[†] The jury is still out on whether or not I've succeeded.

Not only did that short story accidentally turn into a novel, but a minor character, namely Bunny McGarry, turned up and refused to leave. It was like watching a play where one of the lads in charge of shifting the scenery around starts belting out a show tune. Did Bunny make the book better? Yes. Along the way though, he also made it his and seeing as, at the time of writing, I've now produced eleven full novels featuring the big fella, it feels like he and I are in this for the long haul now. Incidentally, as people always ask – yes, I currently envision writing lots more Bunny books. I don't know what it is about him, but every time we get back together, it feels fresh and exciting. Long may our bromance continue!

Even I must admit, one of the notable features of my writing is my frankly shocking disrespect for timelines. I've written sequels to a prequel for God's sake, that's not even supposed to be a thing! There's the McGarry Stateside series which can, more or less, be thought of as 'happening now' with the action following on from the events in The Dublin Trilogy (seven books and counting). Only four of the Trilogy, the aforementioned prequels, take place in the first couple of years of the 21st century. And I've not even mentioned the MCM Investigations series which is happening at the same time as the McGarry Stateside books featuring all the crew left back in Dublin. Frankly, it's just as well that these are published by McFori Ink, the company we created, which is run by my long-suffering Wonderwife, as any other publisher would have throttled me by now. To be fair, I do occasionally wake up in the middle of the night to find her staring at me in a very disconcerting way.[*]

Writing shorter stories has proven to be a wonderful way of getting to know characters. The first couple, 'How to Send a Message' and 'Dog Day Afternoon', were primarily about me doing exactly that. Once I'd finished that first book, I'd realised that I'd created a monster. I needed to take the monster out for a walk and see how he rumbled. They're also excellent ways to explore new environments, like in 'Good Deeds and Bad Intentions.' Then, of course, sometimes

---

[*] I'd like that recorded for posterity in case I should 'die in my sleep'.

I just have a fun idea that I want to spend a couple of weeks with, like 'Bloody Christmas' and 'Escape from Victory.'

The two new stories in this collection come from two very different places, both in terms of their position in the ever-confusing timeline of the Bunnyverse and the reason they exist. 'The Many Deaths of Timmy Branch' is the result of a happy collision between a random fact I found out about the chain of evidence in Ireland and my desire to go right back to the very start of Bunny's career in law enforcement. It's fun to see him long before he's the big dog prowling the streets of Dublin as the unofficial sheriff. We get to see him as a clueless, snotty-nosed kid straight out of metaphorical policing nappies. At the far end of the spectrum, 'Meanwhile in Dublin' came about while re-reading the very first chapter of *Other Plans* after I'd finished writing it. It raised some questions about what was happening back home in Dublin, and they needed to be answered.

Fair warning, if you've not read all the Bunny books then a couple of these short stories contain 'spoilers'*. I say that, but to be honest I've a sneaking suspicion you don't read these books driven by a frantic need to find out what happens next. I like to think you read them for the same reason I write them, because you enjoy the company of Bunny and the rest of the ever-expanding family of misfits and you're happy to go along for the ride. Plus, at this point the existence of a four-book series called McGarry Stateside is in itself a pretty big spoiler for the ending of Last Orders.†

Anyway, thank you as always for your support. The relationship we enjoy with our readers, aka The BunnyMafia, is really special and we treasure it. I hope you enjoy this collection. Personally, I'm excited to finish the project I'm currently writing, as I've got a scene involving Bunny sitting in a sauna that I can't wait to write – and the rest of the

---

* In particular the last two.
† I do wonder if the handful of angry people who e-mailed/tweeted etc when they saw the cover featuring Bunny's gravestone that they were never going to read it and were livid that I'd killed off the big fella have noticed that it hasn't stopped the supply of new books featuring him.

novel that follows that. In the meantime, thank you for your continued appreciation for the fundamentals of the game.

Happy reading!

Caimh

April 2024

THE MANY DEATHS OF TIMMY BRANCH

THIS NEW SHORT STORY, WHICH IS SET IN THE 90S, FULFILS A WISH I'VE LONG HAD TO MEET BUNNY AT THE VERY START OF HIS GARDA CAREER, WHEN HE'S STILL A WET-BEHIND-THE-EARS SCAMP STRAIGHT OUT OF TRAINING. INTERESTINGLY, FOR AN AUTHOR RENOWNED FOR HIS FRANKLY SHODDY APPROACH TO RESEARCH, THIS STORY WAS INSPIRED BY SOME PROPER SOURCE MATERIAL. WITHOUT GIVING ANYTHING AWAY, THE TASK BUNNY IS HANDLING HERE IS AN ACTUAL TASK MEMBERS OF THE GARDA SÍOCHÁNA HAVE TO DO.

RANDOM FACT: THE QUIZ SHOW 'OOPS MOMENT' MENTIONED IN THIS TALE IS INSPIRED BY A SCHOOL FRIEND OF MINE WHO PANICKED DURING A LIVE TV QUIZ AND SAID THERE WERE SIX VOWELS IN THE ALPHABET. HE SPENT THE REST OF HIS SCHOOL CAREER WITH EVEN TEACHERS MAKING JOKES AT HIS EXPENSE.

A, E, I, O, U AND D'OH!

———

Evidence.

That's all it was. Evidence.

Bunny just had to keep thinking about it in that way and he'd be absolutely fine.

Admittedly, it wasn't any old evidence. It was evidence of murder, arguably the worst crime imaginable. Personally, Bunny would rank personalised numberplates a smidgen ahead, but he was a probationary garda, not long out of training, and deciding which crimes should be punished most severely was way above his pay grade.

Watching over evidence was the kind of thing members of the Garda Síochána were supposed to do. It couldn't all be glamour. All right, so far none of it had been glamorous, but it was good, honest work. And somebody had to work New Year's Eve. After all, crime doesn't stop for overpriced piss-ups. Besides, it was a cold night outside and here he was, indoors, sitting down, away from the sleety snow that was forecast. What did he have to complain about? True, it was still pretty cold inside, so he'd left his coat on, and the chair was a hard, plastic one, but things could be worse. In fact, if he wanted to know how much worse things could be, all he needed to do was look over at the evidence – aka Timmy Branch, aka the dead guy.

Timmy had been leaving the gym one evening when someone had run up and shot him from behind. There were certainly better ways to go – being shot on the way *into* the gym, for example. As last thoughts go, thinking that lifting all those heavy objects then putting them down in the exact same spot again and again had been even more pointless than it appeared, was pretty grim.

The moment Timmy ceased to breathe he became evidence, and that's what he would remain until an autopsy was carried out. Admittedly, even as a layman, Bunny would bet that the large hole in the back of the lad's head was an odds-on favourite for cause of death, but that wasn't how the law worked. You needed a clear chain of evidence and an autopsy carried out in the correct manner.

"Could anyone have interfered with the body?"

"No, Your Honour. Probationer Garda McGarry here, a young man in

2

his early twenties, the prime of his life, spent New Year's Eve in the mortuary at Connolly Hospital making sure Timothy Branch enjoyed the kind of protection in death that he could have done with in life."

"Is this true, Probationer Garda McGarry?"

"Yes, Your Honour."

"And am I right in recalling that your friend, Dinny Murphy, obtained for you an invitation to a New Year's Eve party, which he assured you was going to be full of nurses recently returned from a stint working in Saudi Arabia, where many things were in very short supply, if you got his drift."

"Yes, Your Honour."

"And for the sake of the record, what he meant there was that the party would be teeming with women who would be open to the notion of having sexual intercourse."

"Objection, Your Honour. Speculation."

"Overruled. Dinny had staked his reputation on this."

Admittedly, Dinny's reputation had taken a fair battering after Frank's stag do last year, when he'd been found naked on the beach save for a large shell that he'd become inexplicably "attached to" during the night. They never did find out what happened to his clothes, but the nickname "Free Willy" wasn't going anywhere any time soon.

Bunny pulled his coat tightly around himself and shifted in the plastic chair. His left arse cheek was in serious danger of falling asleep. Why had he not brought a book with him? Ah well, too late now. He'd have to soldier on stoically – he was here for the duration of the 8 p.m. till 6 a.m. shift. He just had to keep his head down and plough through. Not long to go now.

He glanced at his watch. Thirty-two minutes! He'd been here only thirty-two minutes. How was that possible? This was going to be the longest night of his life. He was starting to feel more than a little sorry for himself. Luckily, there was nobody else about in need of sympathy. Timmy certainly didn't qualify. He was one of three bastard Branch brothers, a trio of psychos who dabbled in all manner of illegal activities. There were criminals who used violence as a tool, and then there were violent men who turned their proclivities into a career – the Branch boys were definitely in the latter camp.

While nobody was shedding many tears at the loss of Timmy, and his party trick of biting people's ears off, the Gardaí nevertheless needed to find out who was behind his demise, because doing so would invariably prevent a gang war featuring a spiralling series of reprisals. The Brothers Branch were to restraint what your average seagull was to nuclear physics, and predictable assertions of bloody vengeance raining down had already been made. Bunny had caught wind of this information second-hand as someone at his lowly level wasn't ever invited to briefings. He'd gleaned all his knowledge on the subject from two chatty detectives he'd been sitting behind in the canteen.

Bunny hummed tunelessly to himself, trying to focus his mind on anything that wasn't his current situation. It wasn't that he'd never seen a dead body before. Not that he was looking at one now – Timmy was under a sheet. Still, Bunny was dead-body adjacent and not just to Timmy's. A couple of other tables covered in similar sheets were nearby, and Bunny guessed that the big freezers over on the far side of the room were unlikely to be full of ice lollies. The mortuary decor could best be described as impersonal, cold, functional – utterly devoid of any human touches. He supposed it made sense. Nobody who came in to see the remains of a loved one wanted to be confronted by a poster of a cat dangling from a tree bearing a slogan beseeching them to hang in there.

While Bunny had seen corpses before, they'd all been at wakes, where the guest of honour had been done up to look their best, often looking better than they had in life. Mairead Hegarty, who worked at the local undertakers in Cork, where Bunny had grown up, was so good at it that she moonlighted as a bridal make-up artist. She could work wonders, although someone apparently had a quiet word when she gave old Mrs O'Mara a Rachel-from-*Friends* haircut that the woman hadn't sported in life.

Still, New Year's Eve was supposed to be about new beginnings, and here Bunny was, spending ten hours sitting in a mortuary, literally surrounded by nothing but unhappy endings. Bunny was as susceptible as anyone to the odd bout of bleak introspection, and seeing in the New Year surrounded by cold death as opposed to hot nurses would test the morale of any man. It was his own fault that he was here too, in a manner of speaking. Not that he'd shot Timmy. God, no. His crime had been much more subtle than that. He'd made the fatal mistake of carrying out his duty.

He'd been manning a drink-driving checkpoint last Wednesday when he'd pulled over a Merc and breathalysed the driver who, it turned out, was the brother-in-law of a certain minister. The man had found a rather unsubtle way of mentioning that particular fact right before he blew twice the legal limit. Not that anyone had said anything to Bunny, of course. In fact, quite the opposite had happened. He'd been brought in and congratulated for carrying out his duty to the letter of the law. Then, the shift rotas had been updated. Being a young man with no family, being asked to work some of the festive period was to be expected. In Bunny's case, however, the only person working harder over Christmas was Santa Claus himself, and the big guy wasn't spending it breaking up drunken domestic disputes at 3 a.m.

Bunny was being sent a message; he knew that. Despite it all, he also knew they could shove their message where the sun didn't shine. Mrs Clarke, one of his teachers in primary school, had called him the most stubborn boy she'd ever met. Between then and now, only the context had changed. It was funny what context could do.

Right now, he shared a house with three other probationary officers. Before that, he'd been in barracks with over a hundred of them. Statistical analysis was not capable of estimating the vast number of times he'd heard someone pass wind over the last couple of years. Dinny regularly attempted to set his own eruptions on fire, which had indirectly resulted in his best mate, Tony, breaking up with his then girlfriend. At one particular party, Dinny had overexerted himself while attempting to produce the required expulsion of air, which had resulted in Melanie's sofa catching fire and the man in question shitting himself. Melanie and her friends ended up getting evicted from their house and lost their deposit. Happy side note: Melanie was now engaged to one of the firemen who'd turned up to deal with the blaze. Despite the role Dinny played in their meeting, he was still waiting to receive his invitation to the wedding.

The point was, someone farting in Bunny's presence wasn't exactly a novel experience, but he still leaped out of his chair and screamed when it happened on this occasion. The reason for this was that "he who had dealt it" was supposed to be dead.

"Zombie!" Bunny yelled, as he backed into a corner, holding out the chair in defence. The sheet over Timmy wasn't moving, but Bunny had watched enough movies to know he didn't want to be the one standing around telling everyone to calm down during the first wave of the zombie uprising. The "everyone remain calm" guy always bought it in the first act.

A door at the far end of the room flew open and a woman in blue scrubs with tightly cropped blonde hair came rushing out. "What the hell are you shouting about? You'll wake the dead!"

"They're already awake," hollered Bunny, "and farting up a storm!"

"What?"

Bunny jabbed his head in the previously late Timmy's direction. "Mr Branch just let one rip."

The woman put her hands on her hips and shook her head. "For God's sake, ye fool, dead bodies do that."

"What?"

"Corpses – they will often pass wind. Give a sigh. Occasionally they wave."

"Really?" asked Bunny in disbelief.

"Yes," said the woman. "Well, not the waving thing. I should probably clarify that bit, as you don't strike me as a man with a keen grasp on sarcasm."

Bunny lowered the chair slightly. "And you're sure about this?"

"What does that even mean, Guard? Do you think I'm some random woman who runs around covering up for flatulent zombies?"

Bunny set down the chair. "You're really a big fan of the old sarcasm, aren't you?"

"If I was renowned for my people skills, do you think I'd be working the night shift down here?"

"Fair enough," conceded Bunny. Now that his heart rate was slowing from its rabbit-on-a-rollercoaster spike, he was becoming calm enough to feel embarrassed. "Sorry about disturbing you."

The woman nodded.

"I'm Bunny, by the way."

"You're kidding."

"'Tis a nickname."

"Good. Christening a kid with that moniker would technically have been child abuse."

"You really weren't kidding about those people skills."

The woman ran her hand around the back of her neck. "I'm … I'm a little tense. Gary isn't well."

"Oh," said Bunny, "I'm sorry …"

The woman sat down heavily on a chair right beside the still late, if flatulent, Timmy Branch. "He needs an operation."

"Right."

"Three grand. For that and the recovery."

"Jesus. That's awful. Can he not get it on the health service?"

The woman gave him a confused look. "What?"

"The …" Bunny trailed off as something dawned on him. "Gary is … not a person, is he?"

She looked put out by his remark. "So, because he's a dog, he's not important?"

"Oh, that's not it at all," said Bunny, holding up his hands. "I love dogs. Wonderful animals. Man's best friend and all that." He briefly considered returning the favour and offering an assessment of how, if Bunny was a daft name for a man, it was no more ridiculous than calling a dog Gary. However, you didn't need to possess the most heightened conversational sensibilities to realise that such an offering would go down as badly as a fart in a lift from a dead guy.

The woman gave Bunny a suspicious look, as if trying to

7

determine whether he was being sincere, before giving a begrudging nod. Apparently, she'd decided to give him the benefit of the doubt this time. "I love that dog. Such a good boy. Never let me down. Can't say the same for any of the people in my life."

"'Tis a fair point," said Bunny. "Very trustworthy animals. What breed is he?"

"Labrador. He's got bad hips."

"That's rough."

The woman rubbed the heels of her palms into her eyes. "Yeah. It is. I'm going to find a way. I have to find a way."

"Best of luck," said Bunny, meaning it. "So ..." He paused awkwardly. "You never said – what's your name?"

"Veronica."

"Have you worked here long?"

"Five years."

"Do you like it?"

She shrugged. "It's alright, I suppose. I end up doing a lot of night shifts on my own."

"That's a shame."

"No," she corrected, "that's a perk. No managers banging on at you, and say what you want about the mortuary, you very rarely get a customer complaint."

"Right," said Bunny, unsure of what else to say to that.

Another awkward pause followed. Veronica, who was staring off into the distance, lost in thought, looked as if she were happy to let it stretch on until the sun exploded, but it was making Bunny's palms itch.

"Can I ask," he began eventually, "and I'll admit this is my first mortuary, but I get the impression that they're always in the basement – is that right?"

"As opposed to where?" asked Veronica. "Somewhere with nice big windows where anyone can walk by and watch us performing an autopsy?"

"Ah, right. I take your point."

"People get weirdly sentimental about death," mused Veronica, looking around. "It's just a part of life."

"To be exact – the end bit," said Bunny, who didn't share Veronica's obvious comfort in their surroundings.

"Anyway," she said, "I've got paperwork to get back to."

"Right," said Bunny, with a nod. "Give me a shout if you'd like a game of cards."

"Cards? What – like, poker?" asked Veronica.

"You're right," said Bunny. "Sorry. It'd be very disrespectful. Around the dead and all. Forget I mentioned it."

"No," said Veronica, "I was just asking if you'll play poker?"

"Oh," said Bunny. "Sure."

An hour later, Bunny was twenty quid down, but he considered himself to be up in the grand scheme of things, seeing as it was an hour later. As long as Veronica didn't fancy taking a diversion into strip poker, he'd happily keep losing to her all night, as it provided a welcome distraction from where he was and why he was there. Playing cards while on duty wasn't something he'd normally contemplate doing, but then again, seeing as the task at hand could be carried out by a potted plant, he didn't feel like he was taking the piss.

He made a show of looking at his cards. "Do you know what I've just realised?"

Veronica continued to stare fixedly at her hand, as she had done for the last hour. She wasn't the most engaging company, but everything was relative. "That life is ultimately a trudge towards the grave?" she replied. "And all relationships are just a desperate attempt to distract ourselves from the gaping cold chasm of nothingness that is awaiting our return?"

"Jesus, Veronica – you're a shocking loss to the greeting-card industry. No, I had not realised that."

"You should."

"I'll take it under advisement. In the meantime, what I realised is how pro-monarchy playing cards are. The best ones are your Kings and Queens."

"And the King is higher than the Queen. Sexist."

"You're right," agreed Bunny. "Classist and sexist. What's the Ace, though?" he asked, shifting a card around in his hand.

"Ah," said Veronica. "That represents the Illuminati – the secret faceless organisation that actually runs everything."

Bunny gave her a long, assessing look over the top of his cards. "That last bit was a joke," he said finally. "You were joking there."

"You can read me like a book."

"Has anyone ever told you that you've got a very dry sense of humour, Veronica?"

"They rarely put it that politely. Not to rush you, but I think one of the dead bodies just pointed at their watch. I raised you two quid about a decade ago. Are you going to see me, or raise me again in the hope that your transparent bluff, pretending that you've got royalty in that hand of cards you're holding, is going to inexplicably pay off?"

Bunny sighed and threw his cards down on the table. "I fold."

"Was it something I said?"

Veronica turned her hand around to show him the absolute nothing she was holding.

"Ah, for feck's sake. How'd you get so good at this?"

"The other mortuary assistants and I play a lot. Normally, it's for spare body parts, but the principle is the same."

"That's another joke," said Bunny, pointing at her. "I might not be able to spot when you're bluffing, but I'm at least getting better at spotting when you're joking."

She almost smiled. "If only you could find some way of monetising that. Shut up and—"

Bunny jumped as the phone in the corner of the room rang. "Jesus, me heart."

Veronica glanced at the receiver then turned her attention back to Bunny. "Are you dealing, or what?"

"Shouldn't you get that?"

"It's probably a wrong number." She shifted in her chair.

Bunny picked up the cards. "Fair enough. This time, one-eyed Jokers are not wild, because the aristocracy doesn't need any more help in life."

The phone stopped ringing.

"What?" asked Veronica, distracted.

"I said—"

The phone began to ring again.

"They seem pretty insistent."

Veronica bit her lip, then got to her feet. She walked across and lifted the receiver out of its cradle. "Hello, mortuary?"

She turned to face the wall, her fingers fiddling with the cord as she listened to the person on the other end of the line. "I don't think that's a good idea." As she listened some more to whomever the caller was, Veronica ran her fingers through her hair. "Alright," she said after a few more seconds, "I'll ask him."

Veronica turned to Bunny. "Someone's on the line saying that there's a bloke over in maternity, on the third floor of the main building, who's kicking off. They need help dealing with him."

"Right," said Bunny. "I'm technically not supposed to leave my post."

She nodded and put the receiver back to her ear. "He says—" The voice that cut her off was indistinct to Bunny but clearly growing more irate. "Alright, alright!" She turned to Bunny. "They say the guy is getting violent and the station in Blanchardstown hasn't got anyone spare."

"Ara shite," said Bunny, standing up. "OK. I'm on my way."

———

Hospitals had lifts. Course they did. Bunny knew that. They had to ferry people on beds up and down between floors. It was just that in his rush to get to where he needed to be, he'd decided that the stairs would be the quicker option. As he neared the top of the final flight,

11

stumbling on one of the steps and narrowly avoiding becoming the hospital's latest admission, he was regretting the decision. The mortuary was in a separate building to the main hospital, which made sense – you didn't want ordinary Joe Soaps in to get their appendix out, seeing dead bodies coming in and out of the place. It'd be bad for morale. Still, it had meant that Bunny had had to rush across two dimly lit car parks through the sleety snowfall and over a grass lawn in the darkness where the slush was starting to settle. He'd regretted not wearing his boots, but then, guarding a dead body was an assignment that typically didn't involve a whole lot of cross-country running.

He crashed through the swing door on the third floor and saw the sign indicating that the maternity unit was at the far end of the corridor. He ran past a disapproving-looking nurse and headed for the doors to the ward. They were unexpectedly locked, something he discovered only after slamming himself into them, which resulted in him landing in a sprawled heap on the floor. Before he could pick himself up, the doors buzzed open and a nurse in her sixties, with a face like thunder, poked out her head.

She spoke in a snarled whisper. "What on earth are you playing at?"

"I'm ..." panted Bunny, "... a guard."

"Yes, funnily enough, I recognise the uniform. Why are you trying to break down my doors?"

"I'm here about the man ... causing trouble."

"The only man causing trouble here is you. You'll wake up the babies. Get out of here."

"But there's ..." Bunny trailed off and nodded slowly as if understanding. "Right. Of course, Sister." He winked, pointed behind the doors then silently mouthed, "Is he in there?"

She pulled her face into a withering look. "Are you drunk?"

"Am I what? No. I was just ... So there isn't a man in there causing trouble?"

"There are two males in here – Sean, six pounds eight ounces, and Darryl, nine pounds even. He was a bit of trouble but not in the way you mean, and thankfully, mother and baby are both doing fine, which is more than I'll be able to say for you if you don't get away from my ward this instant."

"But there was a phone call?"

"Not from me, I assure you. I think someone is playing you for an eejit, and if I may say, you've been well cast in the role. This is a hospital, not somewhere for you lot to be playing pranks on each other."

Bunny was suddenly struck by a very bad feeling. He took off, sprinting back down the corridor, the words "walk, do not run" echoing off the walls behind him.

As Bunny retraced his steps, part of him began to plot his revenge on whomever was messing with him, but that voice grew smaller and smaller as he ran. He wasn't above a practical joke himself, but this felt different. As he puffed his way back over the slippery lawn area, the thought occurred to him that he might be about to meet a senior officer, who would be standing there awaiting his explanation as to why he'd left his post. A citation as payback for his breathalysing the wrong man. It felt like an awful lot of hassle to pull off, and a weird day to do it, but you could never underestimate the lengths some people would go to when holding a grudge.

Bunny barely slowed as he finally made it through the door of the mortuary. His wet shoes skidded on the tiled floor as he came to a halt and took in the scene before him. The good news, if you could call it that, was that nobody was dead. Or, to be more exact, nobody who wasn't already dead before this juncture, although Veronica was now tied to a chair and gagged. The bad news – as Veronica was indicating by jerking her head and garbling unintelligibly around the gag – was that far from anyone else now being dead, the late Timmy

Branch had made good his escape, along with the trolley he'd been lying on.

"Shite!" Bunny turned and sprinted back out the door, brimming with renewed energy. There wasn't much to be said for watching your entire career in law enforcement going up in smoke, but it certainly gave one's body a whopping great burst of adrenalin.

He crashed through the outside doors into a largely still night. The quietness of a night like tonight was the closest the hospital ever got to shutting down. That would all change later on, though, after the nightclubs closed, and some bozos started off the New Year by trying to kick seven kinds of shite out of each other outside an Abrakebabra. Nothing was stirring apart from a pair of slowly moving headlights over on the far side of the site, opposite the main building. A van, winding its way around the one-way system designed to keep visitors out of the way of the ambulances. Bunny pictured in his mind what he could remember of the route to the exit then set off running at an angle across the lawn. Who said trigonometry never gets used in real life?

———

"Can this thing go any faster?" asked Brendon.

"Of course it can go faster," replied Paudie. "It's a motorised vehicle. If it couldn't go faster than this, I would have stolen a horse and bleedin' cart instead. The reason it isn't going any faster is that there's a ten-mile-an-hour speed limit around the hospital, which we're obeying."

Brendon snorted. "Why do you give a shit about that?"

Paudie shook his head. "Because, ye dipshit, we're trying not to draw attention to ourselves, what with the dead body in the back of the van and all."

"Who's going to see us?"

"I don't know, but that's the point. Control the variables. It's always the little mistakes that trip people up. Like Al Capone getting done for not paying his car tax."

"I don't think you've got that right."

"Yes, I do. I read it in a book."

"When did you read a book?"

"I read! I'm constantly trying to improve myself."

Brendon turned his eyes towards heaven, or to the van's roof rack at least. "There's certainly room for that."

"What's that supposed to mean?"

"Nothing."

Paudie gripped the steering wheel tighter and looked out the windscreen as the wipers slapped back and forth against the steadily falling snow.

Brendon counted in his head. *3 ... 2 ... 1 ...*

"It was a very easy mistake to make," said Paudie right on cue, the words rushing out of him, as they had done many times before.

"I didn't say anything."

"You were thinking it. I know you were thinking it."

For reasons Brendon had never understood, his brother had applied to go on a TV quiz show a couple of years ago, and had been accepted. Brendon reckoned they'd picked him as people from the country loved nothing more than having a thick Dub to laugh at. Paudie had filled the role admirably.

"Everyone thinks they're so clever," growled Paudie. "It's a lot harder under them TV lights."

"Sure it is."

"And the question was worded badly."

Brendon said nothing, not least because they must've had this conversation a thousand times before. Paudie could not let it go.

Paudie continued as he always did. "If Ray D'Arcy had asked, 'What's the capital city of Greece?' then I'd have said, 'Athens'. Course I would have, but that's not what he said. He said, 'What is the capital of Greece?' and so 'The letter G' is a perfectly valid answer. First letter of a country is always a capital letter – Mr Bronson taught us that in school."

Of the many odd things about Paudie's ongoing attempts to rationalise making a tit of himself on national television, his persistent referral to their old English teacher, Mr Bronson, as the highest power, was the oddest. Paudie had been thrown out of school for headbutting him.

"And," continued Paudie, "you're one to talk about people making stupid mistakes, seeing who we've got in the back of this van."

"You told me to shoot him!" protested Brendon.

"Yeah, but not with the same gun you used on that Dutch fella. You're already in the frame for that – using the same shooter? Ye might as well have signed your bleedin' name."

"Yeah, well ... you're ... the dipshit that stole this crappy van. We're supposed to be gangsters – it's got a bloody roof rack."

"So?"

"I bet Al Capone never drove around in something with a roof rack."

"We wouldn't have to if you'd not been an eejit and hung onto a murder weapon. I mean, who does that?"

"If you must know, using a gun once then throwing it in the Liffey is a shocking waste of resources."

"Ah, for ... Is that it? You held onto it because of your stupid obsession with recycling?"

"Stupid?" shouted Brendon. "Stupid? It's gobshites like you that are killing the planet. Carol says—"

"Stop quoting her like she's the bleeding Dalai Lama. Look at you – going vegetarian, using some weird soap, not flushing the loo after you take a pee. She's not coming back, you know. You're going to end up dying alone in a house smelling of piss, if you're not careful."

Brendon's response to this slight on his lifestyle choices was lost to posterity as they were interrupted by a member of An Garda Síochána throwing himself onto their bonnet.

———

Bunny looked through the windscreen at the shocked faces of the two men inside the van. He couldn't blame them; he was rather surprised himself. He wasn't sure he'd even had the idea of jumping on the bonnet of a moving vehicle – it was something his body had done without consulting his brain. He'd been a fan of *Starsky and Hutch* as a child, and it was the kind of thing that happened on that show every other week. Mind you, they also drove through a lot of cardboard boxes, so it probably wasn't the greatest resource for picking up real-world policing tips. If this turned out to be just a couple of plumbers heading home after a highly urgent toilet-unblocking, it'd be embarrassing, but when you're about to become the police officer who lost a dead guy, there's really only so much lower you can sink. Besides, the first reaction of a couple of innocent plumbers whose vehicle had just been leaped upon by a uniformed member of the Gardaí would probably not be to floor it.

"Shoot this pig!" shouted Paudie.

"With what?" Brendon shouted back. "You told me to throw away me gun!"

Well, that disproved the plumber hypothesis at least. "Relief" wasn't the right word, seeing as Bunny now found himself spread-eagled across the windscreen of a rapidly accelerating van like one of those Garfield toys. He didn't have suckers for hands though, so instead, he focused on making sure he had the best grip possible on the cold, wet metal of the roof rack. From his position, he couldn't see the van's passenger, but he was eyeball to eyeball with the driver, whose face wore a worryingly demented look.

"You're under arrest!" shouted Bunny, because he felt as if he should say something in case anyone was in any doubt about the situation.

The driver simply grinned in response. Luckily, Bunny had anticipated what was coming next, so when the driver slammed on the brakes, he'd braced himself for it. Besides, the vehicle didn't come to the dead stop the driver had been hoping for.

All three men screamed as the van skidded and fishtailed across the icy road before ending up facing in what Bunny thought was possibly the opposite direction. He'd closed his eyes for a little bit there, so he couldn't be sure.

"Right," he ordered. "Surrender now or I'm adding dangerous driving."

The driver snarled, threw the van into gear, and slammed his foot on the accelerator once more. "Get this fucker off my windscreen!" he roared while bobbing his head to try to see around Bunny.

The van jolted violently as one of the front wheels hit something, causing Bunny's left hand to lose its grip.

"Jesus!" screamed a voice from his right. "Keep it steady!"

Bunny turned his head to see that the passenger was now leaning out of his window, attempting to grab him.

"Feck off," he roared, endeavouring to swing a kick at his assailant that missed wildly. He was holding on with only his right hand now and his muscles were screaming from the exertion. That was by no means the worst of his problems, though. The passenger now had his own grip on the roof rack and was inching his way across to where he could reach Bunny's remaining hand.

"You're gonna be roadkill, piggy," screamed the man, his face wet with snow and his eyes filled with a wild frenzy.

"Careful," shouted Bunny. "You'll fall out and hurt yourself."

"I'm going to—"

The passenger's subsequent contribution to the witty repartee was cut cruelly short by Bunny's free hand swinging around, having found what it'd been looking for. The look of surprise on the other man's face as the handcuffs snapped around his wrist and the roof rack would stay with Bunny for the rest of his life, which admittedly didn't look like it would be very long. With blessed relief, Bunny managed to re-establish a grip on the metal bar with his left hand.

"He's handcuffed me to the feckin' roof rack," hollered the passenger, confirming he understood what had just happened.

"Why did ye—"

The rest of the driver's question was lost as a siren burst into life behind Bunny.

He watched the driver craning his neck, trying to see the road in front of him.

"You're heading straight for an ambulance!" screamed his

associate, in case he thought they were about to collide with the world's hardest-working ice-cream van.

The driver threw the van into a hard right turn, and Bunny spun around, his left hand losing its grip for the second time, as an ambulance zipped past in his peripheral vision. The van jolted again and suddenly they were heading uphill.

The grip of Bunny's remaining hand on the roof rack was slipping. He stole a look over his shoulder and then he let go, allowing himself to slide off the edge of the bonnet. He managed to tuck himself up a little, to lessen the impact of hitting the snow-covered grass, but the fall still jarred every bone in his body. The back of his head thumped hard onto the ground, sending percussive sparks of light across his vision. At least it meant he wasn't still on the van a second later when it collided at high speed with the trunk of a massive oak tree. In a vivid demonstration of the importance of wearing a seat belt, the driver ended up on the bonnet, semi-conscious and covered in blood. His associate arguably got the worst of it, though, howling in agony for a few seconds before mercifully passing out. The collision had tried to throw him clear, but the handcuffs had other ideas – the man's arm was now hanging at an angle nobody would ever enjoy looking at. He wasn't going to be playing the violin any time soon.

Bunny sat on the snow-carpeted grass. He could feel his arse was wet, which he took as a good sign, given it was the kind of thing your body wouldn't bother telling you about if there were more pressing matters to attend to. His right ankle, however, was starting to hurt like a bugger now that the adrenalin was wearing off.

Downhill, he could see the two-person crew from the ambulance staring up at them in disbelief, and there was activity over by the main hospital building too. Off in the distance, a police siren wailed. A sound from behind Bunny made him turn, and he rolled away just in time to avoid what had been heading towards him.

One glance told him all he needed to know. The van's back doors had been forced open by the crash and poor old Timmy Branch had rolled out on his trolley and was now heading down the hill, picking up speed as he went.

"Ara bollocks," said Bunny, watching Timmy hurtle away from him, gravity's plaything, inevitably trundling straight for the road and ploughing into the second ambulance that had been racing to the scene.

"Jesus," Bunny muttered, to nobody in particular, "that lad is having one hell of a week."

At that moment, the sky over his head lit up with fireworks. Illegal fireworks, mind, because some of Ireland's laws were treated more as suggestions.

Bunny turned back to the van. "Happy New Year, boys."

———

Veronica jumped when she saw the figure in the doorway. "Jesus!"

"Sorry," said Bunny. "I didn't mean to startle you."

He limped in on his crutches and looked around the mortuary. "This place doesn't look any more welcoming in the daytime, does it?"

"I'm afraid not," she said. "I was wondering if you were going to drop back in."

"Sorry, I've been busy. I've spent the last couple of days in a lot of meetings. You wouldn't believe how much paperwork's generated when a dead guy is involved in a traffic accident."

"How are you?" she asked.

"This?" He nodded down at the crutches. "Just a sprain. Got me a fortnight off work."

"It's the least you deserve."

"To be honest, I thought I mightn't have a job any more for a while there. It's considered bad form to lose a dead body."

"Yeah, but you got it back, and you caught the guys."

"I did," he conceded. "They were his brothers, would you believe? They copped to killing him too. Well, they blamed each other, of course."

"Why'd they do that?"

Bunny shrugged. "I dunno. We can't rule out a typical family Christmas being an aggravating factor."

Veronica nodded. "That's all too credible."

"Yeah. Families."

An awkward pause followed.

"Well," said Veronica after a few seconds. "Thanks for dropping in. Glad you're OK."

"Oh, no," said Bunny, "this isn't a social call."

Alarm briefly flitted across her face. "It isn't?"

Bunny fumbled with the crutches for a moment and then took a twenty-pound note out of his pocket. "I always pay my debts."

Veronica laughed nervously and waved him away. "Forget about that."

"No," he insisted, stepping forward and holding it out. "Fair is fair."

"Seriously, I don't want to—"

"Take it," urged Bunny. "Put it towards Gary's thing."

"I ... Right. Yeah." She took the note and tucked it into the pocket of her scrubs. "Thanks."

"How is he?"

"He's ... alright."

"By the way," said Bunny, "we should play again some time. I think I've finally figured out your tell."

Veronica gave him a smile that didn't reach her eyes and another of those nervous laughs. "Really?"

He nodded. "I've been thinking about it a lot over the last couple of days. It was when the phone rang for the first time. The look on your face. You didn't want to answer it because you knew who it was. Then you tried to call the whole thing off."

"I ..." Veronica lowered her eyes and stared at the floor. "I'm really sorry. They're from round my way and ..."

"They scared you and you also needed the money. For Gary."

She looked up at him now, eyes filled with tears. "I really am sorry. It was such a stupid ... I never thought anyone would get hurt."

"Yeah," said Bunny. "I guess we both learned a valuable lesson that night." And with that, he turned and limped back towards the door. "Give Gary a biccie for me."

"Aren't you going to ...?"

He waved without turning around. "Nah." He scanned the room, taking in the selection of bodies covered in sheets, lying under the cold, antiseptic lights. "Life's too short. Happy New Year."

DOG DAY AFTERNOON

THIS WAS THE VERY FIRST SHORT STORY I EVER WROTE FEATURING BUNNY. IT WAS FOR AN ASSIGNMENT I'D BEEN GIVEN AS PART OF A CRIME WRITING MODULE FOR THE MASTER'S DEGREE IN CREATIVE WRITING THAT I NEVER BOTHERED TO FINISH. THE BRIEF WAS TO WRITE A SHORT STORY WHERE AN UNLIKELY COUPLE MET AND FORMED A CRIME FIGHTING DUO. EVERYONE ELSE WROTE ABOUT GRIZZLED DETECTIVES — WHOSE ENTIRE FAMILIES HAD INEVITABLY BEEN MURDERED BY SOME NUTTER — MEETING AN UPTIGHT, BUT ATTRACTIVE, CRIMINOLOGIST WITH A SECRET WILD SIDE. I PAID HOMAGE TO MY FAVOURITE GENRE OF COP MOVIES, 80S-COP-TEAMS-UP-WITH-DOG TROPE WHICH I LOVE WITH ALL MY HEART. THIS SHORT STORY ALSO FEATURES WHAT I'M ONE HUNDRED PER CENT CONFIDENT IS THE GREATEST OPENING LINE I'M EVER GOING TO WRITE.

12:12pm June 18

"I need a dead dog."

People, thought Noreen. People really were the problem. If people were a bit easier to deal with, she'd probably have become a doctor like her father and his father before him, instead of being the unspoken family disappointment of a veterinarian. She really had tried to like people, but it was very hard to based on the available evidence – war, famine and the films of Adam Sandler. Animals, on the other hand, were infinitely more lovable. In fact, their only downside was that they were invariably owned by people. It was the Peter principle on a massive evolutionary scale. Humanity had been promoted to the position of dominant species, a role they managed with utter incompetency.

Take this specimen, for example; standing on the opposite side of the counter in a black sheepskin coat, which smelled like it hadn't been cleaned since the sheep had worn it. His large bulbous face was a shade of red only meant for beetroot and heart attacks, and a lazy left eye only added to the impression of him being unhinged. To be fair, in other circumstances he'd probably have just looked intense as opposed to deranged, but those circumstances would've involved him not bursting into her surgery demanding a dead dog.

"We don't have any dead dogs."

"Have you any that are looking a bit peaky?"

He looked about fifty and was blessed with the kind of Cork accent that managed to lilt and grate at the same time, like somebody was trying to get a tune out of an industrial sander.

"May I ask the nature of your enquiry?"

"I need a dead dog and you're a vet. Now can you help me or not?"

"Absolutely not. I'd like you to leave or I'm going to call the Gardaí."

The man pulled an overstuffed wallet from his inside coat pocket and flipped it open to his official Garda ID. "DS Bunny McGarry at your service. Now about that dead dog; ideally an Alsatian but I'll work with what you've got."

"Sure. Let me just rummage through my extensive collection of corpses out back and I'll see what I can rustle up."

"Really?"

"No."

Bunny sighed heavily and leaned on the counter. "This is no time for sarcasm, Doc. A Garda officer's life is in danger."

Noreen's mouth opened and closed without producing any words. DS Bunny McGarry glowered at her and then looked over her shoulder, presumably for somebody else to glower at. He'd be lucky. Darren had called in sick yet again. People.

"Look," said Bunny, looking at his watch, the anger in him seemingly subsiding, to be replaced by weariness. "I have forty-seven minutes to find a dead dog to take the place of a decorated police officer in front of a firing squad."

"But—"

"I should mention, the police officer is also a dog."

"Ah," said Noreen, getting at least within waving distance of understanding. "You need to – wait – what kind of monster is putting a dog in front of a firing squad?"

"Well, I dunno – they're putting her down."

"That's normally done by a painless injection."

"Well this one will definitely be painless because it's going to be given to a dead dog. At least it will be if you start helping. I tried driving up the M50, but you can never find roadkill when you need it. All I got was half a rabbit and that's gonna be a tough sell."

"Why's this dog being put down?" asked Noreen.

"It's not important."

"It is if you want my help."

"It'll sound bad when you hear it."

"Try me."

"She sort of attacked a few children."

"Oh."

"See, I told ye it'd sound bad. There were mitigating circumstances."

"Which were?"

"Well, she was high on drugs at the time."

"Is that normally a compelling legal defence?"

"She's a good dog. The best on the force until some drug peddling scumbag with a grudge found where she was kennelled and spiked her food with LSD."

"That's awful. Is she OK?"

"Ah she's A1 tip-top, other than the whole being on death row thing. I mean, I've been told she spends quite a lot of time staring at lights but ... look, are you going to help me or not?"

"Isn't there an appeal process?"

He shook his head. "She went mad at the Garda summer barbecue, snarled at a few kids and then shat in a bouncy castle that the Commissioner herself had paid for." He looked at his watch again. "We've got forty-six minutes or else the poor doggie is deader than disco."

"What're you going to do with this dog once she is free?"

"I'd not thought that far ahead."

"I'll only help if you can guarantee her a long and happy life."

"Love, look at me," he said, spreading his arms wide. "If I could provide that to any female, do you think I'd be standing here with a half-eaten kebab in my pocket, begging you for a dead dog? Now are we dancing or not?"

Noreen looked around and then leaned in. "We normally have one or two in the freezer but the crematorium van came around yesterday."

Bunny ran his hands through his hair and puffed his cheeks out.

"Where's the crematorium?"

"Nearest one is out on the Naas Road."

"Feck it, too far. Any other vets nearby?"

"They'd all have—"

"Been collected at the same time by the crematorium van," finished Bunny. "Bollocks!" He pushed himself off the counter with his hands and stared down at the floor. "C'mon Doc, work with me here. Where can we find a German shepherd-sized dead animal in central Dublin in the next forty-something minutes?"

"Well ..." said Noreen.

"What?"

"Never mind. It's a ridiculous idea."

"I'll take it."

"But ..."

. . .

12:54pm June 18 – Kilmainham Garda Station

Garda Patrick Lennox was making Noreen extremely uncomfortable. He didn't mean to, quite the opposite in fact. His teary brown eyes were filled with gratitude and he'd already attempted to hug her a couple of times. Noreen did not like being touched, by anyone in general and tearful men in particular.

"I really appreciate what you're doing and I know how big a deal it is. I mean, you could get in all kinds of trouble for this."

"Paddy," interjected Bunny, "stop saying that, there's a good lad."

Noreen finished filling out the clipboard full of paperwork and handed it back to Lennox. She gave it one last lingering look as she did so. He wasn't wrong. She could be struck off for this. She looked down again at the white sheet under which the body lay. She'd met Bunny McGarry about forty-two minutes ago, instantly disliked him, and was now committing a crime at his behest. She had never had the greatest taste in men.

"And you're sure that the vet you normally use—"

"Relax," interrupted Bunny. "He's been called home by a family emergency."

"Do I want to ask?"

"Best not."

The door opened and a fresh-faced female guard stuck her head in. "Paddy, Mara has just pulled up."

"Oh Christ."

"Is that the vet?" asked Noreen, her career flashing before her eyes.

"No," responded Bunny. "Worse. Feck's sake, you'd think the Assistant Commissioner would have better things to be doing with his time."

"But, you said someone was coming to verify ..."

"Yes," said Lennox, "Someone being Sergeant McCullough, who'd just nod at the sheet and sign the form. Not Mara."

Noreen looked at Bunny.

"He's right, that snivelling little prick would happily take a selfie with a corpse."

"Jesus," said Noreen, "He lifts that sheet and we're all done for."

Bunny started pacing back and forth. "Alright, we're OK. Doc, you just follow my lead."

Noreen nodded; what choice did she have?

Bunny stopped and looked at Lennox. "Paddy, you look terrified, we need grief."

Paddy attempted to make his face a mask of appropriate misery. He looked like Robert DeNiro trying to pass a whole watermelon.

"Christ," said Bunny. "You're not exactly a great loss to the acting profession."

"Sorry Bunny, I'm trying. I just ..."

"It's OK, relax. Take a deep breath ..."

Lennox nodded and obediently complied. The breath exploded out of him a second later when Bunny punched him in the stomach. Bunny gently held him for a moment and then pushed him back into the chair in the corner, where Lennox sat doubled over, unable to speak. Bunny patted him sympathetically on the shoulder.

"Greater good Paddy, greater good."

Bunny looked at Noreen. "Just follow my ..."

And the door opened.

Bunny clasped his hands together as a short, balding man in a dress uniform entered. "As we forgive those who trespass against us; and lead us not into temptation, but deliver us from evil. Amen."

"Amen," responded Noreen. The man, who she assumed was this Mara fella, awkwardly took his peaked hat off and reflexively joined in with them blessing themselves.

"DS McGarry, what are you doing here?"

"I came to console Sergeant Lennox, Sir, he's not taking this well."

Bunny nodded over at Paddy, who did indeed look like a man drowning in a sea of very personal grief. Mara looked down at the sheet.

"This was supposed to happen at precisely 1pm."

"The usual vet, Damian Hickey was called away on a family

matter, Sir. Doctor Richards here kindly agreed to step in."

Noreen added nervously, "Yes, I felt it best if we get things moving."

"Well that's as maybe, but I promised the Commissioner I would verify proceedings properly. How do I know that animal is dead?"

Noreen's heart jumped into her mouth as Mara bent down towards the sheet.

"Oh for feck's sake, Mara," said Bunny, nodding at Lennox, "have a heart, would you?" Bunny roughly nudged the body with his foot. "See ... dead."

"Nobody asked for your input DS McGarry," snarled Mara. "Now, get the hell out of my way." Noreen didn't have to be an expert in reading people to see the obvious animosity that existed between the two men.

Bunny placed himself between Mara and the sheet and then leaned over and poked the body with his finger. "'E's not pinin'! 'E's passed on! He has ceased to be! 'E's expired and gone to meet 'is maker! 'E's shuffled off 'is mortal coil, run down the curtain and joined the bleedin' choir invisible! This – is an ex-parrot!"

Mara attempted to shove Bunny out of his way.

"Are you drunk Bunny? Consider yourself on report. Now get out of my way. I ..." Bunny kept shifting himself to stay between Mara and the body, like a basketball player determinedly holding onto possession.

Noreen took a deep breath and stepped forward. If she was getting struck off, she might as well go down swinging.

"What the hell is going on here?" Her harsh tone caused Bunny and Mara to stop scuffling and look up at her. She pointed down at the body beneath the sheet. "This poor animal has had to be put to sleep due to injuries it suffered in the line of duty. Is this how An Garda Síochána treats a fallen hero? No respect. No basic common decency. Instead you ..." pointing at Bunny, "are using it for some tawdry comedy routine and you ..." pointing at Mara, "wish to parade the poor animal's body through the streets like some deposed third-world dictator. Shame on you. Shame on both of you. I think the press will be very interested to hear about this."

Mara backed away, as if punched in the chest. "I'm sorry ... I just ... I have to verify ..."

Noreen moved forward. "I assure you, this animal is very dead." Technically not a lie. "Or are you now questioning my professional competence as well?"

"No, no ... "

"Good, then if that is all. Excuse me, as I remove this animal and bring it to the crematorium to be disposed of in the appropriate dignified manner."

"Right, I ... of course. Sorry about ... There's no need to bring the press into—"

"Good day, sir!"

"Right I—"

"I said good day!"

5:24pm June 18 – Garda HQ, Phoenix Park

Mara placed his Cajun chicken wrap and his copy of the *Evening Herald* on his desk. It'd been a long day. He'd not eaten since the few biscuits at this morning's policy meeting and he had a Chamber of Commerce reception tonight, standing in for herself. The mess with the dog had been embarrassing. McGarry had been his usual buffoonish self. Ah well, not long now and his retirement would finally come through and the stain of having such a walking anachronism on the Garda payroll would be removed.

He cracked open the seal on his wrap and flicked through the first couple of pages of the paper.

5:27pm June 18 – Garda HQ, Phoenix Park

Health and Safety Incident Report: Garda Maureen O'Sullivan is to be commended for her quick thinking in administering the Heimlich manoeuvre to Assistant Commissioner Justin Mara, who was choking on a Cajun chicken wrap.

. . .

Evening Herald June 18 – page 4

Cat-napped!

The Irish National History Museum on Merrion Square was the site of one of the most bizarre crimes in Irish history today as a stuffed model of a sabre-toothed tiger was stolen from its display case. The theft occurred at 12:30pm when a man, wearing what visitors described as an improvised balaclava made out of a Tesco bag for life, walked in and used a hurley to smash open the display case. The animal was then removed and the catnapper made his getaway.

In an odd twist in the tale, the cat was returned unharmed just two hours later.

The Gardaí are mystified although one unnamed source did point out that it was a reading week at nearby Trinity College.

3:27pm June 18 – O'Hagan's pub, Baggot Street

Tara Flynn surveyed her domain. The lunchtime rush had been dealt with and now there was the mid-afternoon lull, before the post-work crowd barrelled in and messed the place up again. She knew that busy was better but there was still a part of her that enjoyed the quieter moments. It gave you a chance to catch your breath and have a bit of a chat with the customers. She noticed the familiar figure of Bunny McGarry shambling through the doorway and started pouring his usual stout. He was a creature of habit and he'd no doubt been called an awful lot worse than that. He was not a bad sort truth be told, once you got by the bluster. Besides, every good publican knew you could never have too many friends in law enforcement.

Bunny unbuttoned his ever-present sheepskin coat and deposited himself on one of the high stools beside the bar. "Usual please, Tara."

"On its way."

And then Bunny's arse barked.

Tara leaned over the bar to see a German shepherd sitting beside him on the floor. "Have you made a friend Bunny?"

"Something like that. Long story."

"Technically, we don't allow dogs in here."

"I'm legally blind."

"Oh are you now?"

"I must be, otherwise I'd have noticed that those packets of cigarettes behind the bar don't have a custom duty stamp on them."

Tara could feel herself blush, not something she was known for.

"I've got a few sausages left over from lunch if he's hungry?"

"He's a she and you're an angel."

Tara laughed as she topped the pint up and placed it in front of him. "Finally found yourself a woman. What's her name?"

"Maggie. Possibly named after the mad bitch of the same name."

In the corner of her eye, Tara noticed the bloke in the beanie hat and the Captain Birdseye beard, who'd been camped out in the cubby hole with his two friends all afternoon. He was waving a twenty euro note at her from the far end of the bar. Tara rolled out her best fuck-you glare. "The lap dancers start at six love."

"I'm just looking for three Heinys when you're done flirting with your da."

He then turned and leaned back against the bar, basking in his dazzling wit. Tara noticed that little twitch in Bunny's face. This was bad. The last time she'd seen that, some bloke on his Chrimbo party who'd got handsy with one of the waiting staff had found himself with an ornamental Christmas tree shoved somewhere memorable.

"What did you say there, fella?" Bunny actually smiled when he said it. This was very bad.

"Calm down, Grandad, I just ..."

And then he stopped. Tara stopped. Bunny stopped. There'd been no music playing, but if there had been, it surely would have stopped. That's the kind of thing that happens when a German shepherd places its jaws around a man's crotch and growls. It wasn't loud. It didn't need to be.

He spoke in a whisper. "Fuck's sake Grandad, get your dog off me."

Bunny took a slow sip of his pint before responding. It wasn't like the younger man was going anywhere. "Couple of things, firstly ..." Bunny whipped his wallet out, "that's Detective Sergeant Grandad to you. And secondly, that's not my dog. She's just been let go from the force in less than ideal circumstances. I don't think you want me to give her an order right now. She has a bit of a problem with authority." Maggie growled softly as if to emphasise the point. "By any chance, you're not carrying any illegal narcotics are you?"

Captain Birdseye exchanged a worried look with his mates.

"No. You can't search me, I know my rights."

"Fair play. Good luck explaining them to the dog."

"I've nothing on me."

"Right so, must be something else. Have your genitalia recently been in contact with a dead body?"

"No."

"Well then, unless your bollocks are made of Semtex, I'm out of ideas."

"Look, just ..."

The words caught in his throat as the dog tightened her grip on proceedings.

His voice went up an octave. "I might have a small bit of ..."

"I'd get rid of it if I was you."

Slowly, very slowly, Birdseye reached into his pocket, took something out and dropped it on the counter. Tara placed it in front of Bunny. About three joints' worth, by her reckoning.

"Tut tut, young people these days, and he seemed like such a nice boy. Seeing as I'm in a good mood, we'll let you off with a warning."

Nobody seemed more surprised than Bunny when the dog released her grip and calmly padded back to sit beside him. Birdseye nearly collapsed as he staggered for the door, followed by his two friends.

Tara noticed his twenty euro note on the counter and placed it in the charity box. "And a big thank you from the orphans." She turned to Bunny. "Jesus, Bunny!"

"Don't look at me."

As if on cue, Maggie hopped up onto the high stool adjacent to him.

Tara looked at the dog's happy face. She didn't look like she'd hurt a fly. "I'll get them sausages."

Maggie leaned forward and gulped down the lump of hash in one fluid motion, cling-film and all.

"Holy fuck! Ease up there, Janis Joplin," exclaimed Bunny. He turned to face Maggie, who was panting happily away on the stool beside him. She looked calmly back at him. It was accepted Dublin criminal lore that, due to his unnervingly wonky eye, nobody, not even the hardest nutbags on God's green earth, could stay locked in a stare with Bunny McGarry. Until now.

After what seemed like an eternity, Bunny turned back to his pint and took a long pull on it. He then smacked his lips and regarding the half empty glass as if seeing it for the first time.

"Y'know, one of us is going to have to be good cop."

Maggie licked her chops and belched.

"We'll work on that."

HOW TO SEND A MESSAGE

THIS STORY WAS INSPIRED BY THE THING THAT ANNOYS ME SO MUCH IN FILMS THAT MY WIFE NOW GROANS EVERY TIME IT HAPPENS AS SHE KNOWS SHE HAS TO STOP THE MOVIE SO I CAN HAVE A RANT ABOUT IT FOR TWENTY MINUTES.

———

"I'm just saying—"

"Well don't," said Keith. "Alright? Just don't."

Scanner had been 'just saying' things since they were eight. Twenty years later, and he was still full of opinions. He always seemed honestly mystified when his thoughts went unappreciated, often to the point of physical violence. These days he spent a lot of time in the gym. He was now a fully-grown five feet six of bristling muscles and unrestrainable opinions. Keith reckoned Scanner was under the false impression that people picked on him because of his size. They didn't. They picked on him because he was Scanner and Scanner was fucking annoying.

"All I'm saying," continued Scanner as he turned the wheel and took them onto the Cabra Road, "is that us driving over there and posting a bullet through the guy's letterbox, is a bit of a cliché."

"It's a message," said Keith.

"It's a clichéd message."

"And what would you do?"

"Shit in his letterbox."

Keith turned in his seat, truly appalled. "And what message exactly does that send?"

"It says, don't mess with us, we're the kind of people who are capable of anything."

"Does it?" said Keith, "Or does it send the message that we're full of shit?"

"You lack imagination, that's your problem."

"Imagination? Alright, say we do this, Mister Picasso. How would you even go about it?"

"What do you mean?"

"I mean, do we sit there and wait until you feel ready to pop one out or do we do it beforehand and bring it with us?"

"I'm pretty confident I could knock one out as required."

"Impressive," said Keith.

"You could too if you started having proper fibre in your diet."

"Ah, don't start that again," said Keith. "Alright then smartarse, pun intended, what happens if it's one of those up-high letterboxes? Do I pick you up and use you like an icing gun?"

"Nobody has those letterboxes anymore."

"My Auntie Margo does."

"Well, your Auntie Margo is weird."

"Says the man who wants to shit through her letterbox."

"Didn't her husband leave her to go off and live as a woman?"

"Yes he did. He's been going through a difficult life change. We're all trying to be supportive."

"He's a freak."

"And you're a small-minded prick."

Keith turned to stare out the window. He'd had more than enough of Scanner to last him a lifetime. The only reason they were still friends was habit. It was a hell of a lot easier to break up with a bird than it was to break up with a mate. The arsehole had been nice to him twenty years ago when Keith had moved to a new school, and he's been living off it ever since.

They merged onto the Navan Road and Keith looked longingly at the Merc dealership. Even at this time of night, they always had the windows lit up, showing off the goods. He'd gone in there once but the saleswoman had been a bit dismissive when she'd smelled he'd not got the wedge. He dreamed about going back and slamming it down in cash, given her a wink and driving out. That'd show the judgy bitch.

"DNA," said Keith, cutting Scanner off. "They could get your DNA off the turd."

"Bollocks they can."

Keith took out his iPhone and typed it in as he spoke. "DNA in faeces."

"Faces?"

"Faeces, you idiot. It's the medical word for shite."

"Well la-dee-dah. What's wrong with just saying shite?"

Keith scrolled down through the search results. "Cop yourself on. You can't have doctors saying things like 'I'm sorry Mr Williams, you've got bowel cancer, we can tell from your shite'."

"I don't think people would care. If Mr Williams was that concerned, he would have had more fibre in his diet in the first place."

"You're like a broken bleedin' record with the ... Yes! Jog on ye shit cannon, you can even buy a DNA testing kit specifically for faeces."

"Feck off."

"Yep. Your first day in prison would be fucking hil-a-ri-ous. What are you in for? Me? Shitting through a letterbox."

A car in the oncoming lane honked as Scanner tried to look at Keith's phone. "Eyes front. You need to take a right onto Nephin Road up here."

"I know," said Scanner, huffily.

"Yeah, you know everything."

They turned, Keith flicking the required Vs at Cabra Garda station on the corner as they did so.

"Alright," said Scanner, a man utterly incapable of accepting defeat. "You pay a homeless bloke to do it."

"Right, and do we bring him with us or go for the 'here's one we prepared earlier' approach?"

Scanner considered this. "Earlier. You could have him do it into one of them Tupperware containers, so it doesn't stink the car out." Scanner was very particular about his car.

"So, let me get this straight. We're now paying homeless guys to shit in a lunchbox? This is sounding less like a message and more like a cry for help. Take a right up here."

Scanner grumbled under his breath as he turned into the road.

"Alright, stop here," said Keith, pulling on his gloves as he did so. "It's number 26, that'd be that one four from the end I reckon. You come with me. Keep an eye on the surrounding windows and make sure nobody clocks us. When it's all clear, give me the nod and I'll nip in and deliver the bullet. Clear?"

"Could we not..."

Keith opened his door and was out in a flash. He was not in the mood for another one of Scanner's suggestions.

Four minutes later, both car doors reopened and they sat in.

"Job done," said Keith.

"I'm just saying ..." said Scanner.

"D'ye know ..." said a voice that was neither Keith or Scanner, hence the reason that Keith screamed and Scanner punched a crack into his own windscreen.

"Jesus!" said Keith.

"Fuck's sake!" said Scanner.

"You alright there lads?" said the man sitting in the back seat eating a kebab. "You seem a tad jumpy?"

Keith and Scanner exchanged a look. The man, who definitely hadn't been there before, seemed unnervingly calm. He was a large bloke in a black sheepskin coat, blessed with the kind of Cork accent that sounded like a cat in a slow moving blender.

"As I was saying," he continued, "d'ye know what really bothers me? In loads of films, people pop up in the back seat of cars and ye think, how in the hell did you not notice somebody crouching down back there? It's how Grace Jones knocks off Patrick Macnee in that Bond film where Duran Duran did the tune. Happens in the *Godfather* too. One of them *Back to the Future* films. I think it even happens in one of the Bourne things ..."

"Who the fuck are you?" said Scanner.

"It's him," said Keith.

"Him who?"

"Who do you think?" said Keith, nodding back in the direction they'd just come from.

"DS Bunny McGarry," said Bunny, in between messy mouthfuls of kebab. "Delighted to be making your acquaintance. The point I was making is, I didn't think anyone was stupid enough to miss somebody sitting in the back seat of a car and yet here's you two gobshites, proving me wrong." Bunny casually tossed the remains of his kebab onto the floor.

"Ah, for Jaysus's sake," said Scanner, "you're getting it all over me car."

Bunny looked at Keith, who, even panicked as he was, couldn't help but feel a little bit embarrassed.

"I don't think the muscle hamster here has fully grasped the gravity of the situation, has he?" asked Bunny. "Let's recap for the hard of thinking, shall we? You two just made a delivery to my abode. I'm going to guess ... a bullet?" Bunny looked between the two men. "Bit of a cliché, isn't it?"

"I told ye," said Scanner.

Keith felt like slamming his head through the window. "You just confessed, you know-it-all prick."

"Oh dear," said Bunny. "Bit of tension in paradise, is there lads?"

Scanner made as if to speak.

"Don't say a word," said Keith.

"The bullet means they'll have you on at least threat to kill under the Non-Fatal Offences Against the Person Act, 1997. That's a maximum twelve months and seeing as yours truly is a card-carrying member of the Garda Síochána, you'll get the full whack. That's small time to hard men like you though, isn't it?" He looked at them both in turn. Even in the dim glow from the streetlights, the guy had a very off-putting wonky left eye that made it hard for Keith to look directly back at him. "That's not your big problem though."

"Isn't it?" said Keith.

"No," said Bunny. "That'd be the gun."

"What gun?" said Scanner, "We've not got a g..."

There was a loud thunk. Keith didn't need to look to know that the object that'd landed in the rear footwell was a handgun.

"Oh dear, oh dear, oh dear," said Bunny. "You boys are really in over your heads, aren't you?"

"Are we?" said Scanner. "There's another way of looking at it."

"Is there?" said Bunny, a disconcerting hint of glee to his voice.

"Yeah. You're the one in a car with two proper Gs that have now got a gun, ye fat old prick."

"Very true," said Bunny, pointing at Keith. "Your friend here looks like he can handle himself and I bet you'll be invaluable if the situation requires anything heavy being picked up and put down again in the same place. I'm no athlete and as you pointed out, I've got twenty-five hard years on either of you. Plus, as you said, I've now given you a gun. Thing is... wait!" Bunny McGarry held his hand up and then walloped Keith's headrest with it. "Tom Cruise in *A Few Good Men*, that's another one."

"What?" said Scanner.

"Where someone pops up from the back seat. Anyway what was I talking about? Oh yeah. See, you're dead right, you have 'a gun' but I have what could be termed in this situation as 'the gun'."

In the darkness of the car, the click-click of an unseen safety being slipped off and a hammer being pulled back echoed, if only in Keith's mind. It sounded like a coffin lid slamming shut. Bunny grinned widely at him.

"I'll do you a deal, boys. Whichever one of you bleeds first, I'll say he was the one holding the gun."

"What?" said Scanner.

"I do so hate repeating myself," said Bunny. He spoke slowly, pointing to add a visual aid. "I said – whichever one of the two of you, who gets the other to bleed first, doesn't cop for carrying the gun."

"And you think..." said Scanner, who didn't get any further because Keith had just punched him full in the face.

Dessie Kearns was rudely awoken by the doorbell. Actually, he was rudely awoken by his wife's elbow in his ribs, but that had been prompted by the doorbell.

"Fuck's sake!"

"Doorbell," she responded.

"You like it so much, why don't you go and answer it?"

One of the many current sources of friction in their marriage was the cost of that bloody doorbell. Like the house wasn't expensive enough, she'd made him spend four grand on the damn thing. She had seen it on some programme. It felt like every time she turned on the TV or opened a magazine, it cost him money. The stupid thing contained actual bells. Now every time they got a pizza delivered it sounded like Christ Church bleedin' Cathedral.

He could feel her sitting up in the bed beside him, pulling her eye-mask off.

"Let me get this straight..."

He hated when she started a sentence that way, it never ended well.

"... It is three o'clock in the pissing morning, and you want to send your wife, the mother of your children, down to answer the door to God-knows-what?"

"Rapists don't generally ring, love."

She clapped twice to turn the lights on and then slapped him right on the earhole.

"Jesus!" he said, now fully awake and loving life. "Ye mental bitch."

"Tell whichever of your drunken buddies wants you to go out whoring with him that you are unavailable."

He rolled out of bed and grabbed his robe off the floor. As he left the room, he heard her clap again to turn the light off. Like she wasn't going to be sitting there listening, loading up on ammunition for when he got back. Whoever this was, somebody had better be dead or somebody was going to be.

Through the ornate swirling glass beside the door, he could see the outline of two figures in the porch-light. Something wasn't right.

"Who is it?"

"Sorry Dessie," came back a shaky voice. "It's Keith and Scanner."

"What the..."

As he opened the door, the words died in his throat. Keith and Scanner were standing there bollock naked. Scanner was holding a tissue to his bleeding nose with one hand and cupping his nether region with the other. Keith had a swollen eye and both hands covering his modesty. They both sported various other cuts and bruises, and stood awkwardly hunched over like nature wasn't calling so much as hollering.

Dessie looked down the drive and around at the neighbouring houses. Thankfully he couldn't see anyone taking notice. They'd objected to their gnomes at the last resident's association meeting. He glanced back up the stairs; please God don't let her see. He couldn't afford to move again.

He stepped out and pulled the door nearly shut behind him.

"What the fuck?" whispered Dessie.

"We were doing..." started Scanner.

"You – shut up. Keith?"

"We were doing that thing," said Keith.

Dessie nodded.

"And it didn't go well."

"I can see that!" he hissed. "Where the hell are your clothes?"

"He took them."

"And he beat you up?"

Keith averted his eyes and looked down at the rosebushes. "Not exactly."

Scanner removed the hand from his modesty and pointed accusingly at Keith. "This fucker went and..."

Dessie pointed at Scanner without even looking at him. "Keith, what have I said about this dickhead talking?"

"Please, Dessie," said Keith, "can we just come in?"

Dessie glanced back over his shoulder, truly horrified. "No you can not."

"Please. He said as soon as he dropped us off, he was calling a patrol and reporting two naked perverts roaming the area."

"Oh for..."

Dessie looked around again, trying to decide between what would be the lesser of two evils. Out of the corner of his eye, he couldn't help but notice that Scanner's hand had now moved around to his posterior area.

"What on earth do you think you're doing?"

Scanner and Keith exchanged an awkward look. Keith looked between them both.

"Well?"

"He..." said Keith, and then stopped, his voice choking.

"What?"

"He..."

"Fuck's sake," said Scanner. "He made us shove bullets up our arses."

"Jesus."

"Yes," said Keith, again unable to make eye contact with anything but the ground. "And he gave us something to tell you."

"Which was?"

"This is how you send a message."

ESCAPE FROM VICTORY

HONESTLY, I'VE NO IDEA WHAT INSPIRED THIS STORY. I THINK I JUST WANTED TO FIND OUT WHO ELSE WAS ON THE ST JUDE'S UNDER-12S HURLING TEAM, AND I ALWAYS ENJOY MEETING A CERTAIN ASSISTANT-MANAGER SO MUCH THAT I WROTE IT PRIMARILY TO ENTERTAIN MYSELF. SPOILER: THAT'S ACTUALLY THE REASON I WRITE EVERYTHING. YOUR ENJOYMENT IS ENTIRELY COINCIDENTAL.

THIS TAKES PLACE CIRCA 2001.

CHAPTER ONE

Bunny McGarry looked around the corner of the supermarket car park where the St Jude's Under-12s hurling team had gathered. He was unsure what the collective noun for a group of pre-teen boys was – a slouch? A bedragglement? An exhaustion? Regardless, it was a statistically proven fact that if you left eighteen of them to their own devices for more than three minutes, one of them would inevitably carry out a minor act of violence on another.

"Donnacha Aherne," snapped Bunny. "Did I just see you giving Johnny Marsh a dead arm?"

"No, Bunny," responded the perpetrator. "There's no way you could've seen me do that from where you are."

"I didn't. But I heard Johnny scream out in pain."

It tells you all you need to know about the workings of the male mind that after this statement; the puncher gave the punchee a look that had an unmistakable air of betrayal which, in turn, was met with an apologetic grimace from his victim.

"It seems to have slipped your attention, Donnacha, that we have a game this morning and, crazy as this may seem, I think it will be tactically sound if all of our players turned up in one piece."

"To be fair, boss, you did say last week that Johnny would be a better hurler if he only had the one arm." This interjection came from the only non-player amongst the eighteen, the St Jude's assistant manager, one Deccie Fadden.

Bunny glared down at him. "Thank you, Declan. As always, your seeming inability to grasp basic sarcasm is invaluable."

"You're welcome, boss."

Bunny shook his head and handed Deccie the plastic bag full of his purchases. "Here, replenishments for the first-aid kit." Plasters, oranges and a new magic sponge. He'd splashed out, as today was a big game.

Deccie looked into the bag and then looked back up at Bunny. "Where's the can of Coke and two Chomps you said you were getting me?"

This was met with a blank expression.

"Let me guess – that was more of that sarcasm stuff again, wasn't it?"

"See, you're slowly getting the hang of it, Deccie."

"Have you never heard the expression, boss, that sarcasm is the lowest form of wit? Oscar Wilde said that."

Bunny raised an eyebrow. Declan Fadden was full of surprises. "To be fair to old Oscar Wilde, he'd not seen you on the trip home from last week's match doing your recital of all the different fart noises you can make."

"Say what you like," said Deccie, with no small amount of pride, "that absolutely killed."

"It did." Loath as he was to admit it, it had been that funny, Bunny had been forced to pull the minibus over for fear of a traffic accident.

He clapped his hands together. "Right, lads, form a line."

"Actually," said Jason Phillips, "we're already in a line."

Bunny, like every other person in authority, found Jason Phillips alarming. A slight-built skinny kid, who wore thick jam jar glasses and looked like he could blow himself into orbit if he sneezed too vigorously. He also gave off the disconcerting impression of being smarter than everybody else in the room. In fact, quite possibly, that he was smarter than everybody else full stop. What made it worse was he clearly wasn't trying to give off that notion, it was just the way he was. He would be staring off into the distance one minute and then absentmindedly say something the next that you would spend several weeks thinking about. His comments had prompted Bunny to make trips to the library twice in the last three months to try to understand what he said. One of the times he'd wanted to check that Jason's explanation of how black holes worked tallied with what popular science knew already, because if it didn't, he thought they might have to tell somebody. The kid was *that* smart. The fact that he'd come up with it during a training session, when Bunny had been attempting to get the lads to string a few passes together, had been even more perplexing.

Several of the boys assembled in that particular corner of that particular supermarket car park were considered nightmares to teach, but Jason was the only one who actually kept teachers up at night. His was the kind of mind that needed to be properly nurtured, because it could go on to do truly great things. In this regard, it was quite like a big old chunk of enriched uranium. All kids had potential, but his was truly world-changing, in either direction.

Bunny knew how the teachers felt. He worried about putting Jason out on a hurling field in case a flailing stick caught him a glancing blow and cost the world a cure for cancer or the secrets to interstellar space flight, or at the very least, an explanation as to how every call centre is always experiencing higher than average call volumes. He always made sure Jason was wearing one of the team's three fancy new helmets with extra padding and the enormous bars on the front. A few weeks ago, Bunny had asked Jason why he had joined the hurling team and his response had been that he enjoyed the angles. The kid said stuff like that all the time, and nobody could tell if he was joking or not.

Following a disintegrating domestic situation, Jason now lived with his widowed uncle, John-Joe, who dug ditches for the council. Heaven knows what sort of conversations they had over dinner, but the lad appeared to be content enough and was certainly a lot safer than he had been. Bunny knew John-Joe a little; a relaxed, amiable fella, he seemed happy enough to let Jason be Jason while doing all he could to support him. That was a big improvement on what had gone before. Jason's mother had long since disappeared and his father was an abusive alcoholic who was in and out of rehab. The cumulative effect of all this on Jason was hard to read but worrying. How those parents had produced a genius was anybody's guess, and quite probably worthy of serious study.

Last year, after the results of a test given to every kid in Ireland came back, Jason had been offered a full scholarship to attend Belvedere College. To the surprise of everyone involved, he had politely turned it down by explaining that he did not believe in the concept of a private education. Nobody had been able to convince him otherwise. Bunny had even tried to have a word, but the lad had calmly explained that all he needed was a library card, pen and paper. That was the thing – beneath the pre-teen bumbling professor persona, lay something hard and unrelenting. Same as when an opposition player had taken Padraig Brooke out with a horrendous tackle a few weeks ago. Jason, who had shown minimal interest in the game until that point, had needed to be held back from exacting violent vengeance on the perpetrator, a rage bubbling up that was only tangentially related to a teammate getting smashed across the kneecaps. You saw it a lot in kids coming from situations like his, but it didn't make it any less dangerous or easier to cope with. Jason worried everyone because he seemed to be casually sauntering down the line between success story and cautionary tale, and nobody was sure which way things might fall.

Speaking of lines, for all of Jason's undoubted smarts, Bunny knew what a line was, and he was damn sure that the lads were not currently forming one. "With all due respect, Jason, the boys are not in a line."

"Actually," said Jason, not looking up from staring at a spiderweb crack in the concrete, "if we take us to be seventeen individual points, then it is possible to form an infinite array of lines between us."

Everyone in attendance went quiet and looked at each other for a few seconds. This happened a lot around Jason. The silence was broken by the boy himself. "What you mean, Bunny, is that you would like us to form a straight line."

Bunny nodded furiously. "OK, yes – right you are. Form a straight line please, lads." He leaned in towards Jason. "Thanks for the clarification."

Jason nodded and smiled without a hint of malice. "Of course, this assumes we're talking in only three dimensions."

"Let's assume we are," said Bunny quickly, looking at his watch. "We need to be getting a move on."

"But Phil isn't here yet," said Deccie.

"Phil isn't coming."

Deccie's face was a picture of shock. "What are ye on about? Phil Nellis never misses a game. He might be a waste of space, but he's a reliable waste of space."

"Yeah," agreed Bunny, "I've spent the last ten minutes on the phone explaining that to one of my colleagues. Do you remember that shed in Phil's garden?"

"His lab? Course."

"Well, hang onto that memory because it isn't there anymore. It blew up last night."

"How did that happen?"

"Apparently, Phil has narrowed it down to three possible sources. He'll have plenty of time to figure it out. Sounds like he's grounded until he turns eighty."

"Harsh."

"Well, his aunt and uncle aren't over-the-moon about the fire brigade and the gardaí rolling up at 6am on a Sunday morning."

"The cops?" asked Deccie. "Why would they care?"

"Because, while we are in a time of blessed peace on this tortured isle, things blowing up is still something the gardaí take a significant interest in." The part Bunny left out was that Phil's uncle Paddy was popularly believed to be a high-end thief par excellence, one that, bar one early stumble, kept himself so far ahead of law enforcement that he was probably lapping them by now. The incident offered the local constabulary a free go at tearing their house apart and generally going on a fishing expedition. Nobody expected to find anything, Paddy was too smart for that, but they would enjoy inconveniencing him as much as possible. Bunny's assertion that the explosion was invariably the result of a certain curious kid's curious mind had not been greeted enthusiastically by the DI in charge. Still, it happened to be true. As was the fact that they'd lost a player they could ill-afford to. Phil Nellis was useless, but his willingness to stand in front of anyone, or anything, while being so, made him a useful form of useless. If all else failed, the kid would have a bright career as a speedbump.

"Inspection!" said Bunny, clapping his hands together.

The lads had now formed what even Jason would struggle to define as a straight line.

The inspection phase of proceedings, while it looked to the casual observer like a middle-aged man living out his tragic military fantasies, was actually a crucial part of the pre-game process. Bunny had learned this through bitter experience.

"Present ... arms!"

The boys duly held their football boots out in one hand and their shorts out in the other. Bunny took care of washing the jerseys and there was a large pile of hurling sticks and helmets alongside them in the storage compartment on the top of the minibus, but shorts and boots were the responsibility of the individual. He carried a couple of spares, but he still needed the majority of the team to remember their kit. Besides, at least one of the spare pairs of shorts now had so many holes in it that it technically qualified as lingerie. He walked up the line, Deccie falling in to step beside him. "Colm, clean your studs. Johnny, either wash those shorts for next week or take them out and shoot them before they run off on their own. Wayne O'Brien ..." Bunny stopped to take in the magnificent awfulness of what was presented before him. "Right, lads, my position on bullying is well known to all of you. What diabolic dipshit did this to poor Wayne's boots?"

"I did," said Wayne, cheerfully.

Bunny took one of the two offending boots out of Wayne's hands. It was luminous yellow. "What?"

"I used a highlighter to make them yellow."

"Why?"

"Y'know – so I'd stand out."

Bunny hesitated. He was resisting the urge to point out that if Wayne wanted to stand out, managing to make contact with the ball rather than taking divots out of the ground as he swung his hurling stick around like a man who had a grudge against the earth would be a great start. He didn't say that though, as he'd been working on trying to be positive. The team was on an eight-game losing streak and he'd got a book from the library on man management that had been only marginally less confusing than the one on black holes. He'd only read the first three chapters, but he had found himself whole-heartedly agreeing with whoever had written *'this is all bollix'* in the margin of page fifty-seven. Still, Butch had suggested he try positivity, and, for at least this week, he was going to give it a damn good go. With this in mind, Bunny took a deep breath and went with, "What on earth possessed you to do that to your boots?"

"One of them footballers on *Match of the Day* had it."

This was met with a collective wince from the group. Bunny's attitude to soccer was well known by everyone. Or at least everyone who wasn't Wayne O'Brien. The kid wasn't stupid, he just had a perpetually sunny, damn-near-oblivious outlook on life that from a distance looked an awful lot like stupid. Stupid tripped over a tiger because it wasn't paying attention to where it was going. Wayne walked over to nudge it with his foot because he wanted to make friends. Much to the annoyance of more careful souls, this approach to life, against all probability and logical sense, worked for Wayne. Even now, he was beaming up at Bunny with the light-hearted certainty that nothing bad could possibly happen. You couldn't dislike Wayne, and several people had tried.

"Right, well, it's against regulations."

"What regulations?" asked Wayne.

Before Bunny could respond, Deccie stepped forward until he

was inches from Wayne's face. "Are you giving cheek, sonny Jim, m'lad? You'll be running laps of the car park faster than lasagne through a donkey. You mark my words. I'll make you wish you'd—"

Deccie was interrupted by Bunny pulling him back. "All right, Sergeant Slaughter, dial it back a few notches."

"We can't have dissent in the ranks, boss. Not today, of all days."

"Today is just another match," said Bunny, the hint of warning in his voice going so far over Deccie's head that it was a danger to commercial air traffic.

"No, it's not boss. It's the shower of Southsiders from Saint Mungo's, the one's managed by that DI Grainger, the guard you said was your nemesis ..."

"We don't need to—" started Bunny, in a vain effort to stop the high-speed locomotive that was Deccie Fadden's mouth.

"Y'know, the fella who got you suspended off the force there just before Christmas. You said how he goaded you into a bet and whoever wins this game gets his car washed by the other one in front of Garda headquarters. Topless! You said you'd made a terrible mistake and, more than anything, you'd love for us to beat the odds and win this game."

As the Deccie express finally pulled into a station, Bunny looked up and down the line of suddenly concerned faces of a team that hadn't come close to winning for months and who had just been informed that their mentor had bet his dignity on an unlikely upturn in their fortunes.

He threw out an unconvincing smile. "Don't worry about it, lads. Just a bit of craic between two old friends."

"No, boss, you said this Grainger fella was a massive—"

Deccie's attempt to spill what few remaining beans were left was interrupted by Bunny slamming a hand over his mouth. "Right, boys, time's a ticking. Load up."

All of their concerns were temporarily forgotten as seventeen players attempted to grab one of the precious seats in a minibus that was built to hold twelve.

Bunny watched the scramble, checking no actual war crimes were being committed, before he took his hand off Deccie's mouth and spun him around. He bent down to look his assistant manager directly in the eye. "Fecking hell, Deccie. Do you remember the rest of our little chat?"

Deccie crinkled his brow and counted points off on his fingers. "Have to win the game, this peeler fella is a prick, don't tell the lads, topless washing of car ... ah, wait a sec. I see your point. I forgot number three, didn't I?"

Bunny stood up and wiped a hand across his brow. "Jesus Christ and Jackie Charlton! Yes, Deccie, you forgot number three."

"Be fair, boss – I remembered all the other points."

Bunny sighed. "Get on the bus."

"Can I drive?"

"The answer to that question is the same as it was the last million times you asked."

"Do you know what your problem is, boss?"

"You!" snapped Bunny. "Now get moving or I'm not letting you be in charge of the magic sponge."

"How's that positivity thing working out for you so far, boss?"

"'Tis a challenge, Declan. A challenge."

CHAPTER TWO

The minibus descended into an ominous silence as Bunny turned the key in the ignition. The vehicle was unaffectionately known as Bertha. Unaffectionately, as Bunny had only given it that name to stop himself referring to it in more colourful terms. He had long since realised that trying to stop himself swearing entirely in front of the team was unrealistic but, despite the impression given, he did try to keep it to a minimum. The hush was because everyone knew Bunny had no sense of humour whatsoever about Bertha's infuriatingly capricious nature. She could run like a dream for weeks on end only to throw a strop when you really, really needed her to be reliable. They were already running late and, today of all days, Bunny wanted St Jude's putting their best foot forward. They might not win, but at least they could go in and out of there with their heads held high.

The mood was tense as Bunny had already attempted unsuccessfully to start Bertha twice and everybody present knew it was either third time's the charm or half the team had to get back out and push while Sunday shoppers gawped on. Bunny closed his eyes, whispered a prayer to the automotive gods, and turned the key. It was a frozen moment of pause and then, with a cough, a splutter, and a backfire that made a passing greyhound jump into his owner's arms, the engine sprung into life.

The lads cheered and Bunny patted the steering wheel. "Good girl, Bertha. Ye did me proud."

Once she'd started, it was best to give her a few minutes of standing about while she warmed up. In the meantime, there was plenty of admin that needed doing. Bunny looked into the rear-view mirror. The minibus did not have enough seats to carry a fifteen man hurling team, two subs, an assistant manager, and manager/driver/closest thing to a responsible adult. Bunny used to rage about how the makers of minibuses were anti-Gaelic games in that there were just enough seats for a soccer team. Someone had since pointed out to him that there were, in fact, several larger minibuses available, but that was like saying to a homeless person that there was plenty of living space on the moon. St Jude's did not have the kind of budget that could stretch to a fancy new minibus. In fact, St Jude's didn't have any kind of budget. Some parents chipped in when they could, and occasionally Bunny was able to twist some arms of local businesses to throw a few quid in the pot, but mostly he was reliant on whatever grants he could wheedle out of the GAA or putting his hand in his own pocket. They had been approached a couple of times by 'local businessmen' who made their money from less conventional means but, desperate though he was, Bunny had turned those overtures down flat. The whole point of St Jude's was to give him a chance to put some young men on the right path in life and he couldn't preach about staying on the straight and narrow to a bunch of lads running around in jerseys paid for from the proceeds of crime. Morality could be a right pain in the knackers sometimes. The only reason they had Bertha was that two of the leaders of the now-defunct local Cub Scouts had run off together to start a new life in Belgium. It had been quite the scandal, both of the spouses behind whose backs they'd been 'dib, dib, dibbing' had been quoted in a story in the paper. There was talk of a movie.

"Right," said Bunny. "Pre-flight checks ... Has everyone who has a seatbelt clicked it in?"

This was met with a chorus of 'yes, Bunny'.

"And has everybody with a teammate sitting on their lap got a good grip on them?"

This garnered more, if slightly less enthusiastic, confirmations. Technically, they were breaking the rules of the road, but Bunny reasoned whatever danger these boys were in while travelling in Bertha was as nothing compared to the dangers they'd face if left wandering the streets looking for something to do.

"And—"

Bunny found himself interrupted by a camera flash from the seat beside him. "What in the shittin' hell?"

"I'm glad you asked," said Deccie. "I've decided that, as well as being the team's co-manager—"

"Assistant—"

"—I'm also the official photographer and I'm going to document this momentous occasion, boss. I've decided photography is my calling." He held up a hand. "Before you start, Granny already had a word. No nudey stuff, just nice wholesome stuff like wars and that."

"Right, well, that's a relief." Bunny pointed at the disposable camera Deccie was holding. "Where did you get that?"

"I've got like ten of them. Me, Granny and Granda were at Coleen Walsh-from-over-the-road's wedding yesterday and they'd just left a load of these disposable cameras out on the tables."

"You weren't supposed to take them."

"Sure, why did they leave them out then?"

"I'm assuming they wanted people to document the day. Rather than hiring a photographer."

Deccie looked outraged. "As a professional, I'm horrified that they're leaving stuff like that in the hands of amateurs. Not everyone has my eye."

"Oh yeah, you've an eye all right. Just don't take any pictures of me while I'm driving."

"I can't promise that, boss. I have to capture definitive moments wherever they may occur."

"Look at me, Declan." Bunny waited until he did so. "That flash goes off in my face while I'm driving, we are going to have the mother of all definitive moments."

"Noted."

"Speaking of safety, why have you not got your seatbelt on?"

Deccie folded his arms. "I read a thing that says they kill more people than they save."

"Well, we are going to be evening up those numbers a bit because if your seatbelt isn't on in three seconds, you're a dead man."

Deccie mumbled something under his breath, but he complied. Bunny watched carefully to make sure he was completing the process exactly as instructed. The lad had the kind of sharp instinct for loopholes that would make him a brilliant tax accountant, should anyone ever trust him with their money. Only when he heard the definitive click did Bunny turn his attention to the other front seat passenger who was seated over by the window on the far side of Deccie.

Huey Moore had a particularly unfortunate name, given that he suffered from chronic travel sickness. His poor parents had tried everything – tablets, hypnosis, some weird headband thing – but none of it had worked. At this point, the fella looked ill as soon as he looked at a vehicle. For all of that, he was an indomitable little soul who was not going to let his affliction stop him. He was sitting over there right now, his designated up-chucking bowl gripped in both hands, with a facial expression that was equal parts queasy and determined. Interestingly, the rest of the group had long since got past any urge to make jokes and they were now supportive of Huey in his bi-weekly battle with his own body on the way to every away game. It was partly genuine empathy and partly because he took on the thankless task of being the team's goalie. It took a special mind to see a sliotar, a cork core ball covered in leather that could reach speeds of up to ninety miles an hour, and think, 'I need to get in the way of that thing'. The lad had more stoicism than a monastery of Tibetan monks. Bunny had a growing suspicion that Huey Moore was going to go places in life, even if he would need a large bowl and some wet wipes to get there. "Are you all right, Huey?"

This was met with a resolute nod.

"Good man, yourself. 'Tis not that long a drive. We'll be there before you know it." Bunny raised his voice again. "Right so – if we are all sitting uncomfortably, we shall begin."

Bunny threw Bertha into gear and with another smoke-belching backfire that caused a certain greyhound to do irreparable damage to his owner's new jumper, off they went.

As always, for the first few minutes of the drive, Bunny said nothing. He was using this time to listen to Bertha for any signs of impending problems while simultaneously getting re-acquainted with her erratic handling. She was not unlike many governments, in that as soon as she hit a bump in the road, she had a tendency to veer wildly to the right. Besides, something in Bunny enjoyed being enveloped in the cheerful chatter of the lads behind him. Inevitably, the talk quickly came around to slagging off the soccer teams that they each supported. The lads were all too aware of Bunny's dislike for the game, so out of deference to him, they'd come up with a system of replacing team names with fruits and vegetables. It wasn't exactly the hardest code to crack. *Bananas were never going to win the FA Cup two years in a row* – but Bunny appreciated them at least making the effort. The only downside was that Liam Boyle supported kumquats, and Bunny had been unsuccessfully attempting to piece together which team that was for over a month now. It was really getting on his nerves. He'd never admit it, but he did occasionally turn on *Match of the Day* when nothing else was on.

Beside him, Deccie cleared his throat in the way that indicated one of his serious points was coming. "Boss, seeing as this is such a big game—"

"'Tis just another game."

"Pull the other one, boss. You can't big a bigger."

"I think you mean you can't kid a kidder."

"What's that mean?"

"You're the one who said it."

"I didn't, I said big a bigger."

"And what's that mean?"

"It means you can't make a point bigger than my point because my point is already bigger than your point."

"That makes no sense, Deccie."

Deccie threw his hands out. "Makes perfect sense. I'm going to need a ruling on this."

Huey, while he avoided talking as he believed undisturbed regulated breathing helped with his issue, was nevertheless happy to be involved in conversation through the medium of nodding.

Deccie turned to him. "Huey, does 'don't big a bigger' make perfect sense to you?"

He nodded emphatically.

Bunny considered arguing the point, but he decided he didn't have the energy. "Fair enough. What big thing were you going to say?"

"I've been thinking about our tactics."

"Oh, here we go."

Deccie looked at Bunny affronted. "Well, that positivity kick didn't last long, did it?"

"Sorry, Deccie, but before we get into your latest brainwave, let me just temper your expectations. It's a firm no if the plan involves any form of weaponry, sharpening of the hurls or studs, digging a trench or drugging an official. Oh, feck – that reminds me – grab the agenda from the glovebox please, lads."

The agenda was a little notepad that Bunny added to throughout the week, full of lists of things he wanted to bring up on the bus enroute to games. Twelve-year-old boys had the attention spans of stoned goldfish, so Bunny had learned to make use of the time when they were literally a captive audience.

Huey popped the glovebox in front of him open and handed Deccie the notepad and pencil.

"Good, boys. Stick down *referee* please, Declan."

"Are we finally going to bribe a referee like I keep saying?"

"No, we're not," said Bunny, mentally adding that, bar anything else, if they had the budget, Bertha would have a spare tyre. "So, I assume your new strategic masterplan doesn't make it past that test?"

"Actually," said Deccie, "it does."

This caused Huey to glance up momentarily from staring into his bowl.

"Really?" said Bunny. "Well, fire away then."

"OK. Now, this might sound a bit mad, but hear me out. Y'know we have fifteen players on the pitch and they have fifteen players on the pitch?"

"Yeah," said Bunny. "I'm with you so far."

"And how we've got our goalie" – a nod towards Huey – "and they've got their goalie."

"Again, spot on."

"That leaves fourteen players a team out on the field."

"Can't fault your maths. Oh, maths, stick that on the agenda."

"Are you paying proper attention to me?" grumbled Deccie.

"I'm giving you as much attention as I can while keeping us alive and resisting the urge to pullover and throttle the BMW driver that's been flashing his lights behind me for the last two minutes like somehow, he's reserved the road and we're taking his slot. So, my advice, Declan, is stop taking the hump and start making your point."

Deccie tutted. "This is why we need regular management team meetings."

"We would if I had that kind of spare time."

"We're all busy people," said Deccie.

"Really? I'm a member of an underfunded police service who works way more than his allotted hours because otherwise we'd never get any criminals off the streets while simultaneously running this team. You're a young lad who, I know for a fact, doesn't do half his homework because most of the teachers have lost the will to hack their way through your latest jungle of excuses."

"Do you have any idea how long it takes me to come up with those excuses, boss? It'd be easier to just do the homework."

"So why don't you, then?"

"Well, now you're just being ridiculous."

Bunny shook his head. "So, fourteen outfield players per team ..."

"Right, yeah. So, here's my idea. When they have the ball, which, let's be honest, is most of the time" – hard to argue the point on that – "why don't we assign each of our players to follow one of their specific players around for the whole game. Like, you stay with this guy, you stay with that fella, and so on..."

Bunny waited for a few moments, but Deccie said nothing else. "And?"

"And what, boss?"

"What? What you've just described is marking, Deccie."

"You can call it that if you like."

"I call it that. Everyone calls it that. To borrow a phrase from yourself, it's one of the fundamentals of the game. Of all team sports, in fact."

"So why aren't we doing it, then?"

"We..." Bunny took a breath to try to calm himself down. "We are. I mean, we're supposed to be. Are you telling me that you've been the assistant manager for all this time and you've not noticed that?"

"I've not seen any evidence of it."

Bunny couldn't help but clock Huey out of the corner of his eye, nodding in agreement.

"That's as may be, but I'm always telling the lads to do it. What do you think I'm shouting at them throughout the games?"

"To be honest, boss, respectfully, most of us can't figure out what the hell you're saying half the time. With that Cork accent, when you get all wound up, it sounds like someone trying to pull a length of hosepipe out of a lawnmower."

"Are you taking the piss, Deccie?"

"I'm not, boss. It's mainly waving and swearing. D'ye not remember that time at training you got attacked by the bees and it took us all five minutes to figure out what was happening?"

"I..." Bunny found himself speechless, a sense of futility washing over him. Just then, the BMW behind them honked.

"Right, lads," he snarled, "everybody cover your ears and sing *The Wheels on the Bus* now."

"But ..."

"NOW!"

They did as instructed, allowing Bunny to roll down the window and give the honking sod a large piece of his mind, accompanied by a backing track of an unenthusiastic rendition of one of the most pointlessly annoying songs in history. The exchange ended with the other driver flicking Bunny the V's, followed by his face dropping when Bunny flashed his An Garda Síochána ID card in response. He then took great delight in watching the turd's facial expression while Bunny made a great show of taking his numberplate down.

"All right," said Bunny, once Bertha had moved off. "You can stop now, lads."

"Do you feel better after that, boss?" asked Deccie.

"D'ye know what, Deccie? I really do." He guided Bertha up a ramp and onto the M50 motorway. Once they'd successfully merged, Bunny nodded. "Right, Declan. Agenda please."

"What order do you want them in?"

"Surprise me."

"Fair enough. Referee."

"Right, important one this. Lads, pay attention."

The ongoing babble of conversation only abated slightly.

"I said – PAY. ATTENTION." The bus descended into absolute silence. It was so quiet you could hear the various bits of Bertha rattling. "Right. Good. That's the stuff. Now – today St Jude's shall break new ground."

"We're going to actually win?" suggested Wayne O'Brien, accompanied by sniggering.

"Wayne, hilarious as always. I thought you'd be too busy cleaning that day-glow crap off your boots to be sharing your dazzling wit with us."

"You didn't actually say I had to."

"I also didn't tell you not to jump out of the vehicle while it's moving. Some things are just common sense, fella."

"How am I supposed to—"

"You've got a mouth, don't you?"

"You want me to lick it off?" said Wayne, sounding duly outraged as his compatriots laughed and gurned.

"Well, personally, I'd spit on my hand and rub, but I wouldn't like to stifle your creativity. Now, what was I talking about?"

"Referee," prompted Deccie.

"Thank you, Declan. That's right, for the first time today we shall be having a female referee."

He deliberately left a gap and was gratified that nobody filled it. The lads, even someone as unaware as Wayne O'Brien, had been around Bunny long enough to know that he was very hot on certain topics – respect for women being one of the biggest.

"Now," he continued, "I have always said how we must be courteous to all referees—"

Deccie made a scoffing noise. "You said last week's referee was as useless as an umbrella made of bog roll."

"Yes, Declan," said Bunny, through gritted teeth, "but I said it in private, or at least I said it to you, which is, admittedly, a lot like whispering into a megaphone."

"The week before," said Wayne O'Brien, "you shouted out that the referee was half blind."

"In my defence, he was wearing an eye patch, so that was factually correct, although I will admit it wasn't my finest hour, but the point is … all of us will treat this lady with absolute respect."

"Is that not sexist?" asked Wayne O'Brien.

"Should you not be busy licking your boots, Wayne?"

Amazingly, without looking around, Bunny was able to hear Wayne open his mouth to retort and being silenced by the sound of the fifteen heads in the back of the minibus simultaneously shaking to discourage him from doing so.

"Good," said Bunny, "now that is settled, what's next on the agenda, Deccie?"

"Maths."

"Ah, yes. Colm Doyle – please make your way to the front of the vehicle."

This was greeted by a cheer from the rest of the team that was twenty percent at Colm Doyle's expense and eighty percent 'thank God this isn't me'.

Colm Doyle was a tall, thin lad who, despite being only twelve years old, had a look about him like he was going bald. He appeared to have been born at forty and was growing into it rapidly. Somebody moved and Colm took the seat directly behind where Deccie was sitting.

"Now, Colm," said Bunny, "a little bird tells me you're failing maths."

"What?" said Colm.

Bunny sighed. "Not an actual bird. It's an expression."

"Would that be Mrs Geraghty who we have for maths?" asked Deccie.

"We'll make a detective of you yet, Declan."

"No offence, boss, but you shouldn't be calling women birds."

"I wasn't … It doesn't … Ah, never mind."

"Come to that," continued Deccie, "she's not exactly what you'd call little."

"If you don't mind," snapped Bunny, "I'm trying to have a conversation with Colm. So, Mr Doyle, have I been misinformed?"

"Maths is rubbish, Bunny," said Colm, with real feeling.

"That may be the case, but it's very important. How are you going to get a job if you can't add up the numbers?"

"S'alright, I'm going to be a plumber just like my da."

"Plumbers need to be able to add up. How are you going to be able to tell how much pipe you need?"

"That's different. That's measuring. I am dead good at measuring."

Deccie spun around in his seat and held up the index fingers of each hand. "How much is that?"

Colm sucked his teeth, proving that being a tradesman really is hereditary. "I make it about eight inches, give or take."

Deccie looked between his two fingers and then nodded. "Fair play, boss. He's good."

"I'm sure he is," said Bunny, "but you use maths for lots of stuff. How are you going to add up how much people owe you?"

"Dad says you just look at how nice the house is, pick a number, double it and if they don't start screaming, you're golden."

"Well, that's ..." Bunny hesitated. Colm Doyle Senior had fixed his boiler last winter for free, so he didn't want to say anything too judgemental. Luckily, a thought struck him. "What about tax?"

"What is tax?"

"Ask your dad about it."

"As it happens, I did exactly that last week."

"And what did he say?"

"He laughed and said, 'what is tax?'"

"Right," said Bunny, finding himself staring at a conversational dead end. "Still, you need to do better in maths. What did you get in the last test?"

"Twelve percent."

"In which case, I want you to do at least forty percent better in the next test."

"How much is that?"

"I'd imagine figuring that out for yourself would be a great first step towards the new improved you."

"Boss," interjected Deccie, "how long until we get there?"

"We'll get there when..." started Bunny, before stopping himself when he glanced down and noticed the look of concern on Deccie's face. He peered over at Huey, who was now doing the kind of breathing you normally associated with going into labour. "We'll be there very soon. Not long at all now. Not long at all."

The intensity of Huey's breathing lessened slightly, but Bunny reckoned they'd only had about twelve minutes at the very most. Luckily, they were only a few minutes away now. "Right, Deccie, what else is on the agenda?"

"It just says 'inspirational speech'."

"Ara shite." Bunny had been meaning to give it more thought, but work had got in the way. He and Butch had been working every hour God sent trying to track down Ian Hendrix. He was a little scrote who had managed to get hold of a list of vulnerable elderly people from the home care company his girlfriend worked for, and he'd been going around robbing their houses, happy to knock about his victims in the process. Even amongst other criminals, there were those who were considered scum. Bunny had gone to bed every night this week dreaming of dangling the little bastard off the side of O'Connell Bridge by his ever-present ratty ponytail. Despite their best efforts, they'd been unable to locate the arsehole and rumour had it he was getting out of the country for good. While he'd wish it to be otherwise, it wasn't Hendrix's fear of the long arm of the law that had prompted his desire to see the world. Sometimes you couldn't help but wonder if there was a higher power moving in mysterious ways. Of all the grannies in all the world, Ian Hendrix had ripped off the one belonging to one Antonio 'Batshit' Cronin. Antonio had just completed a three-year stint in Mountjoy, and he apparently wasn't too worried about going back. Bunny had personally heard Cronin's description of what he would do to Ian Hendrix when he got hold of him and, while it was probably deserved, if brutal, karma, the bit with the particularly creative use of boiled eggs had put Bunny entirely off his lunch. Still, he couldn't think about any of that now. He needed to pull an inspirational speech out of somewhere, and fast.

Inspirational … Inspirational …

He'd been meaning to rent a copy of that *Any Given Sunday* Al Pacino film from a couple of years ago so he could remind himself of that cracking speech Pacino made at the end. It'd been a lot about inches and now that he thought about it, a fair bit about being a middle-aged man. The second part would not resonate with this crowd and the first he could inevitably see getting bogged down in Colm Doyle measuring stuff.

They passed a sign directing them to the ground. Time was running out. Bunny knew more Shakespeare than most people would suspect, but he thought 'once more unto the breach' wouldn't work on a crowd who didn't know what a breach was. Then Deccie would inevitably ask where exactly King Henry was king of and that'd be a whole thing. Along those lines, *Braveheart* might be more relatable, but odds on it would fire the lads up in the wrong way entirely.

When all else fails, there were a couple of things that remained constant about pre-teen boys. "Right, lads, y'know how we always go for chips after a win?"

"That explains why I've been losing weight," said Deccie.

Bunny shifted down a gear and used the opportunity to give Deccie a warning nudge on the leg that now was not the time for him to interrupt.

"This evening, forget chips. When you win – and I've every confidence you will – I'm afraid we won't be going for chips—"

Bunny left a gap for the inevitable groan that duly followed.

"—because ... we'll be going for pizza!"

This was met with an ooohh. Shop bought pizza was exotic.

"And not just any pizza, we'll be going to that fancy place that has adverts on the telly."

"Deep crust?" asked Deccie excitedly. "I don't even know what it is, but it sounds like something I'd like."

"Sure! And ..." the sense of excitement in the minibus was even getting to Bunny now, "in celebration of this momentous victory, everyone gets ice cream afterwards too!"

The minibus erupted.

It is rare to hear a loud roar of excitement morph into a groan of disgust, but then, it's not every day that someone throws up into a bowl halfway through it.

"Oh shite," said Bunny. "Sorry, Huey."

CHAPTER THREE

Deccie stood behind Bunny, preparing to latch onto the back of his coat to hold him back if he attempted to charge onto the field. He was on a final warning from the league for what had been termed 'excessive exuberance'. It was his fourth such final warning, but one of these days, final might actually mean final. Deccie was also slightly concerned that Bunny could be heading for one of those heart attacks. He'd watched a programme on telly about them. They looked bad, like heartburn, only worse. According to a bit of paperwork Deccie had accidentally seen once while he was definitely not snooping, Bunny was born in 1969 or something like that, which, given that it was now the year 2001, meant he was really old. He was older than mobile phones, colour TVs and women's rights. Deccie was pretty sure they'd only invented science about 20 years ago. True, his granny and granda were technically older, but they didn't get angry, not like this anyway. Granny got angry like an iceberg, slowly freezing you to death. Bunny went off like a volcano, firing stuff everywhere and causing local villagers to run for the hills or away from the hills, or maybe towards a different hill that wasn't the one that had fire shooting out the top of it. Deccie didn't know much about hills and mountains, only that occasionally one of them was a volcano and that those were deadly in all meanings of the word.

If Bunny had one of these heart attacks, then Deccie was going to have to wallop him on the chest, which he was all right with, and give him the kiss of life, which he was considerably less keen on. He'd do it. Bunny was his friend, after all, but he really didn't want to. He was still figuring out the whole kissing thing and how he felt about it, but he didn't want his first one to involve a big sweaty fella from Cork. He knew that sort of thing did it for other people, and good luck to them, but he was pretty sure it wasn't his bag. Besides, the slagging from the lads would be unbelievable. So, all-in-all, he was dead against Bunny having a heart attack. Unfortunately, the team wasn't doing much to prevent it.

"Tackle him, Barney. Tackle him! Don't get out of his way. This is no time for manners. Go on, Stevie! What was that? For feck's sake, that wouldn't have stopped a plastic bag! C'mon, Dermot, impose yourself. Tackle – No, Dermot, no – the fella with the ball. *With* the ball! We talked about this ... Stop him shooting. Stop him!"

The assembled crowd of parents, bored siblings, people who had absolutely nothing else to be doing on a Sunday morning, and frustrated dogs who couldn't understand why they weren't allowed to join in, collectively 'oohed' in sympathy as the ball skipped past the St Jude's goalie's hurl but got stopped by his ribs.

"Ouch! Good man, Huey. Clear it, lads. Don't let him ..."

Another oohhh. This time, Huey stopped the shot with his head, which was thankfully helmeted. The face mask bore the brunt of the force, but it still snapped back in an unpleasant manner.

"Brilliant, Huey. Clear it, lads. Clear it!"

A third oooohhhhh. This one had a distinct undertone of pained masculinity as Huey saved this shot in a manner that could directly impact there being any Huey juniors in the future.

"For feck's sake, boys. Are you even trying to help him?"

Donnacha Aherne decided to do so by dropping his hurl and offering to pick Huey up, inadvertently getting in his way as he valiantly attempted to throw himself across the goal to save yet another shot.

There was a cheer as, not for the first time, Saint Mungo's scored a goal.

"Jaysus, Donnacha, when I said help him, I meant get rid of the ball!"

"Boss," said Deccie.

"Still, though," said Bunny, remembering his pledge to be more positive, "Well done for picking him up. Good ... erm, teamwork, I suppose. Are you all right, Huey?"

Huey shot them an inexplicably cheery thumbs up.

"That kid has balls of steel."

"Iron, actually," said Deccie.

Bunny looked back at his assistant manager for the first time in a while. "What are you on about?"

"I got him a cup made of iron."

"Actual iron?" asked Bunny.

"Of course," said Deccie, offended at being doubted.

"I mean, that's probably not allowed but, fair play, that's a good idea."

"Thank you."

"I wondered what that clanging noise was. Is it not very uncomfortable?"

"Compared to a high-speed sliotar in the knackers?"

"Point taken. What's the score now?"

"Well," said Deccie, "The good news is, we're only one point behind. The bad news is, we are also five goals behind and seeing as a goal is worth three points that makes us sixteen points behind."

"Thank you, Declan," said Bunny gruffly. "I do understand how the scoring system works."

"Right, only you shouted out after their last score that the next goal was important, and, by my reckoning, it isn't."

"I was trying to be inspirational."

"Oh, right. Good one, boss."

Bunny glanced down at Deccie again.

"I'm trying to be positive, too."

"It doesn't suit you."

"Yeah, I felt that as soon as I said it."

Bunny shrugged. "Thanks for trying."

"Look on the bright side, boss ..."

There was a pause as they watched the St Jude's players trudge back into position for the puck-out to restart the game. They looked deflated.

Eventually Bunny said, "Deccie, y'know when you say, 'look on the bright side'?"

"Yes, boss."

"You're generally supposed to follow up by saying what the bright side actually is."

"Really?"

"Yes."

"Shite. I wish I'd known that before I said it. I'm not a miracle worker."

DI Grainger waved cheerily across to Bunny from the other sideline. "I really thought you'd give us more of a game than this."

"'Tis not over yet."

Grainger laughed. "Says who?"

"You're a shining example of sportsmanship, Detective Inspector."

"Can't take a little joke, Detective. Where's that famous McGarry sense of humour?"

"If I want a laugh, I just look up your arrest record."

Deccie pulled at Bunny's coat. "Sorry to interrupt your friendly banter with the gobshite, boss, but ..." Bunny followed Deccie's pointed finger. Johnny Murphy was bent over, both hands on his knees. "Ah crap, Johnny's asthma is playing up." Bunny waved his hand. "Referee."

She glanced over in his direction.

"Substitution please, come on in, Johnny."

He turned to what remained of their bench. He'd been forced to send Dave Blake on for Paschal Quinn in the first half. They could ill-afford to lose him, Paschal being one of the few players on the team who had shown any understanding of where the opposition's goal might be, but he'd been taken out by a brutally high challenge. Bunny hadn't been able to complain about it much, given that it had come from one of his own teammates. Bunny had dropped several hints to Dermot's dad that he might need to get tested for being colour blind, but nothing had been done so far. Still, at least Dermot was tackling people. Besides, St Jude's had so little of the ball that Dermot catching one of his own teammates in possession was really spectacularly bad luck. Grainger, standing on the sideline had attempted to make some hilarious remark about that, but Bunny had deliberately kept talking loudly so as not to hear it. The prick had sent his team out there going for goals instead of trying to score points – a dick move to try to run up the score against an inferior opponent.

Having used Dave early doors, Bunny was left with their one remaining substitute.

"Right," he said clapping his hands together as he turned around, "'tis time to pull out the big guns!"

Rían Stark looked hurt by the remark. Bunny winced. The lad was a sensitive soul, and Bunny had made it very clear to all and sundry that his weight issues were not to be referenced. It didn't help that he was sitting behind them on a deckchair, working his way through a large bag of Tayto crisps. There was something almost magical about Rían. You could be shipwrecked on a desert island and somehow, three weeks in, you'd walk around a palm tree to find him polishing off an ice lolly.

"Sorry, Rían, I didn't mean … I meant you're our secret weapon!"

"I am?" asked Rían.

"He is?" asked Deccie.

"He is," said Bunny, shooting Deccie a warning look. "I'm going to stick you on for Johnny."

"But," said Rían, "Johnny plays on the wing. And he's marking that guy who keeps knocking the ball in for the fella who keeps scoring all the goals."

"Precisely. We stop him. We stop them. And you're the man for the job."

"Really?" Rían's forehead scrunched up in consternation. "But he's way faster than me."

"Exactly. He's faster than Johnny, too. That's why his asthma is playing up. We've been approaching this all wrong. There's no point chasing after someone who's faster than you. Do you know what the definition of insanity is?"

"That fella on Capel Street who throws his own poo at buses?" asked Deccie.

"No," snapped Bunny through gritted teeth. "It's doing the same thing over and over again and expecting a different result. Einstein said that." Bunny jabbed a finger in the direction of the field. "Maybe he's faster than you. Taller than you. Fitter than you. But you've got something he'll never have ..."

"Type two diabetes?" interjected Deccie.

"Heart," said Bunny. "You've got more heart than any two of them Southside soft lads with their correctly fitting jerseys and thirty quid haircuts. Now go out there and show them what you got."

Rían nodded furiously, his face a mask of grim determination. It slipped a little as it took him three attempts to get out of his deckchair, but he appeared to regather himself once he'd found his feet. Bunny and Deccie watched in silence as he ran across the field to take up his position, high-fiving Johnny with more vigour than was necessary as he passed him trudging off the field. It was Deccie who spoke first. "Thirty quid haircuts?"

"I dunno. I had to come up with something."

"Fair enough. Did Einstein really say that, though?"

"Course he did. Famous for it."

"Interesting."

"I'll tell you something about Einstein though, Deccie, that a lot of people don't know."

"What's that?"

"He never had to coach an under-12s hurling team." Bunny clapped his hands together loudly. "Right, c'mon now, lads. All still to play for. The score is nil-nil."

"Nah, boss," shouted back Colm Doyle. "They're miles ahead of us. I've been counting. I make it they're a point and five goals up on us. That's …"

He dropped his hurling stick and looked at his fingers, a look of concentration on his face.

"It was a figure of speech, Colm!" shouted Bunny, before he got to the idea of taking his boots and socks off. "Don't worry about it." A thought struck Bunny. "You see that blonde fella in midfield?"

Colm nodded.

"He's a leak, and I want you to plumb him. Plumb the living shite out of him."

To Deccie's surprise, the young man's eyes lit up, and he nodded intently. "Right, boss." He ran off to find his man.

"Pick up your hurl, Colm," shouted Bunny. "Your hurl."

Colm came back and got it, the fire still burning in his eyes.

"Nicely done, boss," said Deccie. "If you're looking for similar stuff, Donnacha wants to be a butcher, like his uncle, when he grows up. You could get him to chop the legs off that little nippy fella who keeps scoring all the goals."

"Tempting, but no."

They watched as Huey took the puck-out, catching it better than he had all day. The ball hurtled high and long, heading for the left wing. The boy marked by Rían Stark rose and caught the sliotar one-handed. He then looked up to see the considerable bulk of Rían hurtling towards him like a demented boulder of bad intentions rolling downhill. His opponent yelped as he blindly attempted a pass behind him to nobody in particular before diving out of the way.

The ball spilled loose, and the St Mungo's midfielder moved in smoothly, intent on flicking it deftly up onto his hurl, but he never got the chance. Colm Doyle slammed into him with a shoulder charge that left him poleaxed on the ground in front of the opposition bench.

"Referee!" screeched Grainger from the far sideline in protest. The ref tapped her shoulder. "Shoulder to shoulder. Perfectly legal."

Colm, meanwhile, was not waiting around to admire his handiwork. With a determination that had been entirely absent from his play up until this point, he walloped the ball with everything he had, sending it skittering down the field.

Jason Phillips pushed his glasses up his nose, watching the ball coming his way with a look of concentration on his face.

"Oh shite," exclaimed Bunny. Two of the opposition were heading towards Jason from either side, intent on making him the meat in a very unhappy sandwich. Bunny tried to shout something but 'look out you're about to get crushed' was too many words to get out in the time allowed. He only got as far as "Whatchathething—"

The ball reached Jason just before his would-be tacklers. He let it roll onto his hurl and then fell forward, shot-putting the ball high over his shoulders as he did so. As he fell, the two slices of bread slammed into each other in a messy, high-carb, collision.

Bunny watched, mouth gawping, as the ball arched through the air towards the St Mungo's goal. Deccie grabbed onto the sleeve of his coat. "Fucking hell, boss!"

Wayne O'Brien stood in front of the St Mungo's goal, entirely oblivious to the goings on down the pitch. He'd got hold of an orange highlighter from somewhere and he was trying to go for a tricky two-tone design on his boots. The St Mungo's defence, untroubled as they were, had got sucked into watching him work and giving advice. Wayne looked up at the sound of his name being roared to see Bunny and Deccie pointing at the sky.

"What?" he shouted back.

"The ball," screamed Bunny, "the fecking ball!"

Wayne looked up and sighted the ball passing over his head now on its descent. Then his instincts took over. Unfortunately, he did not have the instincts of a hurler, which was why he dropped his hurl, along with the orange highlighter, and he dashed forward towards the St Mungo's goal. The goalie was coming out to meet him, intent on closing down the angle. With a diving lunge, Wayne propelled himself forward, the sliotar meeting the front of his helmet and flying upwards again, arching over the despairing fingertips of the St Mungo's goalie before the two of them collided and tumbled to the ground.

They both watched helplessly as the sliotar dropped, bounced and then, as if in slow motion, trickled towards the St Mungo's goal. The world seemed to stand still as with its very last ounce of momentum it rolled over the line.

The entire St Jude's team erupted into cheering and Bunny realised he was hugging Deccie while they jumped up and down. It wasn't like they hadn't scored a goal before. Back in the golden era when Paul Mulchrone had played for them, they'd been knocking them in for fun. But that felt like a long time ago now.

"Wonderful stuff, lads," hollered Bunny. "Wonderful stuff. That's the spirit! The fightback starts now!"

"Bullshit," screamed Grainger from the far sideline as he stomped onto the field towards the referee. "That's bullshit. You can't score a header in hurling."

"There's no law against it," said the referee.

"Course there is."

"No, there isn't," chimed in Bunny.

Grainger glared across at Bunny. "Shut up, ye fat prick."

"Right," said the referee, "we'll have none of that. Get back to your sideline now or I'll book you for dissent."

"You can't do that."

"Yes, I can. I'm the referee."

"Ah, you're not a proper referee."

"Really?" she said, before shooting her hand into her pocket and producing a yellow card. "Well, this is still a proper card. You're booked!"

Grainger held his hands up. "Whoa, whoa, whoa! Calm down there, love. Can't we have a civilised discussion about the rules?"

"Don't 'love' me," she snapped back. "It's ref or referee."

"Jesus," said Grainger. "Someone's in a mood. That time of the month, is it?"

A weird moment of silence descended upon the field. When the referee spoke again, it was barely above a whisper and yet it carried like a sonic boom across the field. "Excuse me?"

Bunny grabbed Deccie's shoulder. "Pay attention, Deccie. You're about to learn a valuable life lesson."

CHAPTER FOUR

About forty minutes later, Bunny clambered into the front seat of Bertha and slammed the door shut. "Right, lads, who's up for some pizza?"

This was met with a roar of approval from all around him.

"And ice cream?" asked Deccie.

"And ice cream," confirmed Bunny. "I'm a man of my word."

This was met with another roar.

Bunny glanced across at Huey, who was sitting at the other end of the front seat, gripping his bowl as always. "Oh, sorry, Huey, I didn't mean to, y'know …"

"Oh, no," said Huey. "No worries. I just … I mean, can I ask … We didn't actually win the game though, did we?"

Bunny nodded. "That's an excellent question. In fact, pay attention, lads. There are a couple of big life lessons to take away from today" – Bunny held a finger up – "Number one – victory comes in many forms. Sometimes, it's winning a hard-fought battle and doing so with a bit of class. Sometimes it's losing with good grace, especially if the other side are being gobshites about it. And sometimes, and admittedly, this is a bit of a rarer one, but sometimes, victory is having your game abandoned after the referee gives the arsehole in charge of the other team an almighty boot in the bollocks."

This was greeted by another massive cheer. Bunny couldn't help grinning from ear to ear. The memory of seeing Grainger rolling around on the ground was going to warm the cockles of his heart on many a cold night. And it wouldn't just do so for him, young Deccie Fadden having proven that he might just have the instincts to be a war photographer after all, having captured it for posterity. He'd used up an entire disposable camera on it. The shot of Grainger begging for mercy when the referee was being held back by the quickest thinking of the St Mungo's parents would be particularly delightful. It occurred to Bunny that he could pay the no doubt sizeable bill for feeding the entire team fancy pizza if he got a load of copies of those pictures made and sold them around the force. Grainger was not a popular man.

"Which brings me, lads, to important life lesson number two." He held up a second finger. "Now, I assume somebody in school has explained to you what is meant by a lady's 'time of the month'?"

This was met with enough nods that Bunny could choose to interpret it as universal. If not, they'd explain it to one another later on and more or less get the general idea across.

"Right. Good. The big lesson to take away from today is you never ever, ever, ever, bring it up in conversation. I mean ever. This piece of advice should be one of them public service announcement things on the TV, like not trying to get your frisbee out of a power line or the dangers of drowning in a slurry pit. Just, trust me on this; never ever mention it, OK?"

This was met with solemn nods all round.

"Good."

"I have a question," said Deccie.

Bunny sighed. He knew it had been too good to be true. "Go on then."

"What in the hell is a slurry pit?"

"Oh," said Bunny. He hadn't known exactly what he'd expected, but this definitely wasn't it. "It's a thing they have on farms. 'Tis a big container mainly full of animal shite."

"And people drown in that?"

"Yeah, I'm afraid so. There's a case every few years."

Deccie shook his head. "I've said it before, and I'll say it again. People from the country are mental. I mean, why would you go swimming in that in the first place?"

"They don't—" started Bunny before being interrupted by Wayne O'Brien pointing excitedly out the window.

"Boss, boss, boss!"

They all saw where he was pointing. DI Grainger, an ice bag applied to his nether regions, was walking gingerly back to his car.

He looked up at the sound of a detective of his acquaintance pretending to be a bugler, giving a soulful rendition of the 'Last Post' while a minibus full of grinning pre-teens saluted him.

"Oh, piss off!"

CHAPTER FIVE

Bunny wiped a tear from his eye. "All right, c'mon. Stop it now, stop it!"

As he'd suspected, Deccie had clearly spent the majority of the time since their last minibus journey working on his repertoire of fart impressions, and it had not been time spent in vain. Not only that, he'd clearly been paying considerably more attention to current affairs to work on his material, as there were some shrewd political points amidst the gastric fireworks. Bunny guessed most of his audiences didn't get a lot of the references, but the genius of the medium was that even without understanding the nuance, twelve-year-old-boys loved fart noises more than life itself.

"Hang on, boss," said Deccie. "I've got one more."

"Seriously, we're on O'Connell Street now. The pizza place is just up on the corner here. I need to figure out where to park."

"One more. It's a good one."

Bunny shook his head but couldn't help grinning. "All right, one more."

"Grand. This one is a question for you, lads. Who am I?" *Fart* "Oh jaysus, me nuts," *fart* "Oh God, them St Jude's boys ruined me," *fart*.

"Never mention periods." *Fart, fart, fart.* "Oh, that Bunny McGarry is a pain in my arse almost as bad as the one in my bollocks."

Someone behind them honked as Bunny stopped the minibus, unable to trust himself to drive straight. It wasn't the most sophisticated humour in the world, but you could say this for Deccie, he certainly knew his audience. People were falling out of their seats in fits of hysterics. Huey was doubled over with laughter, clutching his bowl hard to his chest.

Someone honked behind them again.

Bunny lowered the window and stuck out a hand to wave them by.

Outside, a light rain had started to fall, adding an additional twist of discomfort to an already bitterly cold Sunday in January. It was nearly lunchtime and town was fairly busy, Sunday shopping now in full flow after the first payday of the new year.

He still had no idea where they were going to park, but ...

Bunny stopped dead. A laugh caught in his throat.

They'd seen each other at exactly the same time. Their eyes locked. What were the odds? Standing there on the far side of O'Connell Street, as real as life itself and twice as ugly, Ian 'Bastard' Hendrix. The granny-robbing scumbag, poised to step into the open driver-side door of a green Peugeot 306, wore an expression of utter shock. There was a roof rack on the top of the car with cases strapped to it. Someone was planning a long trip. In the passenger seat sat Ciara, Ian's girlfriend, who had tearfully sworn on everything under the sun that they were no longer an item. Butch had called that one right enough. Unfortunately, woman's intuition had not been enough to hold her on.

The two men stared at each other; the world frozen around them. "Quiet, lads," hissed Bunny, his hand resting on the door handle. The hubbub only subsided a little. He watched Ian glancing around. They were both doing the same calculations. Could Bunny reach him before Ian was in the car and away?

"Quiet," repeated Bunny. This time, Deccie caught the tone in Bunny's voice and shushed the lads into silence.

He could see Ian and Ciara were having a conversation while Ian kept his eyes firmly on Bunny. He noticed her looking in his direction and then throwing her hands up in the air in exasperation, her *nice young girl led astray* defence having now gone up in flames. Odds on, she was the brains of the outfit, brains having never been something Ian Hendrix had been known for.

Bunny spoke in a low, calm voice. "Everybody double-check your seatbelts and hold on extra tight to anyone who hasn't got one."

"Why ..." started Wayne O'Brien, the rest of his question lost under a collective gasp of shock as Bertha lurched forward. Ian had dived into the driver's seat of the Peugeot. With a squeal of tyres, it took off up O'Connell Street, attracting the attention of passers-by.

"Hold on," roared Bunny as he cut across two lanes of traffic, laying on the horn as he did so. Pedestrians dived out of the way as Bertha mounted the kerb onto the central paved area that divided the two lanes of traffic heading north from the two heading south, causing everyone in the minibus to bounce up in the air. There was an unpleasant scrapping noise as Bertha's undercarriage ground against the stone. With a shuddering thwack, the back wheel mounted the kerb too.

"Sorry," screamed Bunny out the window to the world in general.

"What the hell, boss?" roared Deccie.

"That Peugeot has a very bad man in it."

"And this minibus has a hurling team in it. You're not going to catch him."

The minibus juddered sickeningly as it thumped down onto the south-running side of the street, while the front bumper hit the ground with a screeching protest of metal and a shower of sparks.

"I don't need to catch him," shouted Bunny. "I just need to stay close and Sunday traffic will do the rest. Grab my phone from my coat."

Despite what you see in the movies, running a red light is an activity that rarely goes well. The Peugeot had used its head start to attempt to do just that. Hendrix had struck a Nissan that had been foolish enough to assume a green light meant *go*, and the Peugeot now had to reverse before attempting to weave around the vehicle, its apoplectic driver standing by her car, hands held out in disbelief. Bunny, his own fist still firmly wedged on the horn, wove around the traffic as best he could. They were still too far back. "C'mon, c'mon – he's getting away."

"Who am I ringing?" asked Deccie.

"999 of course."

"Right and—"

"Hang on," screamed Bunny, as, absent any other ideas, he had remounted the central reservation to try to catch up with Hendrix. Every passenger screamed as Bertha's right wheel clanked onto the high kerb. Bunny caught a flash of a hub cap making a break for freedom in his side-view mirror.

"Keep driving like this," hollered Deccie, "and I'd imagine the pigs will be here soon."

"Garda, not pigs," said Bunny through gritted teeth as he jerked the bus left to avoid hitting the pole of a streetlight, leaving them half-on, half-off the paved area, trundling awkwardly alongside the line of traffic, clipping the odd wing mirror as they went. Bunny revved the engine to get the minibus's right wheel over a metal bar that protruded from a bike rack.

The entire minibus yelled in alarm as Bertha begin to tip to the left.

"Shite," roared Bunny, "everybody lean to the right!"

He'd had no idea if that would work, but thankfully, Bertha managed to steady herself. A bloke on a bicycle dived out of their way and Bunny caught sight of the Peugeot up ahead. It had hit a wall of traffic at the lights up on O'Connell Bridge.

"Gardaí please," hollered Deccie into the phone, "and we're probably going to need an ambulance or two as well."

"We've got the prick!" screamed Bunny, now only one block away from their target. They bounced back onto the street again, minus the driver's side wing mirror that had come off much the worse in a collision with the base of a traffic light. On the far side of the bus, there was a scrape of metal as Bertha ruined somebody's paint job. "Sorry," shouted Bunny again.

On the far side of the front seat, Bunny heard Huey throwing up into his bowl. "Better out than in, Huey," said Bunny, not taking his eyes off the prize in front of him. "Better out than in."

Ian Hendrix had now realised he was trapped behind the wall of traffic, because nobody was getting out of his way, no matter how much he honked. A double-decker bus sat to the right of him, further hemming them in. As Bunny headed towards it, the Peugeot was thrown suddenly into reverse. If they could get down Abbey Street, they'd be gone and nothing Bunny could do would stop him.

"O'Connell Street," screamed Deccie into the phone, "there's at least one madman on the loose."

"Oh shite," roared Bunny. "Hang on, lads."

With a crunch of metal, Bertha rammed into the back of the Peugeot. It was like Bunny had told Rían Stark. Speed would only get you so far if your opponent was willing to throw a whole lot of bulk at you. Bertha might not be able to outrun anyone, but the old girl had bulk and a whole lot of momentum. They all lurched forward, and there was a great deal of swearing as Bertha rear-ended the Peugeot into the back of a large van in front of it, wedging it firmly in place.

Bunny turned around in his seat. "Is everybody all right?"

"Are we still getting pizza?" asked Wayne O'Brien from somewhere in the mass of bodies.

Bunny took that as a yes. "Stay here."

He was unbuckled and out of the minibus in time to see Ian Hendrix pulling one of the suitcases down from the roof rack and then making a run for it.

Before he got six feet away, Bunny shoulder charged him into the side of the bus, sending the case flying out of Ian's hand. It walloped against the side of the bus with a jangle. Bunny guessed it contained the valuables from Ian's despicable crime spree that he'd not yet sold. As he landed, Bunny got a brief flash of wide-eyed faces pressed up against the window of the double-decker as they tumbled to the ground. Ian found his feet quickly and his flailing kick caught Bunny square in the stomach, knocking the wind out of him.

He tried to run for it, but Bunny grabbed hold of his left leg and held on for dear life. "Not today, gobshite."

He couldn't see his opponent, but Bunny sensed something in the movement from above that made him instinctively duck away. That was what caused the knife to slice into the shoulder of his jumper instead of his face, where it had been aimed. Bunny reared back and used the side of the bus to regain his feet. Ian Hendrix stood a few feet from him, blood trickling from his forehead, the blade in his right hand and a wild look in his eye. His desire for vengeance having superseded his instinct to run.

"You bastard," he hissed.

"Sorry, Ian. I know you prefer fighting pensioners."

"Come on, Ian!" shouted Ciara, somewhere to Bunny's left. He wasn't sure if she meant that in the 'let's get the hell out of here' or 'get him!' sense of the words, and he certainly didn't have the time to ask.

The thing about fighting someone who has a knife when you don't is that they're thrilled about the knife bit. Like how when you've got a hammer, everything is a nail. When you've got a knife, everything is something you can stick a knife into. That meant as the non-knife-wielder, you just had to worry about the knife, whereas they had to worry about every bit of you. Only, they probably weren't worried enough due to the aforementioned knife-based confidence. This was why when Bunny feinted towards the blade, Ian bought it hook, line and sinker and lunged forward to stab him, getting the sole of Bunny's left boot smashed into the side of his right kneecap for his trouble. As Ian crumpled to the ground with a wail of anguish, Bunny's right fist came around and caught him sweetly on the jaw, sending him sprawling sideways.

All-in-all, it was going surprisingly well. Too well. Bunny caught the flash of movement from the corner of his eye, but by then it was too late. Stupid. He'd been so shocked to see Ian, he'd not clocked the other guy sitting in the back seat. It must have taken him a while to extricate himself from the back of the Peugeot thanks to it being a three-door, but now he had, he'd caught Bunny cold. Something hard and heavy smashed into the back of Bunny's head, and the world lurched nauseatingly out of focus. He stumbled into the side of the double-decker and then dropped to the ground.

His vision came back into focus for a moment, and he looked up to see a big man he'd never seen before standing over him. They had wondered if Ian had an accomplice. He had a shaven-head and was wearing a dark-green bomber jacket. As he raised something over his head, Bunny started to black out.

The last thing he heard before he lost consciousness was a surprised yelp.

CHAPTER SIX

"Bunny," said a soft voice. "Bunny. Wake up. C'mon, wakey wakey ..."

He turned his head, unwilling to leave the soft embrace of sleep just yet.

When the voice spoke again, it was in a lower, less kindly register. "Cork is a shithole."

His eyes flew open to see Detective Pamela 'Butch' Cassidy smiling down at him.

Bunny coughed and then spoke. "Ara, just my luck – I get to heaven and all the angels are lesbians."

"You seriously think you're going to heaven?"

"Well, if you qualify as an angel, anything is possible."

Bunny put a hand to his head and confirmed that there was a large bandage wrapped around it. "Jaysus, who hit me?"

"Would you believe some big sod with a tyre iron?"

"I would, I ..." Bunny tried to sit up as his recollection cleared. "The lads!"

"Relax," said Butch, placing a placatory hand on his shoulder. "Everyone is OK. Well, at least everyone you like. Ian Hendrix and his amigos aren't that OK at all."

Bunny continued to sit up and Butch took a moment to assist him, moving the pillows to support him. He took in his surroundings for the first time. He was in a private room and judging by the view out the window, he reckoned this was the Mater Hospital. "How long have I been out for?"

"It's Monday afternoon."

"God, really?"

"Ah, you're always saying you don't sleep so well. Think of this as a nice lie-in and you didn't even have to get drunk to achieve it."

"Still got the hangover, though." Bunny smacked his dry lips. "My mouth's like the Sahara."

Butch picked up a glass of water from the bedside cabinet and held it in front of him, straw out. He took a sip.

"Ta."

"Happy to serve"

"I still don't understand what happened," said Bunny.

"How much do you remember?" asked Butch.

"We were on O'Connell Street, after playing the game against St Mungo's ..." His eyes lit up. "Did you hear—"

"About Grainger's testicular encounter with authority? Yes, everyone has heard about that. He wanted to press charges, but I believe the commissioner told him to cop himself on and stop attempting to be an even bigger embarrassment to the force than he already is."

"Glad to hear it," said Bunny. "So, I was on O'Connell Street and then, by pure fluke, who do I see but Ian 'Bastard' Hendrix. We spent the last two weeks doing everything we can to find the little shite with no success, and then he just appears right in front of me as if by magic. I couldn't believe it."

"I'd imagine he couldn't either. It's always the way, though. How many serial killers have been caught because of a broken light on a car or an innocuous coincidence? It'd almost make me believe in God."

"To be fair, if this was God, next time I hope he drops something like this in my lap when I'm not driving a minibus full of kids." Bunny winced. "Christ, I can't believe I actually gave chase."

Butch waved a hand dismissively. "Ah, kids love a bit of excitement. Imagine how much they're going to enjoy telling this story for the rest of their lives. You can't buy something like that."

"And they're ...?"

Butch could see where his mind was heading. "Again. Absolutely fine. Not a scratch on them, which is more than can be said for your minibus, I'm afraid."

"Ah, crap."

"I've some good news on that front. He doesn't want it known, but the commish has told the garage boys to sort it out for you."

"Really?"

"Yeah, I guess he reckons he owes you one after a couple of your recent adventures. So, you managed to chase old Ian boy down?"

"I did," confirmed Bunny, "and then ... Well, I think I took him down, but things get a little hazy from there." He noticed Butch's wide grin. "What?"

"Well, as luck would have it, I can fill in the gaps for you from that point as" – she reached into the pocket of her coat and pulled out a pile of photographs – "the whole encounter was captured for posterity by a promising young photographer."

"You're kidding?"

"Nope. Deccie might have found his calling. These are copies, obviously – the originals are in evidence, and I'd imagine several other copies will be doing the rounds for years to come." She began handing Bunny pictures. "There's you tackling Mr Hendrix into the side of the bus. There's the two of you scrapping on the ground. Oh, by the way, worth keeping an eye on the old one there on the bus in the blue anorak. Everyone else is gawping out the window in every picture and, swear to God, she just keeps looking at her watch, like 'Bergerac is on the telly in twenty minutes, can we move this along?'"

Bunny looked at the picture. It was weird seeing himself fighting somebody like this. Butch handed him the next picture. "Here's Ian, the naughty little scamp, pulling a knife on you. Here's you booting him in the knee. Excellent action shot that one ... You're about to throw a dig into his jaw in this one. And there's him lying on the ground. Deccie himself was bitterly disappointed at not getting a snap of the punch landing, but you can't have everything ..." Butch handed him another photo. "Here's that prick in the bomber jacket running in to blindside you. Gary Nolan, by the way, from Tallaght. He's already been inside for assault and he's a proper scumbag. No idea how he and Ian even know each other. There must be some website where arseholes can connect with their soulmates." Butch said nothing as she handed him the next picture. It was of himself pitching forward, having been blindsided with a vicious blow from a tyre iron to the back of the head.

"God," said Bunny, "he could have killed me."

"I know," Butch replied. "Luckily, he hit you on your head, which, as we all know, is thicker than concrete. Speaking as your partner, though, this is why you're supposed to stick to law enforcement while on the job. You don't do well without adult supervision."

"Fair point."

"Anyway, here's the prick standing over you with a tyre iron, and you're about to get your name on a plaque on the wall. And here comes the cavalry ..."

Nolan, the guy in the bomber jacket spun around in shock when the first hurly hit him, but, as the sequence of photos revealed, he quickly crumbled under the sustained assault of a pack of pre-teen, hurly wielding maniacs literally falling over each other to wallop him. It was notable that when he hit the ground, they did not stop. In fact, Ian Hendrix's attempt to limp away in the confusion meant he got in on the action too.

"Jesus," said Bunny. "They're like wild animals. Believe you me, they've never shown this level of teamwork previously."

"Yeah. My favourite is the next one. This is the shot of shots. Ciara, the conniving little witch, tried to grab the suitcase of loot and run." She handed Bunny another photograph.

"Is that ...?"

Butch giggled. "What I am reliably informed is a bowl of warm sick being hurled over her. By all accounts, she did not take it well. There're a few more ..."

Butch handed him a quick sequence of photos. In them, the angle changed as it got closer to the prime figures of Nolan and Hendrix on the ground, both now balled up to protect themselves.

Neither Butch nor Bunny said anything. That way, neither of them had to admit that this was Deccie clearly taking the opportunity to put the literal boot in on both men. The last few shoots were of gardaí in uniform, turning up and dragging wild-eyed hurlers off their opponents.

"The first guards on the scene had a bit of a time of it getting your boys to lower their weapons. They also all wanted to go in the ambulance with you."

Bunny didn't know what to say to that.

"That's the end of it," said Butch, taking the pile of photos back out of his hands.

"Wow. That's … that's quite something."

"Yeah, it's going to make one hell of a flip book."

"The lads aren't going to get into trouble, are they?"

Butch shook her head. "Nah, the dynamic duo got off with way fewer injuries than they deserve. Besides, these pricks put helpless pensioners in the hospital. No defence lawyer in the country is going to be pushing the boat out to get them off. They're going to get the shittiest of shitty deals, and then when they're in prison, well, we all know how nutters feel about their grannies."

"So, all's well that ends well."

"Oh no," said Butch. "You're not getting off that easy. Are you feeling up to visitors?"

"I suppose," said Bunny.

"Good," said Butch, standing up and heading over to the door, "because much to the annoyance of the matron, you've got eighteen of them." She opened the door. "You can—" before she could finish the sentence, the entire St Jude's Under-12s hurling team rushed into the room, led by their assistant manager.

They all spoke at once. "Are you all right, boss? How's the head? Did you brain leak out? We beat the crap out of them fella, did ye see? Huey says he reckons his travel sickness is cured now. Can we beat up some more people?"

Bunny held his hands up. "Lads, lads, lads – a bit of quiet, please. 'Tis great to see you all. I'm grand. Thanks for popping in to see me and for, y'know, helping out yesterday."

"Those were exactly the kind of tactics I've been saying we should use," said Deccie.

"Well, we're not. So don't go getting any ideas. Should you lot not all be in school?"

"It's five o'clock," said Donnacha.

"Oh right. Well, doing homework then?"

"We didn't get any homework," added Colm Doyle. "Not even maths."

"Yeah," said Wayne, "we're heroes now. We've been in the paper and everything."

Bunny looked at Butch. "Really?"

"It's fine," she said. "It got some very sympathetic reporting."

"The lady called us plucky," said Huey.

"Well," replied Bunny, "you've been called worse. And ..." He stopped. "What's that smell?"

He noticed the sea of grins looking back at him and then Deccie, as elected spokesman, spoke up. "Well, a promise is a promise, and it turns out they deliver." He raised his voice and turned to the door. "You can come in now."

The door opened and two smiling nurses came in carrying large piles of pizza boxes, cheered on by the team.

Chaos ensued as the boxes were grabbed and then traded and squabbled over. Butch looked down at Bunny. "The lads down the station all chipped in."

"Thank them for me."

"Do you want a slice?"

Bunny shook his head and smiled. "Nah, I'm all right. This is good for me, though."

"Oh," said Butch, raising her voice, "speaking of which ... Are you forgetting something, lads?"

Rían Stark froze, a slice of pizza halfway into his mouth. "She's not asking us to pray or wash our hands or some shite like that, is she?"

"No," said Butch, nodding her head towards the door, "the other thing."

"Oh right," said Deccie, dropping his pizza box on Bunny's bed. "Donnacha, go get it."

Donnacha nodded and headed back out the door.

Deccie raised himself up to his full height. "We wanted to get you a present for, y'know, stuff, and Donnacha's auntie works in that big shop in town, and she got us a really good deal."

Donnacha pushed back through the door, now carrying an A1-sized frame.

"It's something to remember us by," said Colm Doyle.

"And if I do say so myself," added Deccie, "my finest piece of work to date."

With a slightly awkward flourish, Donnacha turned the large frame around and held it above his head to reveal a picture. They all cheered.

Bunny laughed so hard his head hurt.

There before him was a magnificent shot of DI Grainger getting booted in the knackers by a referee who had taken just about enough of his crap.

Eventually, Bunny wiped his eyes and regained the power of speech. "'Tis perfect, lads. Just perfect."

BLOODY CHRISTMAS

ONE OF THE WEIRDEST THINGS I'VE DISCOVERED ABOUT MYSELF
THROUGH WRITING BOOKS IS THAT I'M APPARENTLY WEIRDLY
OBSESSED WITH CHRISTMAS. YOU WOULDN'T KNOW IT FROM THE
FACT I PUT THE TREE UP ON DECEMBER 24TH LAST YEAR, BUT,
FOR SOME REASON, IT IS MY FAVOURITE TIME OF YEAR TO SET A
STORY. THIS ONE, I THINK, STARTED AS JUST THAT, BUT ODDLY
THERE IS A REVELATION AT THE END THAT I HONESTLY DIDN'T
KNOW WAS GOING TO HAPPEN UNTIL I WROTE IT.

IT IS A STANDALONE STORY BUT FOR CONTINUITY BUFFS, IT
HAPPENS DIRECTLY AFTER A MAN WITH ONE OF THOSE FACES.

DUCK SOUP

Bunny stared hard at the wall. "Can I ask a question?"

"Of course," replied Dr Warwick in that tone of voice that Bunny guessed he practised a lot. The one he no doubt thought made him sound calm yet authoritative and not at all like a smug gobshite with a highly slappable face.

"This wallpaper you've got, is it one of them what-cha-me-call-its ... rickshaw tests?"

"Do you mean Rorschach tests?" asked Warwick.

"Yeah. One of them."

"No, it's just wallpaper."

"Oh right. Did you choose it?"

"As it happens, I did."

"Were there many other options?"

Dr Warwick turned and glanced back at it. "I vaguely recall there being a catalogue."

"Right. And you thought you'd go with this one?"

"Am I to assume that you don't like the wallpaper?"

"It's not for me to say. I mean have ye not noticed at all that the pattern looks a bit y'know ..."

"Like what?"

"Like a lady's downstairs bits, only on fire."

Warwick puckered his lips tightly together. Bunny guessed that unlike the 'psychiatrist voice', he probably hadn't practised that facial expression – not unless he was attempting to mimic a cat's rear end. "I don't ..." he stopped and looked at the wall to his left. He tilted his head slightly. "Well, I didn't see that but now you mention it, I suppose you could see that if you chose to. Nobody has ever mentioned it before."

"Far be it from me to tell you how to do your job there doc, but it seems like a very distracting thing to have on the walls of a psychiatrist's office."

Dr Warwick shifted in his seat. "Well, like I said, nobody has noticed it before."

"Or maybe they have noticed it, and just not mentioned it. Imagine how many people didn't want to say it for y'know, obvious reasons. Think how many poor souls have left this office and got straight on the phone. 'How'd it go?' 'The dude has flaming fannies on his walls. He's mental!' Have you had a problem with patients not coming back for a second session?"

Dr Warwick looked again at the wallpaper and then pointedly didn't look at the wallpaper. Instead, he fixed Bunny with what he considered a penetrative stare. It was surprising he thought this might work, given that he had on his desk a rather thick folder, which contained the career of Detective Sergeant Bernard 'Bunny' McGarry up to this point. His body of work could be interpreted a lot of different ways, but nobody could read that file and come away with the impression that they were sitting across from a man who could be easily intimidated.

The psychiatrist gave what, at a push, might be described as a smile. "Anyway Bernard, you didn't come here today to discuss my interior design choices, did you?"

"My name is Bunny and if we have to discuss something, it might as well be that. Isn't that a picture of Sigmund Freud?"

Warwick gave a laugh devoid of any humour. "Careful. Your mask is slipping."

"How's that doc?"

"You pretend to be this big, loud, simple-minded fool who thinks a Rorschach Test is called a rickshaw test and yet you just correctly identified a picture of Sigmund Freud."

Bunny shrugged. "It might have been a lucky guess."

"I'm a psychiatrist, Bernard. I don't believe in coincidences or guesses."

"Which does rather bring us back to the combustible vaginas."

"This is the third session we've had and I have to say, I don't think you are taking them seriously, Bernard."

"Bunny."

"I'd rather not call you that."

"I'd rather not be here."

"Why don't you like the name you were christened with?"

Bunny rolled his eyes. "Here we go. Nice one doc. You've found another subtle way to get back onto the subject of my parents. Again. You're quite the conversational ninja."

Dr Warwick flicked a non-existent bit of lint from the leg of his suit. The crease in his trousers looked like it could be used to cut cheese. Bunny in contrast, was in jeans and a cardigan. He hadn't dressed to impress.

"Would you say you have a problem with authority?"

"No," said Bunny. "I wouldn't."

"Really? Because a matter of a few weeks ago, you threw the second-highest ranking member of the Garda Síochána off a balcony."

"Allegedly."

"Are you claiming it didn't happen?"

"Oh no, it definitely happened alright. Still, the lawyer the Garda Representative Association got me said I have to keep saying allegedly and him, I'm prepared to listen to."

A flash in his eyes indicated that Dr Warwick had not missed the not very subtle dig. "And still, you believe you don't have a problem with authority?"

"I didn't say that. I said, I wouldn't say I had a problem with authority because us coppers, we're trained to spot an incriminating statement like that from a long way off, and that one was visible from space."

"You're not on trial here, Bernard."

"Bunny. And yes I am, or is the purpose of this meeting not for you to assess my fitness to go back on active duty?"

Dr Warwick sighed. "The purpose of all three of the sessions we've had is to make sure that you are OK."

"Bollocks."

Warwick sat back. "I'm sorry you feel that way. You've been through a lot. I mean, you were shot."

"Twas only a flesh wound. Some proper doctors sorted that right out. Healing grand. Barely feel it."

"But that is only the physical wound."

"Ara c'mon doc, are we really going to keep pretending that this is about me?"

"There's nobody else here, Bernard."

"Bunny, and my parents aren't here either, but you'd like to make it about them. Don't shit a shitter. The higher-ups aren't wild about me returning to work because, while Assistant Commissioner Fintan O'Rourke was as dodgy as a three euro note, he was still one of the chosen and having me knocking about is an unhappy reminder of a rather big embarrassment for the force. 'Tis classic Garda logic – we take a PR black eye when it comes out that the second most powerful peaked cap in the country has been in the pocket of the self-styled godfather of Irish crime, Gerry Fallon, for several decades, and the solution is to shoot the messenger."

"Do you not see how paranoid you sound Bernard?"

"Bunny, and paranoid my hole. Enough people have tried to get rid of me in my life that I know what it feels like."

Warwick leaned forward, a look of excitement in his eyes. "Ah, now that's interesting. I think we've just had a breakthrough here. Talk about that more. This feeling that people have been trying to get rid of you throughout your life."

Bunny leaned back in his chair and blew a large raspberry at the ceiling.

"Bunny?"

"Bernard."

"But … you said you wanted me to call you Bunny."

He looked down and glowered at Dr Warwick. "I did, but I don't like how you say it, so let's go back to Bernard. In fact, feck all that – it's Detective Sergeant McGarry to you. I worked damn hard for that and you aren't taking it away from me." He jabbed a finger at the floor and then at the window. "Either in here or out there."

Warwick sat back. "I'm not trying to do that."

"Really?" said Bunny, fixing Warwick with the patented McGarry stare. "This is why I'm sick of this, because we both know that everybody here is lying."

"Why do you—" Warwick was stopped by Bunny's raised hand.

"Please. Spare me. In fact, to move this along, let's recap some pertinent information, shall we? Assistant Commissioner O'Rourke had his little fall because it was the only way I could get to the truth. He was helping Fallon get rid of two friends of mine and I did what needed to be done to protect the innocent – which is after all, my job. The problem is that everything that happened along the way left Gerry Fallon in a coma. O'Rourke should be looking at a life behind bars for his part in it all but they can't prosecute him until Fallon actually wakes up, which the awkward dipshit is stubbornly refusing to do. Which leaves you and me sitting here on Christmas Eve surrounded by flaming fannies. The higher ups would like me to take retirement and quietly disappear, which is why they keep sending me to you. The GRA says that they've no justification for repeatedly doing that unless you find me unfit. The thing is, doc, you aren't going to find me unfit."

Warwick bristled. "Really? And why not?"

"Because then I'm no good as a witness against O'Rourke or Fallon if it ever comes to court, as his legal eagles will point to me being found a few bricks short of a bungalow and get my testimony thrown out. So you've got a form somewhere in that file on your desk with two boxes on it – crazy and not crazy, and we both know you aren't allowed to tick one of 'em. So tick the other one and then we can both get on with the rest of our lives."

Warwick glanced up at the clock on the wall. "Am I to take it that you wish to terminate this session Bernard?"

"Ha. Nice try but no, I don't. Can't have you going back and saying I walked out now, can we? So I'm here until 11am and I won't be leaving a second earlier."

Warwick made the mistake of trying to lock eyes with Bunny McGarry. He was met with a look that had greeted hundreds of other men who had similarly held the mistaken belief that they had the upper hand. After a long moment Warwick looked away, subconsciously looking at the wallpaper that he would spend the entire Christmas break obsessing over before getting the whole room redecorated in the first week of January. "So what would you like to talk about?"

Bunny smiled broadly. "I spy with my little eye, something beginning with... O."

FINGER FOOD

Tara Flynn looked nervously at the tables lining the wall. Vol-au-vents – what the hell did she know about vol-au-vents? They were a ridiculous food. They were like pies for posh people. There were over a hundred of the buggers with various fillings. Then there were the mince pies and sausages on sticks. There were also these mini vegetarian kebabs which, to her uncultured eye, looked a lot like any old bit of veg shoved on a long toothpick. She was discovering she really hated finger food. It was this kind of nonsense that had previously prevented her from allowing O'Hagan's to be rented out for events.

She had agreed with Mrs O'Hagan, the widow of the original landlord, to take an ownership stake in the pub two years ago with a view to eventually buying her out entirely, something she had kept very quiet. She didn't want the regulars to know – she told herself it was because she didn't want them trying it on to get free drinks but in reality, she felt much more comfortable seeing herself as one of the workers. Being part of the ownership made her feel uncomfortable in ways she couldn't properly explain even to herself, hence she avoided having the conversation with other people. She'd invested her life's savings in this pub and now all of a sudden everything was her problem. She'd been the manager for most of her adult life and really, they'd always been her problems but now, she felt somehow more responsible. It didn't help that just after she'd sunk her nest egg into the place, they'd opened up two flashy mega pubs on the opposite side of the street and suddenly O'Hagan's was in danger of slipping from old world charm to just looking old. This was why she'd committed to trying to improve the place.

"Shittin' Santa on a shiny sled!"

"Jesus!" Torn from her thoughts, Tara spun around. "Oh, it's you."

Bunny waved an expansive hand. "I was only dropping in for a quick one. There was no need to go to this trouble."

"You're hilarious. Did you not see the sign outside?"

Bunny held up the A4 piece of paper that had previously been stuck to the door. 'Closed for private event'. "I took it down. I assumed somebody was taking the piss."

Tara snatched it out of his hand. "For Christ's sake."

"What?" said Bunny, all indignation. "Since when has this place closed for private events?"

"Since now," said Tara, walking over to put the sign back up.

"So I can't get a drink?"

"There are other pubs y'know Bunny."

She turned to look at him. It really shouldn't be possible for a man of his size, age and, most of all, reputation to pull off the wounded puppy look but there he was, all mooning eyes and hurt feelings. "This is my local."

Tara softened her tone. "You don't actually live anywhere near here."

"But this is ... I've been ... where else am I supposed to go?"

"Oh give over Tiny Tim," said Tara, moving behind the bar. "Of course you can have a pint." She started pouring the Guinness through force of habit. "Arthur?"

"Yes please," said Bunny. "And chase him with his good friend Jack Daniels. Some of the fancy stuff."

"Jesus," said Tara. "I know it's Christmas but it's also just gone eleven. Go easy."

"What? I'm celebrating! I have in my possession a piece of paper that certifies that I am 100% grade-A not mental."

Tara expertly killed the pint dead at exactly the top of the harp. "Seriously? Can I get a copy to hang over the bar? It'd be quite the conversation piece. Is this like that newspaper headline Barry got for his birthday saying he'd scored a hat trick for Ireland?"

Bunny slid onto his stool, the one that at least metaphorically had a groove worn into it by his arse. "No, tis genuine. From an honest to goodness head doctor."

Tara expertly pressed a glass to the optic to dispense a shot of Jack while never breaking eye contact with Bunny, then gave him an unasked for double. "Does this mean you're going back on active duty?"

"It does indeed."

She put the glass down. "Thank fuck for that."

"Excuse me?"

"I mean, no offence, but having you moping around in here every day looking like a spare willy at a lesbian convention, it was getting a bit depressing." She began topping up the Guinness.

"Thanks very much." Bunny nodded over at the table. "Besides, it looks like you're taking the pub in a new direction. Like, no longer being a pub."

The pint, poured to perfection, was then disturbed by being slammed down onto the counter slightly too hard, causing it to spill over the lip. "Ah shut up. You were all going on about the gents being crap for ages so I got it re-done. How do you think I'm paying for that? Dyson Airblade hand dryers are expensive y'know."

"How expensive?"

"Expensive enough that Richie is now banned until the new year."

Bunny gave a lopsided grin. "So he—"

"Yes," interrupted Tara. "Despite being expressly forbidden from doing so, he took Barry up on his bet and put his you-know-what into my brand new Dyson Airblade."

"The animal," said Bunny, shaking his head. "Out of curiosity, did he say what—"

"I'm really not in the mood," said Tara, slapping a rag down and aggressively cleaning the already clean counter. "I'm trying to improve this place and you shower of dipshits do stuff like that."

Bunny held his hands up. "Sorry. You alright Tara? You don't seem yourself."

Tara stopped scrubbing and took a deep breath. "Yeah, I'm ... sorry, I'm a bit stressed. We had a lot of bills coming in so when this guy from some place called Cleverly Financials—"

"What's that?"

Tara shrugged. "Some kind of brokerage, whatever the hell that is. This wanker banker in a flash suit came in and asked to take the place over for Christmas Eve. He offered a lot of money and ..."

Bunny took a sip of his drink. "Fair enough. I'll get out of the way. No problem."

Tara shook her head. "Nah, it's not that. I only took two hundred euros as deposit and I've spent three grand on the fecking food. He wanted all the best for two hundred people. I should've asked for all the money up front."

Bunny nodded. "'Tis a great-looking spread though."

"Yeah," said Tara. "Well, you might have to eat it. I've been trying to get hold of this Donal bloke for three days and I'm pretty sure he's dodging my calls."

"Oh."

"Yeah," said Tara. She looked up at the clock. "They're supposed to be in here in an hour and I've closed the whole place down."

"I'm sure it'll be grand," said Bunny.

"I hope you're right. They wanted a free bar and everything. I've got Janice and Ricardo coming in to work, on double time too."

Bunny lowered his voice. "Seeing as you're not open though ..." rather than finishing the sentence, he nodded in the direction of the far side of the bar, where an Asian couple sat in one of the booths. The woman looked heavily pregnant, her hands held to her stomach, her long black hair looking slightly dishevelled. The man, through the thickest glasses Bunny had ever seen, looked only at his wife and spoke softly. She in turn, looked nervously at Bunny and Tara. Bunny was no expert, but he was almost certain they were speaking in Mandarin. He spent a lot of time in a certain Chinese takeaway.

Tara gave the couple a little wave and spoke out of the side of her mouth.

"They came in fifteen minutes ago. I don't think they've much English and they obviously pay no more attention to signs than you do."

"Did you not tell them—"

"Of course I did, but they just kept nodding and smiling. What was I supposed to do?" Tara went back to scrubbing the counter aggressively. "It's Christmas Eve and I literally run an inn. I'm not religious but even I don't want to be the bitch telling the pregnant couple that there's no room. We've heard that story before."

"D'ye know," said Bunny, after taking a slow appreciative sup of his pint, "Some astrologer figured out it was on the 17th of June that Jesus was born because the star of Bethlehem was probably Venus and Jupiter coming together."

"Thanks," said Tara. "I'll explain that to them when I have to chuck them out on the street when the shower of financial fuckwits show up. And FYI, you mean astronomer not astrologer."

"Do I?"

"Ye do. Astrologer is all that star sign nonsense."

"Are you sure?"

"I am," said Tara. "The fight it caused is the reason we stopped having a table quiz."

"I thought that was because of who invented the light bulb?"

"No, that's the reason we no longer have a quiz machine. The clientele of this pub take trivia knowledge far too bleedin' seriously."

Bunny nodded as he finished off his pint. "Ye might well have a point there," He nodded up at a sign behind the bar. "Is that new?"

Tara looked up at the 'Absolutely no mistletoe allowed' sign.

"I put it up last week. I'm not having it. Pissed idiots going around thinking vegetation entitles them to force women to kiss them. Not on my watch."

"Fair enough."

"The next fella who tries to explain how it is a festive tradition is getting a boot right in his Brussels sprouts I can tell you. I'm so sick of it. Have you ever noticed how it is almost always men who are banging on about tradition? That's because the world used to be set up exactly how they like it and things changing doesn't suit them. That's all tradition is: people having no other justification for the stupid way things are done."

Bunny wiped his hand across his lips, belched quietly and picked up his whiskey. "I'll drink to that."

Tara nodded. "You'd drink to anything."

"As a documented one hundred per cent sane individual, I resent that remark. Will you have one yourself?"

Tara shook her head. "No thanks."

Bunny lowered the glass and his voice. "Actually, I've been meaning to ask – how's everything with yourself and Dervla?"

Tara rolled her eyes. "I'm already having a bad day, let's not get into my love life please."

"Fair enough. If you ever need to talk."

Tara patted Bunny's hand. "I appreciate it. Don't tell the other idiots, but you're my favourite. And I'm glad you're back on active duty, this town needs a sheriff."

Bunny raised his glass. "Now that, I'm definitely drinking to!"

A WEE PROBLEM

Bunny pushed open the door to the gents, whistling contentedly to himself as he entered. It was a good day. He had sunk a couple of pints with chasers, but he was right to be celebrating. He was back on active duty. Soon, he'd be doing the one and only thing he was good at. The thing he'd say he was put on this earth to do, if he was ever inclined to speak in such terms.

As he walked over to the old Victorian style urinals, he glanced at the Dyson Airblade sitting beside the sinks and shook his head. "What you've been through, ye poor thing."

As he unzipped and began doing the necessary, Bunny read the newspaper clipping of a match report from the 1965 All-Ireland final that was framed above the urinals, screwed firmly to the wall. He'd won a bet last month with Gary when he had been able to correctly recite the entire article word for word. O'Hagan's had been Bunny's favourite watering hole for a long time and he used the same urinal on the left whenever possible. On every visit he habitually read the article, as there was nowhere else to look, assuming he wasn't so drunk that he needed to use visual guidance down below. Bunny strongly disapproved of people reading their phones while taking a leak. It was firstly rude and secondly, it looked like you were taking a picture of yourself. He was aware that younger lads and even more tragically, some older lads, felt that the height of modern romance was sending a picture of your tackle to a lady, but he found the idea horrific. Bar anything else, he'd never considered that to be an attractive bit of kit. It looked like something you'd find in a butcher's bin. If that made the top five list of your best features, then you needed to take a night class or learn to juggle or something, because you were not much of a catch.

Bunny heard the door swing open behind him, just as he was reading the paragraph about what was described as 'a disturbance in the crowd' – which Bunny had always suspected was code for the first ever streaker at an All-Ireland final. That was how you showed off the goods before the dick pic was invented.

A throat was cleared behind him and then a voice he didn't recognise spoke hesitantly. "Excuse me." The accent was unusual to Bunny, not Romanian or Polish, which you'd hear quite a lot in Dublin. It was obviously 'Joseph' from the couple as there was no other male in the building. "Are you ... Bunny McGarry?" He said the word Bunny like someone who had been assured it really was a name but still didn't quite believe it.

"Yep, that's me." Bunny waved his free hand without turning around. "I can't sign any autographs at the minute, I'm a tad busy."

At a small noise, Bunny's whole body tensed and the smile fell from his lips. He had been told once that stopping yourself mid-pee was dangerous. Mind you, he'd been told that by a heart specialist who he had been arresting after the good doctor had drunkenly stopped his Jag in traffic to take a leak, so the source of the advice was suspect. Still, Bunny did not have a choice. His entire body had tensed up as soon as he'd heard the sound. It was a click. It could have been a lot of things, but it wasn't. What it was, was the hammer on a gun being pulled back.

"I am sorry," said the voice that sounded like it meant it.

"Hang on, hang on." Bunny slowly shuffled himself around, putting his free right hand in the air.

He was confronted by what he'd expected. The man from the

couple, Joseph, stood a few feet away from him, holding a large gun in his shaking hand. It was a .44 Magnum, à la Dirty Harry, or at least some kind of knockoff of it. Revolvers weren't that common in this day and age. Bunny looked at the tip of the gun's barrel and then focused his attention on the face behind it.

"Well," said Bunny. "If nothing else, this is fairly conclusive proof about whether or not I'm paranoid."

The man didn't say anything, just licked his lips. His thick glasses made his eyes look massive but even without the effect, Bunny reckoned they would've been wide with terror. It was odd to say given the circumstances but Bunny felt like he was the least nervous person in the room. "You don't want to do this." It wasn't a question.

"I ... I must ..."

"I don't even know you," said Bunny.

"My son."

Bunny lowered his free hand and instead held it out in a placatory gesture. "Look, whatever this is fella, we can work it out. Somebody is putting you up to this."

"Yes, I ..." the man stopped, blinked a few times and then moved his grip on the gun. "No, I must ... I must." He took a deep breath.

"Hang on, hang on, hang on."

Last year, Tara had got the friend of a friend in to sort out some issues with the plumbing in the ladies' loos. There had been what was described as 'an intermittent flushing problem'. The fix had come with a peculiar side-effect where the cisterns in the gents occasionally released large air bubbles, which resulted in loud plopping noises. They were odd but nothing more than that. In fact, the regulars took turns making the hilarious joke of apologising for them and laying the blame on whatever they'd had for lunch that day. As it turned out, as well as being the basis for a banal running joke, the noise was just enough to cause a terrified man holding a gun to flinch and look in its direction.

Bunny's right hand grabbed at the gun as his left, released from todger wrangling duty, delivered an uppercut, resulting in Joseph's glasses flying across the Gents as his head snapped back. The first thing you learn about grabbing a gun is to do it in such a way that the business end is not left pointing at you, because if you don't, odds on you'll never get to learn the second thing. The gun jumped as it went off, the vibration passing up through Bunny's arm, even as the bullet passed harmlessly away from him. Bunny followed through with an elbow into his attacker's face that sent him sprawling backwards, releasing the gun as he did so. Bunny turned it around and used it to cover the man. He squinted up in Bunny's general direction.

Then, the man pulled his legs away.

"Oh Jesus," said Bunny. "Sorry about that. I mean, I know you were trying to kill me and all, but I didn't mean to pee on your leg. Twas a muscle tension release thing."

The man started crying. Bunny didn't consider himself a proud man but he felt he probably warranted a more impressive hired killer than this one appeared to be.

"Ah there now, less of that."

Now that his heart rate was slowing from speed metal to samba, Bunny became more aware of his surroundings. In particular a new sizzling sound. He turned to look in its direction to see a Dyson hand dryer that had taken a centre mass shot it looked very unlikely to recover from.

Bunny looked down at the weeping man lying on the floor in front of him. "Fuck me, you are properly in trouble now."

The door flew open and Bunny flinched away as a screaming Tara came hurtling through with a baseball bat over her head. Bunny threw a hand out. "Easy there Boudicca!"

Tara stopped the bat still held over her head. "What the actual fuck?"

"Fair question."

Tara looked down at Joseph. "What did he do?"

"He pulled a gun on me."

"He tried to rob you?" The incredulity was rich in her voice.

"No, I think he was sent here to kill me."

The door then flew open again and the heavily pregnant 'Mary' barged through it, terror in her eyes. "No, no, please!"

"Oh Jesus," said Tara.

The couple had a rapid-fire conversation in Mandarin before Mary turned to Bunny. "Please, he have no choice. Our son. They have our son."

"Who?" said Bunny.

"Men," said the woman, her face a mix of frustration and terror. "Men," she repeated. "I don't know who they are. They don't ... they have our son." She blessed herself and looked to the sky, the words rattling out of her recognisable as a raised prayer in any language.

"Bunny," said Tara. "What in the hell is going on?"

He looked from Tara to Mary to Joseph and then he pointed the gun inoffensively towards the roof. "I'm not sure. I don't know what this is all about but I know a terrified mother when I see one." He raised his voice, in the move used by English speakers everywhere to make themselves understood to foreigners. "Alright, I'm going to put the gun away." He slowly put the gun into his coat pocket. "All friends here. Let's get your fella here cleaned up and we can sort all of this out." Bunny reached down a hand to help him up.

Joseph apprehensively took it and gingerly got to his feet. Mary embraced him and the two spoke in hushed voices.

"Bunny," said Tara.

"'Tis alright, I know what I'm doing."

"Yeah, I'm sure you do. I was just going to say ..."

"What?"

Tara averted her eyes and nodded towards Bunny's belt buckle area with a wince. "Ye might want to put that away too."

Bunny glanced down. "Oh right. Good point." He tucked himself away. "Sorry about that."

"Yeah, don't worry about it. It's always good to get my lesbianism refreshed from time to time."

"Here now, no call to be hurtful."

Mary and Joseph flinched as Tara suddenly raised her voice. "Bollocks!"

"What?" said Bunny. "They're not even out." He stopped talking as he followed Tara's eyes. "Oh yeah, that. I'm afraid Corporal Dyson took one for the team there."

Tara pulled in a deep breath, turned and stomped back through the swinging door.

The couple looked at the door and then back at Bunny.

"Don't worry about it."

This time they all flinched as Tara's roar came from within the bar. "Merry Fucking Christmas!"

A CHRISTMAS MIRACLE

It took some time but eventually Bunny managed to calm the couple down enough to get some sense out of them. Tara had put them in the corner booth, giving the mother a glass of water and the father a stiff whiskey and some kitchen roll for the blood. The man who Bunny had thought of as Joseph was in fact called Wang Min. Mary really was called Mary. The Zhaos were from China and they'd arrived in Dublin a week ago. They didn't specify how they'd got there and Bunny didn't ask. He knew enough to know it was unlikely to have been a fun trip. Like millions before them around the world, they'd left their home looking for a better life for their children, both the one on the way and the one they already had. Mary did most of the talking as she had much better English. She'd been a teacher back home.

"Wang Min, he went looking for work. For anything. He is …" she looked around. "How to say, he does maths?"

"Accountant," chipped in Tara.

Mary shook her head.

Tara drummed the table. "I know it, one of them whatchamacallits."

"Never mind," said Bunny. "I don't think it's the most crucial part of the story."

"It's going to annoy me," said Tara and then noticed Bunny's look. "Right. Sorry."

Bunny nodded at Mary encouragingly. "He was looking for work?"

"Yes. Building. Painting. At docks. But he not find anything. Then a man, he said his name was Joe."

Mary looked at Wang Min who nodded. "Joe Bloggs."

Bunny shook his head. "I was afraid of that."

"You know him?" asked Mary.

"It's ... it's not a real name. It's like John Smith or Joe Schmo."

"Oh." Mary looked confused.

"So," said Bunny. "This man Joe Bloggs." He turned to Wang Min. "He asked you to kill me?"

Wang Min nodded his head. "I said no. I don't ... I ..." He shook his head.

Mary placed her hand on her husband's. "He is a good man. He not want to do gun. Then – this man, he come back with two other men. They took Michael. Our son." Tears began to fill her eyes again.

"They kidnapped your son?" said Tara, incredulous. "Jesus Bunny. Make some calls. Get the guards on this."

Mary reached forward and grabbed her hands. "No, no – please. They say, Wang Min do this thing or Michael ..." She left it hanging, unable to finish. "They say, we go to police and ..." She unconsciously placed her hands on her belly, fear for one child transposed to the other. Her voice came out as a strangled whisper. "They took our son."

Tara turned to Bunny. "What are you going to do?"

"What?"

"You need to get their son back."

"That's easier said than done Tara. I've not got the first clue who has him."

"Yes, you do. Who wants you dead?"

Bunny sat back. "Not to blow my own horn, but that's a fairly long list."

"Alright then, who wants it badly enough to do this?"

Bunny shook his head. "This doesn't make any sense."

"How so?"

"If you want me dead," Bunny nodded at Wang Min. "You don't send a half-blind statistician to do it."

Tara slapped the table. "Fuck it, statistician. That was it."

Wang Min nodded and pointed at himself. "Statistician."

"Great," said Bunny. "If his English was better, he could help us figure out the odds on this turning out well."

"Can't you get the Gardai on this?"

Bunny shrugged. "I can ring all the bells alright and they'll roll out. You heard Mary though. Can't be sure it'll be the best thing for Michael."

"What do ..." Tara stopped talking. Bunny didn't want to lay out exactly what he meant by that in front of two terrified parents. It was the truth though. If someone kidnapped the kid and held him as insurance on getting the job done, you probably didn't want them knowing that it had failed and the kid was now a liability. Maybe whoever had him would just let him go, but if you were the kind of scumbag who would kidnap a kid and use him for leverage in the first place, well ...

A thought struck Bunny. "How did you know where to find me?"

"The man," said Mary. "He gave us a bag with gun and then told us directions to come here. O'Hagan's pub. He said you would be here."

"Christ," said Bunny. "That was a bit of a long shot."

"You've been in here every day for a fortnight," replied Tara.

"Alright, but how'd they know which one was me?"

Mary pointed at his left eye. "He say, eye." She twirled her finger at it, indicating Bunny's lazy eye.

"Oh right."

"And," she continued. "He say you are fat."

"Did he?" said Bunny.

Mary's head pumped up and down furiously. "He said you are very fat."

"Ah, here now, 'very' is pushing it."

"You have put on a few pounds to be fair," said Tara, earning a filthy look from Bunny for her trouble. "What?"

"It's the winter. The *Homo sapiens* is supposed to put on a layer of fat to help maintain itself and keep warm through the colder months."

"Is that right? Are you expecting another ice age?"

Bunny's eyes narrowed to slits. "Haven't you got some vol-au-vents to go and arrange or something?"

Tara looked at her watch. "Shit. I forgot about that. They're supposed to be here in twenty minutes. So what's the plan?"

"How have I suddenly got a plan?"

"This is what you do," said Tara. "You sort stuff out."

"I'm technically still on leave."

"My arse," said Tara, standing up. "You might still be on leave from the guards, but you're not on leave from being you." Tara turned to the couple. "Don't worry Mr and Mrs Zhao, it'll all be fine. Bunny is going to get your son back."

Bunny nearly went off the back of his stool as Mary grabbed him in a bear hug. "Thank you. Thank you. Thank you. Good man. You good man."

"He's a great man," chimed in Tara.

Bunny looked up at her, pleading in his eyes. "Could you stop promising people stuff on my behalf?"

"You'll do it. It's why you're my hero."

"Stop taking the piss. And could you give me a hand here."

Tara placed her arms on the tearful Mary's shoulders and guided her back into her seat.

"OK," said Bunny, standing before he could be engulfed in another hormonal hug. "I do have an idea, one idea – but there's a problem."

"Right," said Tara.

"If they sent them in here, odds are someone might be watching. Seeing if they get the job done. I can't be seen leaving or the game is blown. Is there a way out of here other than the front door or the alley at the back?"

Tara thought for a moment and then a smile spread across her lips. "D'ye know how you love *The Shawshank Redemption*?"

FAMILY IS ALSO AN F WORD

Brian Crossan sat in his car and looked out the window. Earlier this week the weather forecaster had teasingly suggested the possibility that there might be a heavy snowfall. It had been his one hope. His great chance.

Nothing.

Not a single bastard flake.

A spike of fear wedged in his stomach as it occurred to him for the first time that it could maybe still come tonight or tomorrow night. The dream had been that the weather would make travel impossible and that his house would just contain him and the wife for Christmas. The nightmare was that the hellish ensemble that now occupied it would have to stay there longer as they'd be snowed in. Not for the first time, Brian wondered about having a minor car crash on the way home. Just enough to require hospitalisation. A few blissful days of grapes and a TV remote all to himself. No – Sheila would know. Sheila would always know. God, he missed work. All he had to deal with there was warring drug gangs.

He jumped as the passenger door of his car opened. "Jesus!"

"Howerya Brian," said Bunny McGarry, pulling the hem of his thick overcoat in and slamming the door behind him.

"For fuck's sake, what are ye playing at?"

"What? I'm just popping in to offer season's greetings to an old friend."

"Even for you, 'popping in' to surprise a man who is allowed to legally carry a firearm twenty-four seven is a bit fucking daft."

"Ara cool your jets quick-draw McGraw."

"How did you even know where I was?"

"I dropped around to your house and the missus told me you'd been dispatched to the shops for some last-minute supplies."

Crossan shook his head. "Aye, right enough. Sheila's auntie Margaret doesn't like salted peanuts and considers our lack of roasted a personal insult. My mother wants metal straws as the ones we had are killing dolphins or some shit. Both the fathers are appalled at the selection of whiskey on offer and apparently our pigs in a blanket could single-handedly ruin Christmas."

Brian became aware that he was gripping the steering wheel rather too tightly.

"Is everything alright Brian?"

He took a deep breath. "No, not really. Myself and Sheila had a big row a few weeks ago. Some things were said. She decided she was inviting her parents for Christmas. I retaliated by inviting mine. She then invited her auntie Margaret and ... long story short, we've got ten people staying for Christmas, every last one of them an insufferable arse."

"Oh."

"Yes. Ye'd think statistically one of us would be related to a reasonable decent human being. I mean for God's sake, just one! But no. Every last one is a whining ingrate bastard. I can't take much more of it, I swear." He looked at his watch and a maniacal unhinged laugh escaped his lips. "They've been here for sixty-eight minutes. Sixty-eight!"

"I see," said Bunny. "Would now be a bad time to mention that Sheila said to hurry back?"

Crossan placed his head against the steering wheel. "I can't ..." he stopped and sat back up, slamming his hand over his nose. "And holy fuck, what is that smell?"

"Sorry. That'd be me," said Bunny. "I had to get out of a pub without being seen, needed to go through the sewers. These shoes might be a write-off."

Crossan pushed the buttons to lower all of the windows. "Oh, would you give me a break? My mother-in-law complained about the smell of the air-freshener when I picked them up from the station, now we've got the smell of shite? There'll be no shifting that."

"Sorry."

"Speaking of things that shouldn't be here, why are you darkening my doorway Bunny? Aren't you still on leave?"

"Not anymore as it happens. I got passed as legally sane this morning." He started slapping the pockets of his coat. "I've got the paperwork here somewhere."

Crossan raised a hand. "Never mind. I'm not saying I wouldn't like to see proof of your possession of the full picnic's worth of sandwiches, but I'm in a weakened enough state to take your word for it. Regardless, the answer is still no, you're not getting on the gangs taskforce."

"That's a tad ungrateful Brian, seeing as it is thanks to me you've got one."

Crossan rolled his head around his shoulders, trying to relieve the knots of tension in his neck. "That is not how I would phrase you putting Gerry Fallon into a coma and creating a vacuum that led to a bloody drug war."

"Well excuse me for arresting a criminal."

Crossan began massaging his temples. "Fine. Whatever. I'll be honest Bunny, if I wanted to have a pointless argument, I'd not have jumped at the chance to get out of my own house."

"I'm not trying to have an argument Brian; I was just wondering how it's going?"

"Excuse me?"

"The war – who is winning it?"

"We are!"

Bunny gave Crossan one of those wonky-eyed looks that he'd always found unsettling. Nobody knew better than he did that what he'd just said was nonsense. The police didn't win gang wars. All they could hope for was making the cost of being in it so high for all involved that eventually it would end. The reality was that law enforcement was on the wrong end of some brutal never-changing circumstance. If the last fifty years had proven anything, it was that the market for drugs was inexhaustible and the profits were so high that scumbags would always be rushing to meet it. You cut down one, and there's another three looking to take their place. Gerry Fallon had been untouchable and a personal insult to every Garda in the country. The dirty little secret though was that he had also meant stability. Now that there was no unassailable king of the castle, everyone thought they'd look good in a crown. After the initial flurry of activity, resulting in several bodies and not enough arrests, things had settled down enough for clear battle lines to be drawn. The three new pretenders to the throne had been the Donavans from the north side around Ballymun, the Clarens from the south side around Tallaght, and the Westies from out in Blanchardstown. And then there'd been the remainder of Fallon's organisation, which his son was doing a piss-poor attempt at heading up.

"What exactly is your interest here, Bunny?"

"Let's just say, I'll be back on the streets soon and as a conscientious member of the force, I'm keen to understand what I should be on the lookout for."

Crossan gave a humourless laugh. "Little tip: if you're going to lie, putting 'let's just say' in front of it is a bit of a giveaway."

Bunny didn't say anything, just gave Crossan what he probably thought of as an attempt at the puppy-dog eyes.

"Screw it, alright fine. If you must know, the Clarens are pretty much a spent force. Two of their main men were found dead in a ditch out by the airport and that raid we hit on last week got their main supply of weapons. As you've seen on the news, this is a shooting war, and seeing as all they have left is their limited wit and charm, they're done, even if they don't know it yet." Crossan looked around and lowered his voice. "This isn't common knowledge, but we have it on good authority that Fallon's crew have brokered a truce with Donavan."

"Really?"

"Yeah. Get this – Gerry Fallon's wife of all people has stepped in. Clearly she's sick of seeing sonny boy screw the pooch. She decided a piece of something is better than all of nothing. She must've run out of outfits to wear to funerals and besides, her son was winning the office pool on being the next one to get a closed casket. Maybe she didn't want to be lonely at Christmas. The Westies are pure rabid dogs whereas, of all this shower, Marty Donavan is the only strategic thinker. At least he's smart enough not to get high on his own supply. Mrs Fallon, it seems, has always had an eye for talent."

Bunny nodded. "I remember Marty back in the day. He was always a nasty piece of work. He started out boosting cars."

"That's a while ago now, he's moved up in the world."

"Isn't he Tom Donavan's young fella?"

Crossan nodded. "Aye, that's right. The dad is gone – cancer, a few years ago now. The son is as fucking ruthless as the father ever was but he's a lot smarter with it. Tom just liked to hurt people; Marty does it with a purpose. Now, if there's nothing else Bunny, I've got four different flavours of ice-cream melting in the back seat."

"Right so." Bunny placed his hand on the handle of the door. "Actually, one last thing."

Crossan gave an exasperated sigh. "What?"

"Any shootings recently where the weapon might have been something like a .44 Magnum? One of them Dirty Harry type jobs?"

Crossan's eyebrows shot up. "What the hell do you know?"

"Nothing," said Bunny.

"Bollocks. We've not even told the press anything about the weapon."

"The weapon in what?"

Crossan shook his head. "No, Bunny. Enough of this shite. What's this about?"

"Honestly Brian, I can't tell you. I promise, as soon as I know something, you'll know it."

"Do you realise I'm your superior officer?"

Bunny nodded. "I do, but I'm also not technically back on active duty."

"Withholding evidence in an on-going criminal case is an offence regardless of who you are. The last thing this situation needs is you sticking your nose in where it doesn't belong McGarry. Not to shock you, but a lot of the higher ups were very keen to take your snout out of the trough entirely."

"Tell me something I don't know, Brian. And besides, while you and I may've had our differences, I'm not picking you as one of those keen to boot me out of the game."

Crossan looked out the window and shrugged. "Let's just say I've always had a begrudging respect for your no-nonsense approach to the job. Besides, I've got bigger fish to fry – something I'll incidentally actually have to do later seeing as Cousin Eric announced an hour ago that he's a pescatarian now."

"A what?"

"I know. I thought he was saying I'd have to drive him somewhere else to go to mass in the morning. Apparently that's a vegetarian who eats fish."

Bunny shook his head. "What in the hell kind of vegetarian is that?"

"An awkward prick of one. My one shining light in this dark day is that *Finding Nemo* is on the BBC tomorrow. I'm going to make that awkward shite sit through every last minute of it."

"Fair play to you. So – where did this Magnum show up?"

Crossan said nothing but gave Bunny a hard stare.

Bunny slapped a hand on the dash. "I tell ye what, Brian – seeing as it's Christmas. You just tell me this, I'll not only leave you alone but I will give you a foolproof excuse to give your missus as to why you won't be home for the next couple of hours."

"Which is?"

"C'mon Brian, you know better than anybody – always get the info first."

Crossan turned and looked out the window. Two men were out of their cars, screaming at each other over a parking space. One of them had reindeer antlers on and the other was wearing a Christmas jumper featuring a drunken snowman. "D'ye know Bunny, I honestly used to really like Christmas."

"Never cared for it that much myself, Brian. Lonely time for a single man like me."

"Lucky sod. Don't rub it in."

Both men gave a laugh and then Crossan turned in his seat slightly. "If you don't mind me asking, how come you never got married? Did you not find the right girl?"

Bunny averted his eyes and said nothing, looking out at the two men who were now bumping chests as they discussed the parking arrangements. He left a long enough gap that Crossan was wondering if he was just going to ignore the question. "Nah, Brian. I found her alright but it wasn't to be. *Que sera*. Besides, I'm married to the job."

Crossan pulled a pack of cigarettes out of his inside pocket, offered Bunny one and had his own lit before Bunny had done waving away the offer.

"Yeah, I'll say this for you Bunny, nobody has ever questioned your commitment. Your sanity? Sure. But not your commitment."

Crossan took in a long drag, held it and then blew the smoke out of the open window. "Alright, screw it but you didn't get this from me."

"Understood."

"And if you get anything actionable, you come to me with it. Got it?"

Bunny nodded.

"Don't fuck me on this, Bunny – I'm not in the mood."

"You have my word."

Crossan tossed his half-smoked cigarette out the window where it hissed as it hit a puddle. "The two lads found out by the airport, they were done with a .44 at close range. Rumour has it, Marty Donavan pulled the trigger on them himself."

"Really?"

"Aye," said Crossan. "Normally, I'd dismiss that as nonsense but in times of war, makes sense to show the foot soldiers that you're willing to get your hands dirty, so it might not be the crock of shite it first appears."

"I see."

"We believe it enough that we've put Donavan under twenty-four seven overt surveillance. Trying to cramp his style to the point that getting the word out to the troops becomes an issue. As we speak, Gar O'Keefe is spending his Christmas Eve following Marty about town as he does his last-minute shopping."

Bunny nodded. "Good to know. I'll let you get on with it." He placed his hand on the door.

"Hey, wait a second. What's this foolproof idea for me getting a couple of hours to myself?"

Bunny hopped out, closed the door and leaned in the window. "Easy peasy. Just tell the missus that I made a pass at you."

"Excuse me?!"

"Tell her I decided to express my undying love for you and that you, while obviously knocking me back, had to take me for a pint and talk me down as I'd been in a very fragile mental state. As a senior officer, you've a duty of care to me and all that. Sure, wasn't I on a psychiatrist's couch only this morning? You'd be a monster to just boot me out the door and be back on your way."

"She'd never believe that!"

"Ah come on now, don't put yourself down Brian. You're a good-looking man." Bunny slapped the roof of the car and then with a brief salute he was off.

Brian shook his head, watching Bunny as he made his way off across the car park. He hopped into the back of a waiting taxi and was gone.

Crossan spoke to himself. "She wouldn't believe that, would she?"

He sat there in a few moments of quiet contemplation of the idea before the action outside attracted his attention. He laid on the horn until the two parking space idiots, who'd moved on to shoving each other, both looked in his direction.

Crossan whipped out his ID. "Both of ye, cop yourselves on or you'll be spending Christmas in the cells."

"What's it to you?" said the clearly stupider of the two.

Crossan waggled his ID. "Garda Síochána sir."

"That's probably fake."

"Yeah, I got it in a Christmas cracker." He pulled a pair of handcuffs out of the glove compartment. "Same as these."

That took the wind out of the mouthy one's sails and he turned around and headed back to his car.

The other fella waved at Crossan. "Thank you, officer. Merry Christmas to you."

"Ah, don't you start."

BAD CHOICES

Bad choices.

If there were two words that summed up Caroline's life up until this point, those would be them. She made bad choices. It was something that she and her parents agreed on, although she'd never admit it.

She meant well. At the time, at least some of the time, it felt like she was making a daring or different move, the kind you read about in those biographies that she'd devoured as a teenager. Be it Janis Joplin, Gandhi, Amelia Earhart – the one thing they all had in common is they had made daring choices in their lives. It had recently dawned on Caroline that the problem with using such people as your role models is that they represented a tiny sample size. It didn't take into account all the other people who'd also made 'daring' choices in their lives and wound up at dead ends or just plain dead. It's like how you could go through your whole life and never meet an unsuccessful parachutist. That didn't mean they didn't exist. They did, but only for as long as it took gravity to prove an emphatic point from ten thousand feet.

Caroline had signed up to do a degree in marketing despite the fact that she had zero interest in marketing. She'd then crashed out of said degree as she had been betting heavily that ska music would come back into fashion, to such an extent that her band could make a go of it, despite the bass player and the drummer refusing to speak to each other, the guitarist refusing to shower and her vocal stylings being based entirely on enthusiasm and shouting the word 'oi' a lot. The band imploded, the guitarist now ran a deli and the rhythm section were married to each other. That was a twist she'd not seen coming.

Caroline had toyed with restarting her educational career but never got around to it. Instead, she floated from dead-end job to dead-end job, doomed relationship to doomed relationship, bad choice to bad choice.

Maybe it was the festive season but recently she'd been thinking a lot about her life. Something in her brain didn't seem to work quite right. She could recall times when she'd known the right choice, one hundred per cent known it, and yet somehow managed not to make it. She'd recently picked up a book called *The Choices We Make* on the bus and while initially sceptical, frankly only reading it to take the piss, a lot of it had hit home. Self-sabotage, low self-esteem, fear of success – these terms had felt like gut punches. Turns out she wasn't unique; she was falling into a lot of the same sorry traps as lots of other people. OK, her little audit had highlighted that maybe she was drinking too much and leaning on recreational drugs a little too heavily. Thing is, unless she was way off, she didn't think that was a cause, but rather a symptom. She didn't have a drink or drug problem; she had a life problem. She needed to get better at having one, or at least believing that she deserved to.

All of this was swirling around in her brain, building to something. At least she hoped so. While it was, she hadn't stopped making bad choices. Case in point – she was thinking all of this while having sex with Craig from work on her break. It was Christmas Eve, they'd both had a drink and work was stressful. Still, she wasn't sure why she was doing this. The job itself was OK, although she'd slagged it off to her friends. She was doing it ironically, after she'd been un-ironically fired from her third waitressing gig in a year. This was the very definition of seasonal work. She was Santa's little helper in the Home shopping centre, and here she was, bent over a crate of faulty Christmas crackers in a storeroom, while Craig, one of the centre's three Santas, banged away. She'd been into it initially but after he'd gone for some ill-judged character-based dirty talk, Caroline was wishing the whole thing were over. She considered stopping it, but it seemed Craig was building to crescendo and it felt easier to just to let him get on with it. After today, they'd never see each other again.

Still, she had that moment: like an out-of-body experience, looking down on herself. She was twenty-six years old and what the hell was she doing with herself? Letting some tedious bloke with a ridiculous monobrow hang out of the back of her making rude remarks about emptying his sack. She was going to make some changes – definitely. This was it. This was finally absolutely bloody it.

The only good thing was thankfully nobody else was here to see this low point. Sure, Craig was – but it was probably the high point of his crappy life, at least judging by the noises coming from behind her.

But at least nobody else would know.

Then, the door flew open and a large, portly man with a wonky eye, wearing a sheepskin overcoat that had seen better days, was standing there looking at them.

"What in the shitting hell are you doing?"

He had a point.

THE WATCHER'S WATCH

Detective Sergeant Gar O'Keefe took the proffered cup of takeaway coffee from Detective Sinead Bonner. He took a sip and nodded appreciatively. "Thanks Sinead, hits the spot."

"That's your fifth one today. You'll never get to sleep for Santa tonight."

"I won't be allowed to sleep. After we're done, I've to go home and build a table football thing for the boys and a doll's house for Keira. You would not believe how many pieces there are in a fecking doll's house. It's ridiculous. Ye pay a fortune for the thing and then you do most of the work assembling it yourself."

Bonner leaned back against the wall, keeping an eye on the queue through the throng of passing shoppers. "I'm sure the kids will appreciate all your hard work, Sarge."

O'Keefe gave a harsh laugh. "I don't share your confidence. Last year was a disaster. If you ever consider popping out sprogs in later life, know that there's every chance you'll spend six months saving for the perfect Christmas and there's still a strong chance that everything is going to be 'lame' – wherever the hell the kids got that from. Well, the boys got it from their sister, but heaven knows where she picked it up. Ye can't be right for being wrong sometimes as a parent."

Bonner smiled. "Are you going to tell me next how when you were a kid you only got an orange for Christmas, Sarge?"

O'Keefe took a sip on his coffee to hide a smile. "Cheeky bitch, I'm not that old."

"Or that fond of fruit."

O'Keefe rolled his eyes. "Let's not take this lull in the action as an opportunity for you to give me another reading from your bible of healthy living please, Detective Bonner."

She held her hands up. "Alright boss. I just want to see you live long enough that you become a burden on your kids at Christmas instead of the other way round."

"Ha," said O'Keefe. "That's the dream."

Bonner nodded over to the queue in front of Santa's grotto. "How much do you think Mr Donavan has spent on Christmas presents so far today?"

Marty Donavan stood in the queue, holding his daughter's hand. From a distance, he looked just like any other parent in the queue, laden down with bags and trying to keep a six-year-old girl interested as they waited to meet Santa.

O'Keefe whistled. "Got to be north of a grand, including the stuff he dropped back to the car earlier."

"She's going to be quite the spoiled brat."

"Well Sinead, buying a child's affection isn't cheap. Especially when daddy dumped mammy while she was eight months pregnant with you."

"He's a class act our Marty."

As if on cue, Donavan waved over at them. O'Keefe and Bonner offered no response. He knew they were there. The idea of covertly following him was pointless. Never mind what you saw in the movies, doing that to someone who was expecting it was virtually impossible, unless you had drones or some such science fiction stuff. While the guards had a little bit of that kind of kit, they didn't go flying it around Grafton Street. So instead, given the recent events in the bloody drug war that had the city in its grip, and Marty Donavan's role in them, it was decided by the higher ups that overt surveillance would be deployed.

Bonner rolled her head around her neck in a practised fashion. She'd gone hard on the weight training last night, one last blowout before the Christmas break. "Can I ask, Sarge – what are we doing here?"

"Well, speaking for myself Sinead, I'm collecting over-time to pay for the trip to Euro Disney the missus wants."

"Right. It's not called that anymore by the way."

O'Keefe looked at her. "What?"

"It's Disneyland Paris now."

"When did that happen?"

"Ages ago, I think. They let you drink there now too."

"Really?"

"It's a big concession to the French way of life. I remember reading a thing about it somewhere."

O'Keefe shrugged. "Great. I imagine I'll enjoy meeting the giant rodent even more when I'm half-cut."

"Right. To go back to my question though boss—"

"Yes," said O'Keefe cutting her off. "Why are we following this scumbag about when he knows we're here?"

"Yeah."

"Because the higher ups think that we're curtailing his operations. He can't meet with his band of merry men and organise wholesale slaughter and drug deals if we're standing fifty feet away."

Bonner went to speak but O'Keefe silenced her by raising his hand. "And yes, you might well ask isn't this entirely pointless in this modern era of WhatsApp and what not, where secure encrypted communication is available to the modern gangster about town. In fact, he could well have been organising the next St Valentine's day massacre while standing over there queuing up so that his little angel can sit on Santa's knee for all we know. Meanwhile, we're standing here like idiots watching him do it. Is that your question Detective Bonner?"

Sinead shrugged, already regretting asking it. "Yes, Sarge."

"Well, I'm afraid the answer is, that while senior management have no doubt attended numerous symposiums, away days, conferences and who knows what else where experts explain the lay of the land in regards to modern criminal communication, in typical force fashion, it's not really sunk in. Whereas, what we're doing now has worked before and, when in doubt, they'll always go back to doing it again and again, regardless of how effective it now is."

"I'm sorry I asked."

"Ah, look on the bright side."

"What's that?" asked Bonner.

"In just over six months, I'm hoping to see my over-excited young fella accidentally head-butt a French teenager in a rodent suit right in the knackers. The lad is a crotch-butter par excellence. It's a sight to behold."

Bonner held up her bottle of water and touched it against O'Keefe's coffee. "I'll drink to that."

They both stood in silence for a few minutes before Bonner spoke again. "What was that call earlier?"

"What call?"

"As I was heading off on the drinks run."

"Oh that," said O'Keefe. "That was Bunny McGarry."

"Who?"

"I keep forgetting you're a recent transfer to the capital. You'll meet him eventually. Everybody does. He's the man who we have to thank for Gerry Fallon taking his extended nap."

"That guy?" said Bonner, realisation dawning. "Why do they call him Bunny?"

"Fuck knows. He's ... well, he's what we could call a 'character' – with all the shit that comes along with that. He was probably pissed. Kept telling me he was waving at me and that I was a prick for not waving back."

"What?"

"I know. I said I couldn't see him and he got argumentative. I told him I was in this god-forsaken temple to commercialism and he said, sorry – must be someone else and hung up."

"Weird," said Bonner.

"Not for him."

"Really?"

"Really. I could tell you some stories."

Bonner looked about. "Well, seeing as there's a good thirty minutes at least left in that queue, I'm not going anywhere."

O'Keefe shifted his feet. "I was once at this wedding, I forget whose, but McGarry got into a fight."

"With who?"

O'Keefe smirked. "A swan."

"Fuck off."

"Seriously."

GROTTY GROTTO

"So," said Bunny. "What's the story here then?"

Caroline blushed again, or rather her blush deepened. She doubted at any point in the last twenty minutes had she technically ever stopped blushing. The sheer mortifying embarrassment of it all, you probably could have fried an egg on her face.

"Look," she said. "It was a one-time thing, alright? I made a mistake and ..." She slammed her hand over her own mouth and closed her eyes for a moment, disappointed when she reopened them to have it confirmed that this wasn't all a horrible dream. She really had been caught shagging Craig bastard Murphy in the storeroom while they were both still in costume. "Sorry. You meant how does this work," she said, waving her hand in the air to indicate the 'grotto' that they were now standing in. A Christmas tree sat in the corner, under which sat a massive pile of entirely empty presents. Drifts of fake snow covered every surface while an animatronic reindeer stood in the corner. It'd gone a bit funny after one of the older and particularly shitty kids had decided to roundhouse kick it in the head on the way out the door last week. Now, instead of bobbing his head up and down, poor Dancer just sort of shook like he was suffering from PTSD. Caroline could sympathise.

"Well," she said. "There's three Santas to keep the queues manageable, although Rita and Dexter next door are on break now as we've just come back from ours." Well, Caroline had. Craig was sitting in the storeroom in his underwear as the big fella had taken the suit off him and was now wearing it. He'd got him out of it through a mix of stuff about it being a Garda operation and the heavy implication about what need not be mentioned to management if he played along. Craig was a children's entertainer for the rest of the year and the last thing he needed was the whiff of impropriety. "The elf," continued Caroline. "i.e. me, goes out and lets Mrs Spring—"

"Is that the woman outside in the funny hat?"

"It is."

"Who is she supposed to be?"

"I'm not sure. I think she was supposed to be Mrs Claus."

"She's still wearing her name badge with assistant manager on it though."

"Yeah," said Caroline. "I'm guessing her need to feel important sort of superseded her character work."

"Poor form."

"Be that as it may, she's in charge. I go out and tell her we're ready, then I take the next kid in the queue in to see Santa, who stays here on his throne." It was actually an armchair with a shed load of tinsel on it sitting up on a wooden plinth. "Each kid gets two minutes. I have to time it. The little ones sit on your knee, the big ones don't have to. You ... y'know ask if they've been good and then hear what they want for Christmas. Always look for signals from the parent and don't promise them anything." Craig had got the mother of all bollockings from Mrs Spring after he'd told a kid on the first day that he would be getting the PlayStation he was after. "Can I just – sorry but, can you explain again exactly how this is a police thing?"

"That would be on a need to know basis."

"Right," said Caroline. "Well, I think I kind of need to know."

"How's that?" asked Bunny.

"I mean, you come in here and tell me you're a Garda called Bunny. Not the most police-sounding name if you don't mind me saying. And ... look, I'm not cool with you interviewing a child under false pretences."

Bunny gave her an assessing look. "Fair play to you. That would be totally out of order. It's also not what I'm doing."

"Isn't it?"

"No, I just need a word with the parent of a particular child that happens to be in the queue outside."

"Right," said Caroline. "I see. Actually no – I take that back, I don't see. This makes no sense. Can you not just talk to them outside?"

"No," said Bunny. "They're being followed."

"By who?"

Bunny gave her a tight smile. "As it happens, other members of the Garda Síochána."

"Right." Caroline stood there, staring at the man who was now dressed as Santa, deciding if screaming for help might be a sensible option.

"Look," said Bunny. "If I was up to no good, would I have told you that?"

She rubbed her hand across her forehead.

"Are you OK?"

"No," she said. "To be honest, your logic on top of a hangover is wrecking my head."

"OK, look. Let me tell you this. It is not overly dramatic to say that I'm here trying to save a child and get them back to their parents."

Caroline pointed at the door that led to the queue outside.

"No, not that child. Look, it's going to take too long to explain and the clock is ticking here. You're just going to have to trust me."

"The thing is," said Caroline. "I think I can trust you which is worrying as honestly, I always trust the wrong people."

Bunny inclined his head back towards the grotto's rear entrance.

"God, no – not Craig. That was just, let's call it the latest in a long line of bad decisions."

"'Tis not for me to judge."

"Really? That's not the impression I got from your little chat with Craig."

"Well, no offence, but he seemed like an arse."

Caroline nodded. "He is. You've nailed that."

"Right, so why did you ..."

"We definitely don't have the time to explain that either. So, either I do this or you tell the management how you found us?"

Bunny shook his head. "Actually, no. Wouldn't be right. I implied it to put the wind up lover boy but I'm not actually going to do that either way."

"Doesn't you confessing that sort of give up your leverage in this situation?"

"I suppose it does, but well," he gave her his version of a winning smile. "I dunno. Doesn't seem right. Your business is your business although for what it is worth, I'm fairly sure you can do better for yourself than that sack of shite in the storeroom."

"I dunno. I'm not exactly a prize myself."

"And you can cut out saying crap like that for a start."

Caroline sat on the throne and looked at Bunny. "If you don't mind me saying, you are a very peculiar man."

"Sane though. I've got a piece of paper."

Caroline gave him a long assessing look and then threw her hands in the air. "Screw it – I'm going to trust you because, well – I've got to be right eventually. What does this kid and parent you need to talk to look like?"

"He's a tall lad, late 20s. She's in a pink dress."

"What age?" Asked Caroline.

"Oh God," said Bunny. "I dunno." He held his hand about three feet off the ground. "About yay old."

"Right. We can't pull them out of the queue as trust me, you don't want that." There'd been a near riot when Rita had tried to fast track her nephew. "But I can tip Mrs Spring the wink, say the girl is a friend of mine, make sure we get her."

"OK," said Bunny.

"Right," said Caroline, jumping down. "Hop up on the throne there. Remember, you're Santa. Don't break character, listen to the kids, be jolly, all of that. I'll hand you the present to give them and most importantly, keep it moving."

"Right."

Caroline took a deep breath. "OK, here goes nothing."

———

She was shocked to discover over the next twenty-five minutes that the wonky-eyed copper was a natural at the Santa-ing game. He got the scared little fella to go from clinging to his mammy to happily sitting on his knee. He listened patiently as the little girl explained how she wanted a pony and then deflected that expertly, much to the relief of the mother standing behind her. He even dealt with a couple of the awkward 'too old for this crap' kids who were only there because they wanted a present. Everyone got the chat about behaving themselves and thinking of those less fortunate and he really did deliver it well. Both kids and parents left happy.

Caroline came back in. "Right – the target is two away in the queue. Mrs Spring is going to let the next two go into number 3 so we don't miss them."

"Excellent," said Bunny. "Thanks."

Caroline stood beside his throne awkwardly as they both looked at the door. Bunny drummed his fingers on his knees.

"Can I say – I'm sorry if I was rude before. Tis not my place to judge you."

Caroline waved his concerns away. "To be honest, maybe I need a little judgement in my life. I've not got a clue what I'm doing. I'm a mess."

"You seem alright to me."

"Really? I was having sex with a guy I don't even like when we met. And look at me." Caroline flapped her hands. "I'm doing this to make my rent, and I've no idea how I'm making next month's. I have no clue what I'm doing with my life."

Bunny scratched under the fake beard. "What would you like to do?"

"Since when has that got anything to do with anything? I pissed a decent education up a wall and now I'm an elf. I'm twenty-six. Too late to start again."

"Pardon my French but that's bollocks."

Caroline turned to look at him.

"It is. In ten years' time you'll look back at twenty-six and wish you'd realised you had your whole life ahead of you. And at forty-six you'll look back at thirty-six and think the exact same thing. The world is full of people killing time because they think they've no time left." Bunny reached across and put his hand over her eyes. "Quick as you can, tell me what you'd like to be more than anything else in this world."

"I can't just—"

"Ye can. Three … two … one … go!"

"Psychology!" Caroline managed to be simultaneously surprised and completely unsurprised by the word that just came out of her mouth.

Bunny pulled his hand away. "Right, by the power vested in me as Saint Nicholas, patron saint of screaming brats and office party mistakes, you can go work in psychology."

"I can't just …"

"Ye can. Do a night class. You can keep doing crappy jobs to support yourself but at least you'll be doing them for a reason. You can work your way up. Certificate. Diploma. Degree. Doctorate or whatever. It's all there if you want it, now stop pissing about thinking about what you want to do and just go and do it."

Caroline stared into the face of the man who wasn't Santa and, in that moment, she couldn't come up with one single argument as to why he was wrong.

Bunny broke away and looked at the door, the Santa voice kicking in. "Ho, ho, ho – and who do we have here?"

———

Bunny sat the little girl in the pink dress up on his knee.

"Hello little lady, and what's your name?"

"Tamara."

"And what do you want for—"

She started speaking before he'd finished, rattling off a list while counting points off on her fingers. "I am getting a Barbie playhouse, a big doll house like they had on the Late Late Show, a trampoline, an iPhone ..." She looked up at him pointedly. "... one of the new ones, a new laptop, a tablet, a new wardrobe, three new dresses, a big teddy, a makeup kit, a big mirror, a new duvet, a stereo and a special dressing table."

Bunny looked at Caroline and then back at Tamara. "Right, I see. Golly – that's a lot isn't it? Well if you've been a good girl, I'm sure you'll get some of the things from your list."

Her face scrunched up and her eyes beamed lasers of outrage up at Bunny. "I'm getting all of it."

Bunny glanced up at Marty Donavan for the first time; he was looking at his phone. He spoke without taking his eyes off it. "She's getting all of it."

"Right. Well aren't you a lucky girl?"

"And," continued Tamara. "I want Suzie Doyle to get nothing because she is a basic bitch."

Bunny pulled back. "Ah here now, that's an awful thing to say."

Donavan shoved his phone in his pocket. "Mind your manners."

"See, listen to your daddy."

"I was talking to you."

The two men locked eyes briefly before Bunny returned his attention to Tamara. "Well, I can see where you get it from. Still, good girls shouldn't talk like that."

Donavan glowered at Bunny. "Like I'm going to take advice from some loser in fancy dress." He turned to Caroline. "You. Present. Now." He looked back at Bunny. "And you, tell my little girl that you're bringing all she asked for because she is daddy's little angel."

Bunny looked back down at Tamara. "Oh, your daddy is very mean, isn't he? I think he's going to end up on Santa's naughty list if he's not careful."

Donavan stepped forward and snatched the present out of Caroline's hands. "C'mon Tamara, we're going. We've got your present. Don't mind this smelly loser, he's not the real Santa."

Bunny gave the jolly laugh. "Ho. Ho. Ho. Someone needs to find his happy." Bunny turned to Caroline. "My elf is going to take you outside, Tamara and help you open your present. Daddy and I need to have a little chat."

Donavan stared daggers at Bunny and then he spoke slowly, "Yeah. You take a seat outside, sweetie. Daddy is going to double-check Santa has got your list right."

"But I want to go home—"

"Outside. Now."

Caroline took the little girl's hand as Bunny stood up and stretched out his back. "C'mon Tamara, we've got a big bag of sweeties and you can pick your favourite."

The little girl looked at her father huffily and then begrudgingly headed towards the door of the grotto with Caroline.

Donavan watched her leave before turning back towards the throne. "Now you F—"

The rest of the sentence was lost as Donavan felt the barrel of a .44 Magnum being shoved up under his chin. Santa's face moved close to his and then he pulled off the fake beard. "Howerya Marty. Merry Christmas."

Donavan's eyes narrowed and then widened as realisation hit. "McGarry?"

"Shush. Don't be giving away my secret identity."

"Jesus, your breath stinks."

"That's an awful thing to say, especially to a man holding a .44 Magnum somewhere that allows him to give your head a sun roof with just a twitch of his finger."

"This is harassment."

"You'd know. I'm not here as a copper though Marty."

Donavan for the first time looked nervous. "How much are they paying you?"

Bunny took a step away and moved the gun away from Donavan's chin, pointing it at his bellybutton instead. "Relax Marty, I'm not here to kill ye. I'm actually here to save your sorry arse."

Donavan rubbed a hand on the skin where the gun barrel had been pressed. "You've a funny way of showing it. I'm not hiring right now but—"

"Shut up," said Bunny. "We don't have much time. Last week, when you killed those two lads ..."

"I don't know what you're—."

"Save it." Bunny held the gun up. "I'm going to bet this is the gun you used. Quite distinctive, isn't it? Bit Clint Eastwood."

Donavan said nothing, instead he glanced around, clearly wondering what this was.

"Funny thing happened this morning, Marty. Some poor eejit was given this gun and sent into my pub to shoot me. Into *my* pub though? Is nothing sacred? I'm not going to lie, that proper put a dent in my Christmas spirit."

Donavan did nothing more than raise an eyebrow. Bunny found himself having a grudging respect for the man's ability to at least shut up and listen. He really was smarter than his dad.

"Now," said Bunny. "A little bird tells me that you have made a deal with the Fallon family. I mean, the members of it that aren't having an awful long nap thanks to yours truly. So, if I got taken out with this gun – how would that look, Marty? Christmas Eve. Cold-blooded assassination of a copper. That'd get you some attention, wouldn't it? Six and nine o'clock news. Hand wringing in the papers. I'm honestly not that popular but nothing fixes a bad rep quicker than a bloody death. So imagine then, when the ballistics come back and prove the gun used was the same one used in the killing of the two lads from the Clarens gang. You know, the pair whose executions dogs in the street are saying were carried out by you personally. It'd start to look like my untimely death was you sealing your deal with the Fallons by taking out the man who fucked everything up for them."

Donavan folded his arms. "This is all bullshit."

"D'ye know," said Bunny. "I'm inclined to agree. It struck me that somebody here is trying to paint a picture. You're too smart for this. I mean, not killing a copper. We both know you'd put a hit on your own granny if it served your purposes. But having somebody use the same gun, that'd be stupid. You'd have every cop in the country gunning for you. It'd be very bad for business."

"So," said Donavan. "If you reckon this is crap, then what are you doing here?"

Bunny took a step forward. "Ah, here's the thing Marty. The poor gobshite who was sent to kill me, somebody took his kid. Forced him into it."

"I know nothing about that."

"Probably not, but let me speed things up for you as we're on the clock here. Let me ask you the question now that'll pop into your head in a few minutes' time. Somebody gave the poor sod this gun. That someone has the kid I'm trying to get back and, here's the kicker – he had access to this gun." Bunny waggled it in the air. "Unless you're a lot dumber than I've been led to believe, you gave this to someone to dispose of. That person I'm betting has made a deal with the Westies to set you up and bring the Garda Síochána down on yourself and the Fallons like a tonne of bricks. The question is, who is that person?"

Bunny watched as Donavan gritted his teeth. "That sneaky little bollocks."

"Ah good, I thought you might have a name. Care to enlighten me?"

"I'll handle it."

Bunny stepped forward and blocked Donavan's route to the door. "No, you won't. Whoever it is has an innocent kid held as a hostage. You're giving me the name and I will take care of it."

"I want him dead."

"I don't work for you."

"Then get out of my way."

Bunny stepped back and waved a hand at the door. "Fine, off you go."

Donavan took a step forward.

"Of course, I'm going to start screaming about you having a gun if you take two more steps. I'd imagine that'll bring your police escort running."

"Nobody is going to—"

"A gun that matches the one used in a killing you've been linked to."

"You'll never make that stick."

Bunny smiled. "I know. You'll walk, but only after spending a fair bit of time helping the guards with their enquiries. Did you have plans for Christmas Day Marty? Then of course, Tamara's mammy will have to come pick her up. She'll be traumatised. Will that go down well d'ye reckon?"

Donavan pulled a face. "You'd use a kid?"

Bunny nodded. "To save one, you'd better believe it. Give me the name and give me two hours. Then, you can do what you like."

Donavan gave Bunny a long hard look.

Bunny stared back. "Well?"

SING, SING A SONG

Bunny sighed. "Alright, one more time from the top."

This was met with groans and exasperated mutterings. Gathered in front of him were five members of the St Jude's Under-12s Hurling Team that he coached. They wouldn't have been Bunny's first choices for his current course of action but they were the ones he was able to get hold of in the shortest time possible. His skills as a hurling coach were questionable, relying as heavily as he did on screaming and extolling the virtues of getting stuck in. It had quickly become apparent that his abilities as a singing coach made him look like a hurling genius.

Pete Roach, aged twelve going on forty and heading for a life as a criminal mastermind or union organiser depend on which way the next couple of years fell, held his hands up. "Alright Bunny, we've all had enough of this. You asked us to help with something, you did not mention there'd be singing."

"In the name of baby Jesus, the donkey and the cow, how is it that none of you five lads can sing 'Jingle Bells'?"

"It's not that we can't sing it, it's that it was not part of the terms of our agreement re vis-à-vis assistance in a matter of law enforcement."

"Vis-à-vis?" said Bunny. "You know the phrase vis-à-vis but you can't sing 'Jingle Bells'? Are they teaching you anything at all in that school?"

"It's a waste of time," chimed in Stevie Marks. "That's why I'm thinking of chucking it in."

"Shut up, Stevie. You're going to school."

"Says who?"

"Says me!"

Finding himself on the wrong end of the patented Bunny McGarry stare, Stevie Marks folded faster than an origami tent in a typhoon. He averted his eyes and shuffled his feet, addressing his next sentence into his scarf.

"What was that?" said Bunny. "Speak up Stevie, there's a good lad."

"I said I'm going to school."

"Course you are. Good boy."

Pete Roach raised a hand. "If we could get back to the matter at hand ..."

"Seriously," said Bunny. "Where are you picking up the fancy talking?"

"He's been watching this *Rumpled of the Bailey* TV show," said Pete's younger brother Sean. This was a surprising interjection as Sean was one of those kids who gave the distinct impression that reality was of no interest to him at all. He followed the other lads around in a permanent daze, exhibiting as much drive in life as a shopping bag in the wind. In the match they had played the previous Sunday, Bunny had caught Sean colouring in his hurling stick with markers while on the field. It said something about the state of their team that he was still one of their best players.

"Really?" said Bunny.

"Rumpole is the man," said Pete. "Don't be dissing Rumpole."

"Now there's a sentence I didn't expect to hear today."

Pete steepled his fingers together under his chin in a way Bunny would've found hilarious if he was in the mood to find anything hilarious, which he wasn't. "While we negotiated our fee of ten euros a man in good faith, there had been no mention of singing at that juncture."

"Yeah, it's a bleedin' liberty is what it is," chimed in Denny O'Brien.

"Denny, you mind your language. What've I feckin' told you about cursing?"

"But you just cursed."

"I did feckin' not. You shut up or I'll be having a word with your granny."

Denny lowered his eyes to the ground. "Yes Bunny."

"I would like to redirect the conversation back to our negotiations if I may—"

"Fine," said Bunny, raising his hand to stop Pete Roach going into any more barrack room lawyer nonsense. "Twenty euros."

"Thirty!"

"Roach, look at my face."

Pete did and then nodded. "Twenty is fair."

"Well played. As the man said, ye got to know when to hold 'em and know when to fold' em."

"What man?" asked Stevie.

"Never mind," said Bunny. "It's from a song which, judging by what I've heard over the last ten minutes, is a medium none of you have ever come across before. Now – this isn't my area of expertise lads but there's things called keys. I don't know how they work but if you find yourself accidentally sounding like you're singing in the same one as one of the other lads, stick with that. As for tempo, I'll count you in. Let's all try and stay in some kind of synch. I'm just glad the options available to you boys in certain areas have expanded, as if any of you ever had to rely on the rhythm method ..."

"What's the—"

"Never you mind Stevie Marks. Here we go. A one, a one, a one ... two ... three ... four."

If anything, the next ninety seconds were even worse than their previous attempts. Eventually, Bunny couldn't take it anymore and he waved them into silence, at which point two of them were somewhere in the chorus, two were attempting a verse and Sean appeared to be doing a saxophone solo without being encumbered by a saxophone.

"Right. Enough lads. Enough. That was perfect."

"Really?"

"Jesus Stevie, no. It was dreadful. In fact, there's a very good chance any arrest I'm about to make will be thrown out due to it involving cruel and unusual punishment from having to listen to you lot, but we've got to get moving so I'm afraid we won't be able to improve your performance levels above their current level of shite."

"Isn't that a—" started Denny.

"No, Denny. Nothing I say is a swear. But if you say something I have said, then it can and almost certainly will become a swear when it comes out of your mouth."

"That's not fair."

Bunny nodded. "You're exactly right. Welcome to the real world. Life isn't fair. Merry bloody Christmas." Bunny clapped his hands together. "Now lads, ring the doorbell and if they don't answer, keep ringing."

"But—"

"This one time, you're allowed to do that. Go to town on it. As soon as they answer, start belting the song out. If they close the door, start ringing the doorbell again. Come hell or high water, I want this to be a compelling performance."

"What do we do when we've finished the song?"

"Start again."

"Ehm," said Denny. "I've actually got a song I've been working on myself."

"No solo material. This group does 'Jingle Bells'."

"What about dancing?" asked Barney Moorhouse, speaking up for the first time. He didn't talk much because he said it affected his asthma. Bunny thought that was an excuse to cover shyness but given what the other four were like, having one member of the strong silent brigade along for the ride was welcome.

"Dancing? Really?" Bunny looked down into a face full of earnest excitement. "Sure, why not? Don't give yourself an attack though."

153

Barney waved his inhaler cheerfully in the air. "I've got me puff puff."

"Grand. I'd probably stop calling it that, but that's a conversation for another time."

"Any final tips?" asked Pete.

"Yeah. Don't go all in on two queens, never trust a builder who says he'll be back first thing, and if someone tells you that they want to see other people, they already are and they're almost certainly shagging them, probably your builder."

Bunny looked at the five fresh faces gawping up at him. "Sorry, that last one may've been inappropriate for this audience. It's been a long day."

"I actually meant tips on our performance," said Pete.

"Oh right," said Bunny. "Loud. Let's just aim for really feckin' loud."

IF YOU DON'T LIKE WHAT YOU SEE HERE

Frankie didn't like this.

He didn't like any of it. When Darren had asked him to help out on a job, he'd have thought it might be nicking something or making a delivery of some gear. Maybe even roughing somebody up. Frankie wasn't much of a fighter but he'd not need to be. Darren was a Donavan, younger brother of Marty, and since they'd been kids together on the estate, nobody had ever fucked with the Donavans. The only people who'd ever given Darren a beating was his brother or his da. Darren had then passed it on to other kids. All he'd need Frankie for was as a witness or someone to hold his coat. They had ended up being mates as they'd been stuck sitting beside each other in school and being Darren's mate was way better than being his enemy. Not that being his friend meant you were spared his temper; the lad could go off at anything.

Still, this – this was really bad. Frankie hadn't known what they were up to until they'd met that Chinese family and taken their kid off them. Frankie had to pull him away from his pregnant mother kicking and screaming. It was seriously bad karma. They'd shoved the kid in the boot of the car and took him to the house up in Corduff. Frankie had tried to talk Darren out of whatever the hell this was, but he wasn't a good listener at the best of times. Instead, Darren had sat in that armchair all day, skulling cans and doing the odd line while Frankie had sat there watching TV and quietly freaking out. Darren had started talking in between checking the new phone he had every couple of minutes. He said he was waiting to hear if something had been handled. He said he had Paidi out doing surveillance for him, keeping his ear to the ground. Darren said he was going to be the man now and that he'd make sure Frankie was taken care of. Marty was going to be out of the way and Darren would be running things. Frankie had nodded and said nothing. The kid was under the stairs, bound and gagged. Frankie had given him a sandwich and a can of coke, told him it was going to be alright. The kid didn't look like he believed that any more than Frankie did. He didn't speak much English, which was probably just as well. Darren had referred to 'dealing with' him in a way that left Frankie fearing the worst.

The doorbell rang. "What the fuck is that?" asked Darren.

"I dunno Daz."

"I told you not to order a pizza."

"I didn't."

"Ignore it then."

The doorbell rang again.

And again.

"Fuck off!" roared Darren.

The doorbell was then pressed constantly. After thirty seconds or so, Darren stood up, sending empties flying as he stormed out of the room. "I'll deal with this."

Frankie heard the front door wallop open and then singing broke out. Well, sort of. It sounded like a bunch of deaf kids had formed a choir and they'd not been given any guidance.

Frankie winced as Darren hollered at them. "What is this shit?"

That was it. Screw it. Frankie wanted no part of whatever this was. Scary as Darren was, his big brother Marty was scarier. Frankie knew he was a fuck-up and that he had been for most of his life, but he still wanted nothing to do with hurting a kid. Everyone has a line.

He opened the door as softly as he could. Darren stood at the end of the hall roaring abuse at a group of five kids who seemed entirely oblivious to it as they belted out 'Jingle Bells' for all they were worth. He slipped into the kitchen and, leaving the light off, headed straight for the back door. He thought he heard the sound of metal on metal but it was hard to make out given the din coming from behind him. Just as Frankie reached for the handle, the door opened. It was supposed to be locked. He'd checked it.

Frankie froze, somehow terrified that he'd been caught mid-escape.

A man came through the door.

"Howerya."

Frankie recognised the man's face, right before it hurtled towards him at high velocity and butted him hard. Frankie fell backwards and felt hands catch him and lay him softly down. Screw it – he was going to have a nap.

He was dimly aware of the sound in the room changing as the door to the hall opened and closed quietly.

The last thing Frankie heard before losing consciousness was somewhere in the distance, somebody breaking into a saxophone solo without the assistance of a saxophone.

A TALE TO TELL

Pete Roach looked around at his audience. There were now nearly twenty kids from the estate gathering around him and the other four members of the carolling crew. The crowd was growing bigger and bigger as word spread around the estate. Pete was telling the story for the third time. He 'remembered' more details with each rendition, along with other members of the crew adding in new details each time that may, or may not have happened. "So, we're singing ..."

"'Jingle Bells'," said Denny.

"Yeah, 'Jingle Bells'. Bunny said it was his favourite song."

"Really?" asked Cara King.

"Oh yeah," said Pete. "He's mad about 'Jingle Bells'." Pete had no idea if this was true but this was the longest he'd spoken to a girl that wasn't his sister since that became a thing he'd decided he'd like to do. The way Cara was looking at him as he told the story would stay with him for a long time. He wanted it to last as long as possible. "He likes any song with bells in it. 'Ding Dong Merrily on High'. That's another one."

"Dead right," interjected Stevie. "He's got a CD of all these bell songs in his car."

Pete glared at Stevie. He was aware that he was trying to muscle in on Cara's attention and he didn't like it.

"How would you know what he has in his car?" asked Denny, unwittingly winning himself a warm place in Pete's heart for the rest of time. "Bunny doesn't let nobody in his car. Everybody knows that."

Even the girls nodded. Everybody really did know that. Stevie had blown it. Pete's spirits soared as he saw Stevie's face redden. "Well, yeah. Obviously. But like … I heard it when he drove by."

Nobody reacted to this, instead turning their faces back to Pete.

"So anyway," he continued. "Bunny says to me, 'Pete – I need you and the lads to cause a distraction for me'."

"No he didn't," said Stevie.

"Yeah he did," said Sean, without looking up from staring at his own fingers as he clicked the ones on each hand in turn. It was like he'd just got hands and was excited to see what they did. Sean might be away with the fairies but brothers still backed up brothers.

"He did," confirmed Pete, as Stevie folded his arms getting all in a huff. "He pulled me aside and had a quiet word." Cara looked impressed. Quiet words were things grown-ups had.

"And you went up to the house?" asked Cara. "Like, knowing there were baddies in it?"

"Oh yeah," said Pete.

"I rang the doorbell," said Denny.

"He did," agreed Pete, because he had to be judicious in not taking all the credit. "He held it down too."

"Proper fucking hard," said Denny.

Cara wrinkled her nose, she didn't like what her ma called 'language'. Pete liked how her nose did that.

"So then," said Pete, picking up the narrative. "This fella opens the door and he's like – massive!" Pete puffed himself out and pulled a ferocious face. "Eight foot tall he was, muscles bulging on him everywhere. His eyes were all red and bloodshot." This was a new detail but Pete instantly decided he liked it. He made a mental note to keep it in.

"Yellow teeth too," said Stevie.

Pete nodded. He didn't want to make Stevie feel too bad and besides, that was a good new bit too. "And he's roaring at us and we're standing there just singing."

"And dancing," said Barney.

"You were dancing?" said Cara, half-laughing.

"Only Barney was dancing," said Pete quickly.

"Yeah," agreed Stevie.

"You can dance?" Cara asked Barney.

"Oh yeah," said Barney, before breaking into thirty seconds of body popping. Pete had to begrudgingly admit he was pretty good. As he finished, the crowd cheered and Barney gave a bow. Sneaky sod, he came out of nowhere.

"As I'm singing," continued Pete, keen to regain control of the situation. "This fella is roaring, foaming at the mouth he was." All of the lads nodded, in silent agreement that this should be part of the story now too as it made them all sound *even braver*. "And I spy Bunny sneaking up behind him. He nods at me like, keep it going Pete."

"Then," said Denny. "This massive bollocks was about to turn around and see Bunny, but luckily Sean did his thing."

"He did what?" said Cara.

"His thing," repeated Denny.

"He does a saxophone solo," clarified Pete.

"He has a saxophone?" asked Cara.

"No."

Then, Sean broke into one of his saxophone solos unencumbered by a saxophone. Cara watched him, enraptured. When he was done, the entire crowd broke into serious applause. Sean went back to looking at his fingers entirely oblivious to the ovation.

"And then," said Pete. "Bunny slams this guy's head into the wall."

"Wow," said Cara.

"And he takes a swing at Bunny but he ducks and knees him right in the bollocks."

At this point, Stevie and Denny started re-enacting the fight complete with sound effects.

"Lads," Pete protested. "I wasn't finished telling the story!" But there was no stopping them. Pete tried to intervene and then became part of the fight. It was all a bit confusing, as everyone appeared to be playing the part of Bunny.

When Pete eventually turned around, he saw Cara standing beside Sean watching in awe as he did another of his saxophone solos.

Pete learned a valuable lesson. Bravery is one thing, but girls really dig musicians.

THE GIVING OF GIFTS

Brian Crossan took a deep breath.

This had been a terrible idea. He was now out of options. He needed to make a deal, even if it meant giving a sworn enemy what they wanted.

"Alright," he said. "I'll make it two fifty."

"No."

The woman was impossible.

"Look, we're at the very edge here. We need to come to an understanding or we're both doomed. Would you rather take the mutually assured destruction option?"

"Fine by me."

"OK."

They locked eyes. He couldn't blink first. Everything hung in the balance.

Eventually Uncle George cleared his throat. "Right then, if you two are done – can you give me the dice please, Margaret, it's my go."

Margaret didn't move. "I want your railway stations."

"I can't give you my railway stations."

The doorbell rang.

Sheila's shout came for the kitchen. "Brian, can you get that?"

"I'm in the middle of something, sweetheart."

The kitchen door slammed. "Right, of course. Well, I'm only sitting in my sunbed topping up my tan while the staff cook a meal for twelve people. Ye selfish …"

She opened the front door. "Oh hello again, just a second." Sheila's voice rose to a holler. "Brian, your boyfriend is back!"

Brian shoved his fist in his mouth and bit the knuckle. In a moment of weakness, he'd managed to convince himself that McGarry's idea of pretending he'd made a pass at him was believable, and he'd gone for a quiet pint alone in the Stag's Head. As soon as he'd ordered it, he realised it was a terrible idea. As he had the second pint he had been trying to come up with a Plan B. Nothing had come to him. Instead, he'd gone home and gone all in on the "Bunny McGarry says he loves me" angle. It had not gone well.

Sheila had burst out laughing as soon as he'd tried it. He'd attempted to double down. "C'mon now Sheila, I can't believe you're being so dismissive of the man's private turmoil."

"Oh pull the other one. Bunny McGarry is the least gay man on the planet."

"What's that supposed to mean?"

"Everything about him: the shoes, the hair, the entire way he carries himself."

"That's just lazy stereotypes. Gay people come in all shapes and sizes."

"They do, all except Bunny McGarry's shape and size. There's more chance of him being an alien than there is gay. Don't get me wrong, if he was gay, I'd be nothing but supportive. But he isn't."

"How do you know that?"

"I just know. A woman knows."

"You didn't know about my nephew."

"Fergus? Oh please, of course I did. I knew since he was twelve."

"What? You never said."

"That's because it's not my place to say, is it? It's his own affair."

"Still though."

"Still nothing." She'd placed her hands on her hips in that way he

163

hated and given him that smile that had no smile in it. "Tell you what, if you'd like to spend a romantic evening in a luxury hotel somewhere with Bunny, I'm fine with it. Go on, enjoy yourselves."

"You're being very juvenile."

"Says the man who went and hid in the pub and then came home with this cock and bull story. Pathetic."

Since then, there'd been a frosty truce. Brian knew he was rumbled and that he was going to no doubt pay for this error of judgement at a later date. He was probably going to quite literally have to pay for it – they'd be getting that new paving in the back garden Sheila wanted. He had started the game of Monopoly as Auntie Margaret had been veering very close to having one of her chats about "foreigners" and Brian had doubted his own ability to hold his tongue this time.

Still, the last thing he needed was Sheila being reminded of the McGarry debacle again so soon. He stood up from the table, stopped and picked up his money before leaving. He wouldn't put it past them to all have a nibble, thieving so-and-sos.

Sheila met him at the living room door. She had that smile again and then she spoke in a gleeful whisper. "My God Brian, I'd no idea the two of you had started a family. How long has this been going on?"

"What on Earth are you ..."

Instead of answering, Sheila walked back towards the kitchen, chuckling to herself. Shite. They might have to get that sunroom too.

───────

Brian opened the door to see Bunny McGarry standing there, looking sheepish. "McGarry, what in the hell are ..." Brian stopped speaking as he noticed they weren't alone. He realised what Sheila had been on about. "Eh, Bunny – why is there what appears to be a small Chinese boy attached to your leg?"

"That's a very good question, DSI Crossan. As it happens, he was kidnapped this morning and I rescued him. He's developed a bit of an attachment issue. I'm hoping it'll stop when I get him back to his parents."

Brian looked down at the boy's tearstained face. "Yeah, otherwise it'll really start to cramp your style. Why do I have the feeling you're about to ruin my Christmas?"

"I thought it was already ruined. You said—"

"Shush! Keep your voice down for Christ's sake. You've done more than enough damage already."

"What did I do?"

Brian just looked at him. Bunny's eyes went wide. "Oh for fuck – you didn't seriously try that thing about me making a pass at you, did you?"

"You told me to!"

"I was joking."

Bunny reflexively took a step back, correctly judging that Brian was a hair's breadth away from swinging for him.

He held his hands up. "Ok, sorry. Relax, Brian. I have some good news."

"Really?" Brian could feel that twitching near his temple that meant he had a whopper of a headache coming on. The muscles in his neck felt like steel cables.

"Absolutely," said Bunny. "Here." He handed Brian the bag for life he was holding.

Brian looked inside, did a double take and then looked up at Bunny.

"Is this ...?"

"The murder weapon from that double murder last week, yes."

"How did you—"

"I'll explain everything. You see, this morning, I went for a pee in O'Hagan's ..."

It took Bunny nearly ten minutes to lay out the events of the day, omitting names of anyone who might get into trouble for their role in proceedings. Well, everyone but his own – there was no way he could avoid that trouble.

"... and that's how we ended up here."

Crossan didn't say anything for several seconds. "Seriously, is this a wind-up?"

"No."

"It must be."

"It isn't." Bunny crossed his heart. "I swear it on the Holy Bible and the 2006 Cork hurling team."

"Right." Brian's voice rose several decibels. "Are you fucking insane?"

A man walking his dog on the path outside looked up. Crossan was past caring.

"Keep calm, Brian."

"Calm? Calm? Calm he says!" The kid scooted around behind Bunny's legs and Brian felt a moment of guilt. He leaned against the doorframe and returned to a steadier tone of voice. "Let me see if I have this right. This morning there was an attempt on your life." He waved the bag for life containing a .44 Magnum in the air. "Using the alleged murder weapon from a double homicide carried out last week. Instead of immediately reporting it, you decided to aid the perpetrator in his attempts to save his son who had been supposedly taken hostage. You threatened Marty Donavan with a loaded weapon …"

"I wouldn't say—"

"Doesn't matter what you'd say. It matters what that prick of a lawyer of his will say. And then, again, instead of informing your colleagues in the Garda Síochána of the situation, you stage a one-man rescue mission to get this boy back with no warrant, dodgy probable cause and inadmissible evidence up the wazoo. Have I got all this right so far?"

"More or less."

Crossan closed his eyes for a second and ran a hand across his brow. "OK, am I missing something? Where exactly is the good news here?"

"Well," said Bunny. "I've got Darren Donavan in the boot of my car."

"Oh God, now you've taken a hostage. How is that good news?"

"Because, once he had come around and calmed down, I explained the situation. Now that he knows big brother Marty is aware of his failed coup and his deal with the Westies, he is mad keen to turn state's evidence."

Crossan's eyelids shot open and he took a step forward. "You are kidding?"

Bunny shook his head. "Merry bloody Christmas."

Crossan ran his fingers through his hair. "Holy shit, we need to get him into protective custody."

"Shouldn't be a problem," said Bunny. "He was going to go to Marty's for Christmas dinner tomorrow but I think he's lost his appetite."

"I'm going to have to ring the commissioner. This is big." Crossan fished his mobile out of his back pocket.

"Grand," said Bunny. "While you're on the phone to her, I have a couple of demands."

Crossan looked up from his phone, his tone incredulous. "You have demands?"

"Well, requests. You know, season of good will and all that."

Crossan shook his head. "C'mon – you two better come in. Wipe your feet."

"I don't want to intrude."

"Yeah. I think that horse has already bolted. Does the young fella like salted peanuts by any chance?"

THE COMEBACK KID

Tara smiled nervously across the table. Nobody tried to smile back. Bunny had been gone hours and they'd not heard anything from him since that afternoon. The last message had been that he was making progress but his phone was short of charge so relax and he'll take care of everything. Relax. Like two parents are going to relax while their son is in harm's way. The father's English was nearly non-existent but she'd still noticed the tendency to look down at the table every few minutes. She could see the pain on his face as his mind tortured him, running through worst-case scenarios again and again. Grief was not contained by language barriers. The mother kept doing her breathing exercises and clutching her husband's hand. Did stress bring on early labour? Tara wasn't sure. She knew that sex and curry apparently did. In the case of her cousin Cheryl, they'd also played a fairly big role in conception.

Tara considered offering her guests another vol-au-vent but decided against it. She could tell the last time that it had irritated them. She had hundreds of the buggers to get shot of. She had inevitably been screwed over by Donal the wanker banker, and upsetting as it was, the predicament of the Zhao family meant it was hard to get too upset about it. She'd just have to find the money somewhere else. Could you freeze vol-au-vents? Maybe she could eat nothing but finger food for the whole of January? God, that'd be grim.

She jumped as there was a pounding on the door.

"For fuck's sake, we're closed!"

"Bollocks ye are! I'm not coming back through the damn sewer."

Tara leapt up to her feet. The Zhaos started talking furiously to each other.

"OK, relax," said Tara. "I'll let him in."

Tara rushed over and slid the bolts on the top and bottom of the door across and then opened it. Bunny McGarry stood there in the pouring rain.

"Christ."

"It has gone ferocious wet Tara."

"C'mon in."

Bunny walked in, a slight hitch in his step. The source for this was revealed when he pulled his coat back and Tara saw the young boy who had his arms locked around Bunny's leg.

Mary screamed. The young lad released his grip on Bunny and ran to his parents. Bunny leaned against the bar. "Thank fuck for that. If he was going to be staying there long term, I was going to have to get another child to hang onto the other leg to even me out."

"What the hell happened?" asked Tara.

"'Tis a long story. Oh, before I forget ..." Bunny took a thick brown envelope out of his pocket and threw it on the bar. "There's the money the wanker banker owes you."

Tara snatched it up. "How did you get this?"

"My colleagues in the Garda Síochána helped out."

"I don't need charity."

Bunny laughed. "Oh, it wasn't charity. We found out where the wanker banker had moved his bash to and a couple of lads from the drugs squad had a quiet word. Turns out they might have had more than vol-au-vents laid on, as they were suddenly ferocious keen to pay their tab here to avoid any awkward questions about their recreational supply."

"You're kidding!"

"I'm not. All five grand of it present and correct."

Tara looked in the envelope. "Ehm Bunny, he only owed me three."

He looked honestly surprised. "Really? Hand on heart, I got that wrong. Ah, screw it – I'm sure he can afford it. Besides, I'd imagine that Dyson in the bathroom might be drying the hands of the angels in heaven by now, so it'll cover a new one."

Tara felt her eyes start to water. "Oh Bunny, this is incredible."

Bunny shifted uncomfortably. "Hey now, none of that."

"Seriously though, how can I ever thank you?"

"For feck's sake woman, you own a pub!"

Tara wiped a hand across her eyes. "Pint of Arthur's finest coming up." She moved behind the bar and got it started.

"And his friend Jack can come too. It's been a long old day."

"Right you are."

Bunny glanced over at the reunited Zhao family.

Tara followed his eyes. "Not for nothing Sergeant McGarry, but that's a hell of a day's work you did there."

Bunny smiled. "Yeah. Not too shabby. Actually," he said, drumming his hands on the bar. "Seeing as the wanker banker won't be needing them, what do you reckon to us taking all this food down to the homeless shelter?"

Tara nodded, putting the pint aside to settle as she went for the whiskey. "That is a fantastic idea."

"'Tis the season and all that."

Tara poured them both a large and they clinked the glasses in toast. "Sláinte," said Tara.

"Merry bloody Christmas."

"You, Bunny, are my very own secret Santa."

"Would now be a good time to confess it was me that broke the jukebox?"

"Did you really think I didn't know that?"

Bunny laughed. "Tara, you're a shocking loss to law enforcement."

He stretched out his back and yawned. "I tell ye, I'm not as young as I used to be."

"Says the man who saved the day again."

"Still though, I'm taking the retirement."

Tara nearly dropped her glass. "What?"

Bunny nodded. "For reasons I won't go into, I needed to have a chat with the commissioner earlier. I have taken their generous offer of retirement."

"But just this morning ..."

"Ah," said Bunny. "That was them pushing me out. I've never been the sort that likes to be pushed. This way, it's my choice. And besides, I'm getting too old for all these forms and rules they've got now. They were going to get me out eventually, this way I go on my terms."

"Are you sure about this?" asked Tara.

Bunny shrugged. "I dunno, ask me in a year. Besides, turns out I have more tricks than being a guard. I'm actually pretty good at being Santa Claus."

Tara patted the envelope. "Ain't that the truth."

"Speaking of my terms." Bunny turned to address the Zhao family and raised his voice. "Sorry to interrupt folks but you'll be pleased to hear, in acknowledgement of the ordeal you've been through, the Commissioner of the Garda Síochána shall be ringing her old friend the Minister for something or other next week and pleading your case."

They all looked at him blankly.

"You can stay here. Welcome to Ireland. Céad míle fáilte."

Mary gasped and then quickly started talking to the others.

"You're welcome."

Bunny held his hands up but that didn't stop the trio rushing towards him. Joseph hugged the top half of him, while little junior clamped back on to his leg again. Mary started slowly making her way over to him too. She smiled at him and then stopped in the middle of the floor.

"Oh boy," said Bunny. "Erm, Tara?"

"Just a sec," came the shout from the back, where she'd disappeared to. "I'm just looking for cling film for the food."

"Right. We'll need a mop too."

"Oh. OK."

"Actually, we'll need an ambulance and a mop."

"What?"

"I think Mary's water just broke."

Wang Min rushed back to Mary's side and guided her back into a chair.

Tara reappeared behind the bar. "Jesus Christ!"

"That'd be a good name for him alright, given the timing."

"I'll ring the ambulance."

"Good woman." Bunny turned to the Zhaos and spoke loudly and slowly. "The ambulance will be here soon. Relax."

Mrs Zhao nodded, while taking deep breaths.

"While we're waiting," said Bunny, "does anyone know the words to 'Jingle Bells'?"

GOOD DEEDS AND BAD INTENTIONS

THIS IS ANOTHER STORY SET AT CHRISTMAS, BUT IT'S CHRISTMAS IN NEW YORK. I'D LIKE TO TELL YOU THAT I HAD SOME FANCY INSPIRATION FOR THIS BUT HONESTLY, I MAY HAVE JUST STARTED WITH THE IDEA OF BUNNY, AS SANTA, RECEIVING A SERIOUS DRESSING-DOWN FROM A PRECOCIOUS LITTLE GIRL AND WORKED BACKWARDS FROM THERE. I ALSO POSSIBLY HAD THE IDEA THAT IN THE ABSENCE OF BEING ABLE TO FIND A *CERTAIN* LADY THAT HE'S LOOKING FOR; BUNNY MIGHT FILL HIS TIME DOING GOOD DEEDS IN HIS OWN INIMITABLE STYLE — AS IT'S EITHER THAT OR GETTING INTO TROUBLE SOME OTHER WAY.

TWAS THE NIGHT BEFORE CHRISTMAS

"You ain't nothing but bull."

Bunny looked down to see a face, scrunched up with anger, glowering up at him from between pigtails. He wasn't exactly a leading expert on children, but he reckoned the girl was eight or nine at most.

"Excuse me?" said Bunny, trying to give what he hoped was a winning smile.

The girl pointed up at him. "You heard me. Ain't no such thing as Santa, and this whole thing is a scam! A straight-up scam!"

Bunny glanced around and noticed that they were getting noticed by passers-by. Seventh Avenue had no shortage of foot traffic, and while he had come to appreciate just how good most people were at ignoring anything going on around them, a little girl standing on the sidewalk hollering at Santa Claus on Christmas Eve was the kind of thing that'd pique the interest of all but the most insular of New Yorkers.

"Are you OK, little girl?"

"Don't you 'little girl' me. I'm sick of all this nonsense. You're fake. I bet even that belly is fake."

She poked Bunny in what was very definitely his real belly.

"Ouch! Go easy, would ye? That's all me."

"Oh. Well then you should lose some weight."

"Thanks for the advice. And before you rip it off my face, this beard is mine too." He gave it a tug to emphasise his point. None of these facts seemed to do anything to take the angry wind out of the little girl's sails.

"None of that makes you Santa Claus. You're just some fat old guy with a beard!"

Bunny looked around, hoping to see a parent, but while several people were now paying attention, none of them had that parental air about them. "Jesus, love, is your charm school on a day off or something?"

She wrinkled her nose and wafted her hand in front of it. "And you smell of booze. I know that smell."

Bunny tried to smile. "Santa has been out here all day in the freezing cold, ringing this bell, raising money for the homeless..." He pointed at the bucket next to him, which contained mostly coins. "And he may have taken a little nip of something to take the edge off."

"Stop calling yourself Santa. You ain't Santa."

Bunny scratched his beard. She had him there. He wasn't the real Santa. In fact, he wasn't even the real fake Santa – that guy was in a bar down the block getting wasted. Bunny had needed an excuse to stand around on this street corner and not look suspicious. This had seemed like a good idea at the time. It turned out the other guy was doing this as part of his community service for a public urination citation, and he'd been more than happy to be liberated from his bell-ringing responsibilities.

"OK," said Bunny, lowering his voice and leaning down to look at the little girl. "You're absolutely right, sweetheart – I'm not 'the' Santa. I'm a friend of his, and he let me borrow his suit so I could raise money for charity to help homeless people have a nice Christmas."

"So you're a friend of Santa?"

"Yes."

"OK, then explain this: there are, like, two billion children in the world – how is he delivering presents to all of them?"

"Well," said Bunny, "his reindeer can fly, and—"

"Yeah," she interrupted, "but to visit every house, they'd have to be clocking at least 650 miles per second. At that speed, reindeers are gonna spontaneously combust. BOOM!" She threw her arms out in an extravagant gesture to emphasis the violence of this untimely end. "I googled it in the library at school. The top speed of a reindeer is fifteen miles per hour. Per hour! They reach 650 miles per second and Santa's hurtling towards the earth with a face full of fried reindeer, and that's gonna leave a big old fat-white-guy-sized crater. That's science! You can't argue with science."

"Right," said Bunny. "Well, that's very impressive. You know a lot about science, don't you?"

"Yeah. I like science. Science don't lie to you, unlike everybody else." She pointed around them. "Look at all this. Spirit of goodwill? It's all rich people buying other rich people fancy things."

Despite the cold weather, Bunny was sweating. Down the block, amidst the throng of tourists, last-minute shoppers and pickpockets, he could see two members of the NYPD looking in his direction.

"So, are you going to be a scientist when you grow up?"

The little girl folded her arms and narrowed her eyes. "I'd like to be, but I ain't gonna be. I looked that up too. To do science, you gotta go to college. That costs a lot of money, and I'm an orphan. Where am I gonna get that kind of money? Ain't gonna happen."

"Oh," said Bunny.

"Yeah," said the girl. "I'm gonna end up in some crappy job where I don't get to use my brain. I'll probably end up standing on a street corner ringing a bell."

"Ouch."

"No offence," she said, with the air of someone who was aware she had an inadvertent tendency to cause an awful lot of it. "I saw some comedian guy on TV talking about how angry the staff are at the DMV. I bet that's because they couldn't afford to be scientists either. Life ain't fair." She nodded – agreeing with herself emphatically.

Bunny was floundering. The little girl had a relentless line of argument, which he was having a hard time countering. "Santa's reindeer are magic?" He could hear the disbelief in his own voice as he said it. He knew it was futile, but he felt the need to at least attempt it anyway.

"Oh, please," said the little girl, throwing her arms up in disgust. "If Santa has all this magic at his fingertips, what's he doing with it? Take a look around – world needs a hero, not some fat dude who works one day a year."

"Annabelle Watson!" The shout came from a large, sweaty white woman who was rushing down the sidewalk towards them, her face a mix of panic, relief and outrage. "There you are!"

The little girl looked back at the woman. "What? I wasn't doing nothing."

"You weren't doing *anything*," said the woman, almost on automatic.

"See, you agree with me."

"No, I..."

The lady reached them, her breathing now heavy and laboured. "You most certainly were doing something, and you know it was something you weren't supposed to."

"Make up your mind," said the little girl, just quietly enough to not be heard.

"What was the one thing I said before we left Saint Augustine's this morning?"

"Pee now as we can't—"

"Not that! I said don't wander off. And what did you do, missy? You wandered off. We will be having some serious words about this when we get back."

The woman leaned down and took Annabelle's hand, and then she looked up at Bunny, her face full of apology. "I am sorry, sir. I hope she wasn't a bother?"

"Oh no, not at all. We were just having a nice chat."

She gave a tight smile. "Thank you. She's a smart child, but she is a handful."

"But Mrs Tandy—"

"Not another word, missy. Not one word. Well, at least you got to meet Santa."

Annabelle pointed at Bunny with her free hand. "He ain't Santa; he's just some fat dude in a suit."

"Annabelle!" Mrs Tandy exclaimed, her voice full of genuine outrage. She looked at Bunny. "I do apologise, sir."

Bunny waved it away. "Ah, don't worry about it. She speaks her mind – not enough of it about."

Mrs Tandy leaned in. "I'm sorry – she's acting out. We brought all the children into Manhattan on a day trip. Danelli's department store gives us a free visit with Father Christmas on Christmas Eve – you know, as a PR thing. The kids really look forward to it."

"Ah, right," said Bunny. "That's nice of them."

"Yes, it would have been, only we turned up to find out they'd bumped us. Some NBA team is in town to play a game tomorrow and they brought their kids to see Santa instead."

"Oh," said Bunny.

"Yes. The PR woman said orphans at Christmas were a bit depressing. They'd rather have Santa taking free throws with millionaires." Despite giving it some effort, Mrs Tandy failed to keep the anger from her voice. "We load twenty-seven kids onto the subway from Queens because the home's bus has broken down – again – only to get here and find that. Not exactly the most Christian thing, is it?"

"No," agreed Bunny, "'tis an absolute disgrace."

"Yes. As if that wasn't bad enough, the woman gave us discount vouchers for toys, like that's some kind of a thing. Giving orphans money off on toys – might as well be giving me free parking for my Ferrari. I don't know how some people—"

Mrs Tandy's cell phone interrupted her. She fished it out of her pocket with her free hand. "Hey, Samantha... Yes, I found her. We'll meet you over by the station... What? Anthony needs to go again? You'd think with all that crying, he'd be tapped out. OK, I'll be back over in a second."

She hung up the phone.

"Come on, Annabelle, we have to be getting back. Say goodbye to the nice man."

Annabelle shot a begrudging nod in Bunny's direction.

Mrs Tandy shook her head again. "A merry Christmas to you, sir."

Bunny nodded. "And to you too," he said, raising his voice, as the duo were already hurrying back down the sidewalk.

Bunny watched them go, Mrs Tandy weaving in and out of the torrent of pedestrian traffic, a truculent Annabelle dragged in her wake. He stood transfixed for a full minute, until, from the corner of his eye, he saw an object arc its way into the bucket that dangled from the stand beside him.

His hand shot out on instinct, and grabbed the source of the object around the throat: a blond guy in his mid twenties, wearing a suede jacket and a smug grin – although the grin didn't survive a coarse hand wrapping itself around his body's primary avenue for oxygen consumption.

"What the—"

The rest of the sentence was lost as Bunny tightened his grip. The tosser found himself eye to eye with Father Christmas, whose right eye glowered at him while the left seemed to be gazing off in an entirely different direction. "'Tis the most magical time of the year, fella. And to prove that, a couple of miracles are about to happen. In particular, the soda can you just tossed into the bucket – which you know is there to collect money for the homeless – is going to magically transform itself into all the cash in your wallet."

The guy went to push Bunny away, but this resulted in a firm grip being applied to his right wrist, sending pain shooting up his arm. He gave a strangled yelp.

"And if that miracle does happen," continued Bunny, "then the other miracle will be you walking away from here with the same number of bollocks as you came with. Are we clear?"

Five minutes and an ostentatious donation of two hundred bucks later, Bunny was back to ringing his bell and trying not to attract attention. Then he saw Helena Martinez step out of the side door of the theatre where she worked, just as she had done for the last three days. Everything around her wasn't the same though. You'd have had to know what to look for to see it, especially in the Christmas rush of people moving in all directions. Still, Bunny knew what to look for. He hadn't been watching Helena Martinez so much as he'd been waiting to see who else was watching Helena Martinez. A large man with a shaven head, who, despite the just above freezing weather, was only wearing a black hoodie, walked quickly out of a nearby coffee shop and, with his eyes fixed on her, followed her down the street.

Bunny took the burner phone out of the pocket and hit speed dial.

"We got a bite."

A WALK IN THE PARK

Helena checked the bench was clean and then sat down. In reality, it really was far too cold to be sitting in Central Park eating her lunch, but she didn't care. Even as a kid, she had weirdly loved the cold weather. Everyone else longed for summer, but not her. There was something about that bite in the air that made her feel alive. And so it was that, at the same time every day, rain allowing, she would nip out of the theatre and hurry the three blocks up to Central Park, so she could sit there in the closest thing you could find to peace and quiet on the Island of Manhattan. When Helena was a child, her momma had often joked that, seeing as she loved the cold and the quiet so much, she should go live in Alaska with the penguins. Helena had known there weren't any penguins in Alaska outside of a zoo, but she hadn't corrected her momma, as then she would have had to admit that she had not only looked it up but studied it in embarrassing detail. Everyone else dreamed of Hollywood; she was the little girl who had gone to bed every night dreaming of Alaska. She'd grown into a woman who had never even left New York. With a sigh, she pulled the package of sandwiches she had brought from home out of her bag and unwrapped it. A few pigeons swooped down as she did so. She recognised the one with the unusual white and brown markings – he was a regular who knew she was an easy mark.

She was halfway through her second sandwich when a red-headed woman sat down at the other end of the bench. Helena let out an involuntary yelp of surprise. The woman held out a hand.

"Pardon me, honey – didn't mean to frighten you."

Helena blushed. "Oh no, not at all. Sorry. I was engrossed in feeding the birds."

The woman nodded. "I can see that. They sure do love you."

Helena gave a polite laugh. "They love anybody with bread. Not many people sit around feeding them this time of year."

The redhead gave a warm laugh and hugged her arms around herself. "Ain't that the truth. Too damn cold. I'm from Texas – we don't keep our iceboxes this frosty."

Helena smiled in response.

"Still," continued the woman, "sitting here, we got more space around us than you get anywhere else in Manhattan, huh?"

Helena nodded. "That's why I come here."

"Yeah," said the woman with a nod. "It's broad daylight and we've got plenty of wide-open ground around us. I want you to remember that."

Helena's head whipped around to look at the woman.

"Oh gee, I'm sorry. That came out wrong. Didn't mean to sound quite so stalkery. Apologies." The redhead held her hands up. "I'm kinda new to this."

"New to what exactly?"

The woman gave her a smile. "I promise you, I'm here as a friend. Relax, Helena."

Helena sat up ramrod straight. "How do you know my name?"

"That's what I'm here to explain. My name is Cheryl, and I want to help you."

"I don't need help."

Cheryl nodded. "I'm afraid you do. Try not to look, but there's a big, muscly dude with a shaven head over on the far side there, on the left, at the treeline. He followed you here."

Helena tried to look casual as she looked around. She could see the man now, staring over at them.

"Oh God." She said it to herself as much as anything.

"It's OK," said Cheryl.

"It's not. You don't understand."

"I do. I really do. You think that man has something to do with your ex-husband, and you're right – he does."

Helena grabbed her bag, ready to stand and run.

"Wait, wait – please. Just give me sixty seconds. I swear to you, honey, I'm here to help."

Helena eyed the woman suspiciously, but she didn't move.

"Thank you," continued Cheryl. "I'm helping out a friend of mine. He got hold of a list of women like yourself who are trying to get away from abusive partners."

"How would you get that? They don't just hand that kind of information out."

"No. I know somebody who works in an emergency room. Let's just say he got tired of seeing a certain kind of injury."

Helena said nothing, instead looking down at her hands clasped in her lap.

"We," continued Cheryl, "well, mainly my friend – he keeps an eye on these ladies, just in case the abusers show up again. We know the law doesn't offer enough protection, and we're just trying to fill in the gaps."

"And what's in it for you?" The fear in Helena's voice was turning to anger now.

"First and foremost, we want to stop bad things happening. I get you being suspicious, I really do. That's why I'm approaching you like this. We want to help you. Also..." The woman shifted in her seat. "Also," she repeated, "to be completely honest with you, honey, my friend... he's trying to find a bunch of nuns that operate in New York, helping women in situations like yourself. We figure we help out enough people, somebody might know them, put us in contact."

Helena shook her head. "I don't know any nuns."

"OK, not a problem. Like I said, we want to help regardless, and we can. Believe me. We've done this a few times now."

Helena gave her a suspicious look. "Why can't you just go talk to these nuns?"

Cheryl shrugged. "He can't find them. He's been here looking for them for like..." She took a moment to think. "Damn, nine months now. They don't officially exist. It's complicated, but if they're here at all, they don't want to be found. So this is what we came up with."

"It doesn't make any sense."

Cheryl pursed her lips. "You might be right, honey, but – to be straight with you – this is his last hope. He's kinda desperate. And besides, he likes helping people – people who need help. And no offence, but that is you."

Helena ran her hand over her brow. "Jonny said he'd kill me if he found me. I've got to run."

"You do that, he'll find you again."

She shook her head. "You don't understand. He's a dangerous man."

"Jonny Risbury, suspected lieutenant for the Los Zetas Cartel, on the run after skipping bail in Miami on two serious assault charges. He was previously charged but not convicted in three first-degree murder cases and was a person of interest in several more investigations."

Helena gulped and put her head in her hands. "Oh God."

"He's a dangerous man alright. The good news is so is my friend."

Helena looked into the distance and didn't speak for about thirty seconds. Finally, she pushed her hair back behind her ear and spoke in a soft voice. "You're probably wondering how I could ever go with a guy like that?"

Cheryl shook her head. "No, I'm not. I know as well as anyone, sweetheart, the evil bastards can be just as charming as the good guys – sometimes even more so, precisely because they are the evil bastards."

Helena nodded, tears in her eyes now. "He wasn't always... When we met, he was just a nice guy working in a bar. Mostly."

"His actions are his actions. None of this is your fault. If you'll let us, we'd like to make it so he'll never bother you again."

"I've got a son."

"We know. If it makes you feel better, right now my beau is outside his school, making sure he's safe."

"This guy you work with," said Helena. "The one looking for the nuns, he is your...?"

Cheryl laughed. "Oh no. Lord, no. He's a friend. Me and my man just help him out."

"How do you know him?"

Cheryl smiled. "That's a long story. Let's just say the crazy Irishman dropped into our—"

"He's Irish?" asked Helena with such abruptness that Cheryl sat back.

"Ehm, yes."

"Big guy? Beard?"

It was Cheryl's turn to look surprised. "You know him?"

"He has a..." She waved a hand at her face. "Y'know, a sort of 'off' eye?"

Cheryl nodded. "You really have met him."

Helena shook her head. "No, but I got a friend. Well, I mean, I know her. We're in this support group together. Her name's Marcia. She lives out in Brooklyn somewhere, I think."

"Ah. Right."

"Her old boyfriend came looking for her. Came after her with a baseball bat."

Cheryl nodded. "Like I said, we've done this before."

"Your friend? That was the guy who bust in and...?"

Cheryl nodded again.

"Is it true they found her ex hanging upside down from a street light?"

"My friend has a... Let's call it a certain sense of flair."

"Carol told us it took them hours to remove the bat."

Cheryl tried to suppress a smile. "He ain't a big fan of baseball."

Helena bit her knuckle and then turned back to Cheryl with a very different look in her eyes. "What would I have to do?"

SMILE – IT CONFUSES PEOPLE

Jackson Diller leaned against the lamp post and smiled. He was a young black guy standing on a street corner in one of New York's nicer suburbs, and that made people nervous. People being nervous because a black dude was just standing doing absolutely nothing really shouldn't be his problem, but it was. Rather than taking steps to bring about meaningful social change at 8pm on Christmas Eve, he was smiling just to stop the white people from calling the cops. Smiling had been Diller's preferred mode of defence since birth, and that had seen him through more challenging situations than this. He had been stationed here for over two hours now and it was getting cold. He'd found a thick duffle coat in a thrift store a few weeks ago and it was proving to be a superb purchase. It was two sizes too big for his skinny frame, but Diller loved it. He clapped his hands together to keep the blood flowing. An old lady looked at him nervously and Diller upped the wattage on the smile.

"Happy Christmas to you, ma'am."

The woman nodded, smiled and noticeably increased her pace. Diller was between meaningful positions of employment. He wondered if he could get a gig as a personal trainer for the elderly? He'd had two weeks of acting work booked in, but that had gone south after the one-act play's opening night turned out to be its closing night too. Not only had there been only one performance – well, there hadn't even been that, really. Their leading lady/director/writer/backer had shimmied down a drainpipe mid-performance and disappeared. It turned out she had stolen a painting from her psychiatrist's office and had been shocked to see him sitting in the audience – although not as shocked as he was to see his painting hanging on the back wall of the set. Diller had finished the play by performing both parts. The consensus was that it had improved it greatly.

Diller returned to watching the six-storey brownstone about a hundred yards away on the opposite side of the street. It was the building where Helena Martinez and her son lived, up on the fourth floor. He had followed them home earlier that day. Actually, he had followed the guy who was following them home, and then watched as he'd checked their precise address before leaving. The theory was that he and his boss, Helena Martinez's ex, would be back later tonight, which was why Diller was standing on a street corner smiling at nervous strangers. His job for this part of proceedings was to be lookout. They had a plan. He personally felt that at least one part of it was terrible and another part was verging on the suicidal, but nobody seemed keen to hear his thoughts, and besides, his mom had always told him that if you can't say anything nice...

Diller's upbringing had been, to say the least, unconventional, but his mom had always made a big effort for the holidays. They'd never had much, but she had done everything in her power to make something out of it. Looking at all of these apartments, their windows aglow with warm lights, snapshots of lives festooned with decorations and presents under the Christmas tree, felt like looking into a different world, one he'd only ever seen on TV.

He heard a noise and glanced behind him, then he turned again, executing a textbook double take.

"Is that a pig?"

The slight woman in a bobble hat and thick-rimmed glasses did nothing to hide her eye-roll. "Yes, it's a pig," she said, before adding with a sigh, "just once it would be nice to bring him for a walk without people asking us questions."

Diller pulled back. "Sorry, but you're walking a pot-bellied pig in New York. I think you're going to have to get used to the fact that people will have questions." Diller gave his best winning smile which still lost.

"Honestly, you'd think people haven't seen a pig before."

The woman would have undoubtedly liked to storm off, but the pig had taken this moment to engage in a large dump.

There was an awkward silence – or at least there would have been, but for the sounds of the pig popping out a prodigious poop. Diller wasn't a big fan of silences.

"So what's his name?"

"Mr Oinks."

"Right. Hey, Mr Oinks!" Diller gave a wave in the pig's direction, but the pig seemed preoccupied.

His owner shuffled her feet. "Sorry about snapping before. It's just... It's my last day with him."

"Oh," said Diller, before lowering his voice. "Is he...?"

"What?"

"Going to be Christmas dinner?"

The woman reared back in outrage. "No! I am a strict vegan, as is Mr Oinks."

"Right. Sorry," said Diller, who happened to know pigs were omnivores by nature and Mr Oinks was very unlikely to be vegan by choice, but elected, rightly, not to mention it.

"It turns out that *technically*" – she said "technically" like it was a very bad word – "it is illegal to keep a pig as a pet in New York City. It's fine to slaughter them en masse, of course."

"Right," said Diller. He glanced over at the building he was supposed to be watching, aware that he was getting dragged into a distraction he could not afford.

"One of my neighbours complained. Bitch! So now Mr Oinks has to go live with my Uncle Jeffrey in Jersey. I'm taking him over there tomorrow."

"I see. Is it legal to keep him in Jersey?"

"Have you been to Jersey? It's barely fit for human habitation."

The woman bent down before storming off, or at least as much as it was possible to storm off with a pig's lead in one hand and a freezer bag full of pig poop in the other.

In the opposite direction, Diller noticed a yellow Mustang pulling up to park. The man Diller recognised from earlier got out of the driver's side, and another man got out on the passenger side. They had a brief discussion over the hood and then the driver stayed with the car while the other one headed towards the building's front door.

Diller casually took his mobile out of his pocket and sent a group text.

THEY ARE HERE.

THE MAN COMES AROUND

Jonny Risbury stepped back as a hassled-looking guy, laden with too much luggage and with his phone clamped to his ear, emerged from the building's front door.

"No, Mom, Janice said she was getting the cranberry sauce. I don't even eat it. Why would I... No, I'm not... I have... Alright, fine, I'll get it. I'll ask the Uber driver to stop on the way. OK."

He dropped his bags and looked at Jonny, who gave him a polite smile in return.

"So, where are you parked?" He looked at Jonny expectantly and then, after a few moments of blankness, looked mortified. "Oh my God, I'm so sorry. You're not my Uber driver, are you?"

Jonny shook his head. "No."

Designer leather jacket, Rolex on his wrist – this guy obviously thought the people-ferrying business paid really well.

"Sorry, dude. Sorry. I'm a little stressed out, y'know – family!"

Jonny gave him a big grin and caught the door before it closed behind him. "Yeah. Tell me about it." Then he moved inside and headed for the stairs.

NO GOOD DEED

Rolo sat in the Mustang and fiddled irritably with the heater. It somehow managed to blow a lot of hot air around without making the car warm. He'd already spent most of the day trudging around New York following the boss's ex, and he was getting royally sick of this. Not that he'd say anything. Jonny was real friendly and amicable, right up until the point he wasn't. Rolo had been there the night Jonny had messed up Xavier Fuentes bad, when they had been playing cards. Jonny was alright with losing, but Xavier had had to go twisting the knife, making it all personal. Xavier wouldn't be running his mouth off like that again – the dude spoke with a permanent slur now, like his tongue was too big for his mouth. Last Rolo heard, Xavier had got himself deliberately arrested robbing a five-and-dime, because he couldn't cope with being outside since he was all messed up. These days he pushed a broom up in Rikers and didn't say nothing to nobody.

Rolo didn't like this. If it was up to him, Jonny would just forget about his ex-wife and kid, but it very definitely wasn't up to him. They were supposed to be making money for the bosses. Jonny got a lot of rope because he was an earner, but that only went so far. They had something they were meant to be doing, and this wasn't it. Rolo knew better than to bring it up though. Jonny was full-on crazy on this particular subject – like he took the whole thing as a personal insult. Rolo didn't get it. it wasn't like Jonny didn't have plenty of women, and it wasn't like he was a contender for dad of the year either. He had another kid he never saw. This was all because she had walked away from him and the man couldn't take losing. It was messed up. Rolo wasn't sure what the endgame was supposed to be. Did Jonny think they were going to see each other again and it'd be happy families? Did he just want to scare her? Or worse? Rolo had plans for the night; the last thing he wanted was to have to go dump a body in the river on Christmas Eve. He had surf and turf at Marco's booked in.

A van pulled up in front of him and a blonde got out. She was cute, and not exactly dressed for the weather. Leather miniskirt and a mirrorball top that clung in all the right places. She had legs to die for. She looked around, searching for something that wasn't there. Rolo watched as she twirled around and then pulled out her phone. She rang a number and swore into somebody's voicemail. Rolo looked up from checking out her body to find her eyes on him. He felt himself redden, but she gave him a big smile and headed straight for him. As she reached the window, he pressed the button to bring it down. She leaned in with a big smile and Rolo tried to look without looking at what was on display below the smile.

"Hey, baby, I'm real sorry to bother you. I'm supposed to be meeting my friend but he ain't here. I've got to drop a sound desk just over there to my girl Janice's apartment. Is there any chance you could help me lift it?"

Rolo looked up. "Sorry, I'm just waiting for somebody."

"Please?" She gave him a little pout. "I'd be real grateful. It's just over there. We're in a band. I'll give you tickets to a show we got coming up at the Roxy."

Rolo thought about it. Jonny was likely to be a while yet.

"Please, baby. I'll make sure you get the VIP treatment too."

She said it with a sly smile that won him over.

"Alright then."

"Oh, thank you. You're such a sweetheart."

Rolo got out of the car and moved around.

"It'll just take a second."

"Sure, no problem. So what's the name of the band?"

"Shocker. We're funk metal."

"Right," said Rolo. "Sounds cool." It didn't, but Rolo was warming to the idea of the VIP treatment and what exactly that might entail.

"Can you get the doors there, baby?"

Rolo opened the van doors. "I ain't been to the Roxy for—"

He stopped talking because, upon opening the van doors, he'd seen it was empty. A flicker of suspicion flashed through him a millisecond before the 1200 volts of electricity. He fell to the ground. As Rolo's scrambled brain tried to process this unexpected turn of events, he was dimly aware of the woman's knee digging into his back and then a hand pressing a material with a sweet chemical smell to his face.

Diller moved over to stand beside Cheryl as she kneeled on top of the big guy's back. He looked around.

"Are we cool?" asked Cheryl.

"Yeah. I don't think anybody saw."

"Excellent. I told you this would work."

Diller nodded. "You did. Don't take this the wrong way, but you would make an excellent serial killer."

Cheryl looked up at him and smiled. "And what exactly is the right way to take that?"

Diller shrugged.

"How long do I have to hold this chloroform over his mouth?"

"I'd give it another minute. People think it acts instantly because they've seen it go down like that in movies, but it doesn't."

"OK," said Cheryl, pulling her blonde wig off with her free hand and tossing it into the back of the van. "Damn, I'm freezing my ass off."

Diller nodded. "You should've worn a thick coat."

Cheryl laughed and shook her head. "Dill, honey, for such a smart dude, there are some big things you don't understand – like if I was wearing a big warm coat, this guy would still be sitting in his car. Anyway, do you think that's enough?"

Diller looked at the big dude's face. "Yeah, he looks out of it. Besides, too much chloroform could kill him."

Cheryl pulled the rag away. "Jesus, Dill, couldn't you have mentioned that before?"

"Sorry. I thought I had?"

"Nope, you definitely didn't." Cheryl stood up and glanced around. "C'mon, let's get him into the back before somebody sees."

They bent down to the unconscious man and each grabbed an arm. "This dude is heavy," said Cheryl.

"Yep," said Diller through gritted teeth.

The man's face hit the tow bar on the van.

"Oops," said Cheryl. "Where did you get the chloroform from anyway?"

"I made it."

"You're kidding?"

With a heave they got his upper body in the back of the van.

"You just need some acetone and a gallon of six per cent sodium hypochlorite bleach. I'll get the rope and tie him up. I'm good with knots."

"Right," said Cheryl. "And remind me again why *I'm* the one who'd make a good serial killer?"

LIKE THE FELLA ONCE SAID...

Jonny stood to the side, out of view of the peephole, and then knocked politely on the door.

"Amazon delivery."

He waited. He'd been careful to disguise his voice, going for an inoffensive Midwestern accent like all those companies used in their adverts. Apparently it was the most trusted – they'd done a study or something. He'd read a thing in a magazine once while waiting in a doctor's office.

Nothing happened. There was no sound from within the apartment. He had checked the windows from the street; there had definitely been lights on.

He knocked again, more loudly this time.

"Amazon delivery for a Helena Martinez." He knew she had changed her name. It should be Risbury, but even if you accepted this bullshit divorce the judge had granted, her maiden name was Ortega. She had changed it again when she'd run and taken his son away from him. It had made finding them harder, but not impossible. Not when you knew the right people.

There was still no noise from inside. Jonny reached inside his jacket and checked the Glock holstered under his left armpit. Then he stood and listened for a full minute to make sure nobody was coming. He glanced up and down the hallway. He could hear a TV from across the hall, and a selection of festive tunes sung by a choir could be made out playing elsewhere in the building, but there didn't seem to be many people moving about. He put his hand in his inside pocket and pulled out the picks. This had never been his greatest skill, even in his early days, but the lock didn't look like much. As long as nobody disturbed him, he'd be fine.

He placed his hand against the door and was surprised to feel it give. The crazy bitch had left it open. She'd never been the smartest. Jonny slipped his picks back into his pocket and then discreetly withdrew the gun. He took a deep breath and moved inside, closing the door behind him. The apartment was now in darkness save for the wan light spilling in from the street outside. He listened but he still couldn't hear anything.

"Hey, baby. Daddy's home."

He was about to reach around for a switch when the lights came on.

"Howerya, Daddy."

Now illuminated, Jonny could see it was a studio apartment. There was an open-plan kitchen to his left and a bunk bed pushed against the far wall, with a small dining table and chairs beside it. A raggedy couch faced an old-looking TV to his right, behind which sat a small Christmas tree. At the far side of the room, about twenty feet from where Jonny stood, a large man in a Santa Claus outfit was sitting in an armchair giving him an amused look. Jonny pointed the gun at him.

"Who the fuck are you?"

The man raised his eyebrows. "Really? Jolly fat lad, red suit, beard? You're not exactly the world's greatest detective, are you?"

"Hilarious. Where's my wife?"

"You don't have a wife."

Jonny stepped forward. "You've got a hell of a mouth on you for the man who ain't holding the gun."

The man shrugged. "Well, I've been standing on a street corner for a lot of the day and I may've had a couple of nips against the cold. Sure, 'tis Christmas."

"She's picking up drunk Scottish bums now?"

"Scottish? Scottish?! I'm Irish, ye cloth-eared gobshite."

"I don't give a fuck. Where is my wife?"

"If you mean your ex-wife, then she and her son are miles away."

"Our son. I'm his father."

"Only in the sperm-donor sense."

Jonny looked around. There was a door that presumably led to a bathroom. Maybe they could be in there?

"And what are you doing in my wife's apartment?"

The man stretched his arms out and yawned expansively. "Well, appropriately enough, you're on my naughty list."

"Who do you work for?"

The man gave Jonny what he may have thought was a smile. One of his eyes was messed up, making him look more than a little crazy, even before you factored in the suit. The beard was real, although it looked like he'd made a half-assed attempt to make it whiter. "I don't work for anybody. Think of me as a freelancer."

"Well, I ain't and believe me, you don't want to mess with who I represent."

"What? Amazon? Just leave the card saying you tried to make the delivery and feck off, there's a good lad."

"You got jokes. Ain't that sweet. You really need to shut up now, old man."

"Ohhh, there's no need to be hurtful, ye drug-peddling, wife-beating shiteburger."

"Your mouth is gonna get you into a world of pain."

The man shrugged. "To be honest with you, it wouldn't be the first time."

"I don't know what she told you, but my wife…"

"Ex-wife."

"Has put you in the middle of somewhere you shouldn't be. You're in my way. Bad things happen to people that get in my way."

"Yeah, I read the hospital report. You left her with a broken collarbone and a cracked—"

Jonny raised his voice. "You better mind your goddamn manners."

The man scratched at his beard. "Fecking weird moment to break into a lesson on etiquette there, fella."

"I'm done with your bullshit. You either tell me where my wife and son are or the first bullet goes through your leg. And that's just the first one."

"They want nothing to do with you. This is your last chance to walk away."

Jonny looked around. This fat a-hole seemed inexplicably confident, given the circumstances. Either Jonny was missing something or the guy was straight-up insane.

"My last chance? My last chance?" repeated Jonny. "There's a word for someone who comes between a man and his wife."

All pretence of jollity left the Irishman's voice, which dropped to a low, growling register. "And there are lots of words for someone who raises his hand to a woman, and none of them are 'man'."

"Alright, that's it. Which leg do you want first, motherfucker?"

"Yeah, you're a big man with a gun, aren't you, Jonny? You only go toe to toe with women, is that right? Macho. Why don't you dance with someone your own size for a change?"

"You are one dumb son of a bitch."

"Tell you what there, John-boy. You beat me one-on-one and I'll tell you the exact address of where they are."

"Like I can't get it out of you anyway?"

"Yeah, but where'd be the fun in that?"

Jonny was twenty years younger, sixty pounds lighter and in considerably better shape. He'd gone to the state championships as a boxer in his teen years, and since then his fast hands had ended a lot of fights quickly.

"Stand up."

Santa Claus did as he was told, rising slowly from the chair.

"Show me you haven't got any weapons."

"Only my dazzling wits." The Irishman opened the stupid red suit and lifted it up as he turned slowly around. As he did so, he hummed 'It's Beginning to Look a Lot like Christmas' happily to himself. Jonny wanted to wipe the smile off this idiot's face. Rotation completed, Jonny pointed at the legs of the Irishman's Santa Claus outfit. He raised each of them in turn to show there was nothing strapped down there either. Then he rolled up his sleeves.

"I've also got nothing up me arse, but you're welcome to check?"

"No, thank you."

"Suit yourself. People have made that mistake before."

Jonny stood and looked at him for a long moment before placing the Glock down on the kitchen island. He could take this asshole easy, and if something went wrong, he still had the 22 strapped to his ankle. It'd feel real good to smash his face into the floor. He deserved a little Christmas treat.

The Irishman gave a sarcastic clap. "Fair play, Jonny. I would say I misjudged you but I haven't."

Jonny took his jacket off and tossed it on the floor. "Let's do this," he said, moving forward.

"Hang on a sec," said the Irishman, raising his hands. "Before we do – no knocking over the Christmas tree, it's bad luck."

Jonny cracked his knuckles. "Whatever."

"And, as it's Christmas, what do you say to no bollock shots?"

"Stop talking."

"Also" – the Irishman pointed back over towards the counter – "any disputes will be decided by the referee."

"What the...?"

Jonny glanced behind him. Standing beside the counter was a dwarf, holding Jonny's gun and pointing it at him.

"Fuck!"

"Yep," said the Irishman, before addressing the dwarf. "You owe me ten bucks, by the way." He turned back to Jonny. "I bet him I could make you give up the gun, and bless your fucking stupidity, you did. It was either that or he'd have used that stun gun thing he has. Thing is, that'd make you have a muscle spasm – never the cleverest thing to do to somebody holding a gun."

Jonny prepared to dive for his ankle holster.

"Don't," said the dwarf. "Just don't. I will if I have to."

Jonny looked at him and then relaxed his body. Nothing about the little guy indicated he was bluffing. "You better let me walk out of here. You think I came alone?"

"No," said the dwarf. "But the big dude outside in the car has already been dealt with. I got a text. Looks like you're having a bad day."

Jonny looked between the two men. "What's the plan here? You want me to leave Helena alone? Fine. You have my word."

"Well," said the Irishman, "if you can't trust a wife beater."

Jonny was just about done with this nonsense. "Who the fuck do you people think you are?"

The fat man held his hands out. "Sure, didn't I tell you. I'm Santa and he's my…"

"Don't say it," said the dwarf.

"I'm not. I didn't say it."

"You said you wouldn't say it."

"I haven't said it," pleaded the Irishman.

"You both need to listen to me," said Jonny, "and listen good. Anything happens to me, the people I work for will come for you. You'll meet your end begging for death. I've seen it. They get real creative." He pointed at the Irishman. "Believe me, they'll come for you, Santa Claus." He said it with a sneer. "And your little helper."

"That's it," barked the dwarf.

"I didn't say it. He—"

Jonny didn't hear the rest of the conversation. He watched as the dwarf pulled a yellow device from his pocket and fired it at him. Time slowed as Jonny watched the two metal probes arc through the air. He tried to run, but that just meant he got hit in the back. He went down hard. The last thing he remembered was seeing Santa's boot heading straight for his head.

CHRISTMAS AT BERNIE'S

They'd be fine.

Cheryl sat behind the wheel of the van and looked up at the apartment window. The light had come on a few minutes ago. She looked at her phone again: no message from Smithy. She'd give it another five minutes and then she would go and check. If it had gone south, she'd ring the cops and they would just have to deal with the consequences. She'd felt OK about her part of the plan, but now it was over, she was starting to realise just how many flaws were in the other half of it. If she had to explain to a cop why some hired muscle was hog-tied and unconscious in the back of the van, then so be it. OK, it wasn't her van, which was awkward, but her friend Carol could just say she hadn't known what Cheryl was using it for. She drummed on the steering wheel and looked at the clock on the dash, trying not to think of Smithy and Bunny bleeding out on the floor of an apartment. Smithy hadn't wanted her involved in this, but Bunny's little side project being what it was, he needed a woman more than he needed Smithy or Diller, not least because Diller was a non-combatant. Although the guy certainly had his uses.

Cheryl jumped as Diller's face appeared at the window right beside her. "Jesus, Dill!"

He waved apologetically as she wound the window down. "Sorry, didn't mean to startle you."

"Any sign of...?" started Cheryl.

"What? Oh, no."

Diller didn't seem worried. He appeared to have complete faith that Smithy and Bunny would be fine.

"Y'know how you said to take the keys and check their car?"

"Yeah."

"Well, I found something in the trunk."

"What did you...?"

Cheryl never finished the thought, as the door to the apartment building opened and three drunks exited. At least that was what it would look like to any passers-by. Santa Claus and a dwarf messily carried an unconscious man between them. They passed a female jogger making her way back into the building.

"Sorry, m'darling, sorry there. Jonny here is a bit worse for the drink."

"I told him," added Smithy in a slur, "you can't go drink for drink with an Irishman."

The jogger gave them a tight smile as she moved past them.

As she watched them make their way down the steps, Cheryl laughed, as much from relief as anything. Diller, for his part, applauded appreciatively. "They're *Weekend at Bernie's*-ing it. Gotta respect that. Quality touch."

GIFTS OF ALL KINDS

Sergeant Marlon Watts punched his fist on his chest and issued a resounding belch. He didn't know when this obsession with baking had hit the precinct, but it was reaching epidemic levels. Since two weeks before Thanksgiving, people had been bringing in all manner of homemade cookies and confections and it was becoming a nightmare, albeit a delicious one. Everybody knew he had a sweet tooth and that he was in charge of setting rotas, and this had led him to eating his own weight in baked goods over the last month. It was getting to the point that he had found himself craving a salad earlier. Well, craving may have been too strong a word; he hadn't been moved enough to actually go and get one. Still, as the doctor had said at his last physical, his feet problem was really a weight problem, and every other problem he would have in later life would end up being a weight problem too. Looking at life from the wrong side of fifty, Marlon couldn't take such things lightly anymore – not when his stomach was so large that he could lean it on his desk to get a little relief. His belt was also digging into him more and more. Damn it – come January first, he would go back to that gym he had been paying for every month for two years now. Marcia joked that he went religiously, in the sense that like church, he went a couple of times every year, usually around Christmas.

The doors flew open and Marsden and Gianelli came charging in. "Sarge, Sarge, Sarge – you gotta come outside!" insisted Gianelli.

Marlon didn't look up from the arrest reports he was scanning through on his desk. "I don't know if you're familiar with the chain of command in the sainted New York Police Department, Officer Gianelli, but I, like everyone else on the force, do not have to do anything you say."

Marlon didn't like Gianelli. Not even an Italian family could have as many uncles as he'd had 'die' over the last two years. If even half of them were real, he should have set up his own undertaking firm.

"C'mon, Sarge," chimed in Marsden. "I'm telling you, you do not want to miss this. It's a little Christmas treat."

On the other hand, Marlon actually did like Marsden; she was a good kid. She once judo-threw a tweaker across the receiving area after he'd lost it and tried to fight his way out. The woman was a pocket rocket.

"If it's carollers, then I'll give it a hard pass."

"It's better than that," said Gianelli. "I swear, Sarge."

Marlon stopped and looked at both of their faces. He'd not seen such eagerness since his own kids were youngsters on Christmas morning.

"Alright then, what is it?"

Marlon Watts stepped out of the back doors of the Precinct and into the car park. He didn't need to be directed as to where his attention was required. Two men sat tied up and gagged in the back seat of a yellow Mustang. The Mustang was wrapped in a massive bow. "Well, I'll be. There's something you don't see every day."

Unsurprisingly, the two men looked less than happy with their lot in life.

"There's a note, Sarge, there's a note!"

Marlon turned to Gianelli. "Yes, thank you, Officer Gianelli – having not lost the use of my eyes, I can see there is a note."

Marlon took two steps down to look at the note displayed on the Mustang's front windscreen, because, while he hated to admit it, his eyes weren't as good as they once had been.

He read the note aloud.

"Hello, I am Jonny Risbury, a lieutenant in the Los Zetas Cartel. I am a wanted man after skipping bail in Miami on two assault charges. Odds-on my colleague here is also of interest to the authorities. A merry Christmas and God bless us each and every one. Yours sincerely, Santa Claus and his merry men and/or women. PS There are about ten kilos of cocaine in the trunk of this car."

Marlon Watts looked around the car park. "Is this some kind of Christmas prank?"

"No, Sarge."

"Because if it is, Gianelli, then you should know the rumours of me having a sense of humour have been greatly exaggerated."

"I swear it isn't, Sarge."

Marsden interrupted. "Well, if it is, it has nothing to do with us, I swear."

"Alright then," said Marlon.

"How come you believed her and not me, Sarge?"

"Because, Gianelli, her relatives don't all die on Fridays. So where's the coke?" Marlon looked at the two rookies. "Oh, for... Open the damn trunk then!"

IN THE ABSENCE OF CHIMNEYS

Smithy tapped the screwdriver against his chin, stared hard at the circuit board in front of him and took a deep breath. "Can both of you please stop watching me?"

"What?" said Cheryl.

"We're not watching you," said Bunny.

"I can feel your eyes on me and I'm trying to concentrate."

"You're sounding a bit paranoid there, sweetheart," said Cheryl.

"We're on the roof of a building we're trying to break into, and I'm trying to disable an alarm system. This is exactly the place where being paranoid is a good idea. Can't the two of you just talk amongst yourselves?"

They were indeed on top of a building, and while nobody was drawing attention to it out of politeness, it was bitterly cold. There was the threat of snow in the air and Cheryl was regretting not wearing her woollen gloves over the plastic gloves she was already wearing in order to not leave fingerprints. As Christmas Eves went...

"Alright, Smithy boy," said Bunny. "You relax and take your time. Cheryl and I will talk to each other, alright?"

"Excellent."

"So, Cheryl, do you think your fella can disable this alarm?"

Cheryl pursed her lips. "Don't ask me. I didn't know he had any skills in this area until an hour ago. This is yet another part of his mysterious past that he doesn't talk about."

"When I said talk amongst yourselves, I thought not talking about what I'm doing kinda went without saying?"

"Sorry," said Bunny. "You should have said."

"If I wanted to answer a lot of questions, I'd have brought Diller up here with me."

"Alright, alright," said Bunny. "Relax. Jesus, breaking and entering makes him fierce grumpy."

A low growl issued from Smithy, causing Cheryl and Bunny to exchange a look that said 'maybe we shouldn't push this anymore'.

Cheryl turned to Bunny. "Besides, is this even a crime?"

"It is," said Smithy.

"Well," admitted Bunny, "technically, yes. Although, as a big believer in law and order, I'm fine with it, which is an indication of the level of seriousness."

"Hmm," said Cheryl. "On a related note, is taking the twenty grand from the trunk of Jonny's car a crime?"

"It is," said Smithy.

"Again, technically, yes," said Bunny. "Although, once again, I'm absolutely fine with it. Plus, we did make a citizen's arrest there of sorts."

"You're not a citizen," said Smithy.

"Can I ask," said Cheryl, pointing at Bunny's clothes, "why've you not changed your outfit? I mean, I did." She had, otherwise she probably would've been dead from hypothermia by now.

"What?" said Bunny. "It's Christmas Eve – this suit is the perfect disguise. Who's going to shoot Santa on a rooftop on Christmas Eve?"

Smithy sighed. "You still haven't got your head around America, have you? You're going end up mounted above someone's fireplace."

"I thought you were supposed to be concentrating?" asked Cheryl. "Why do you keep talking to us?"

Smithy said nothing, instead putting the screwdriver back into his small toolkit with more force than was necessary and taking out a slightly smaller screwdriver and tapping that against his chin instead.

"Actually," said Cheryl, turning to Bunny, "I did want to talk to you. How come you've turned down our gracious invite to come over for Christmas dinner tomorrow?"

"Ah, thanks but no thanks," said Bunny. "I don't want to intrude."

"Really?" Sarcasm dripped from Cheryl's voice as she held her arms out. "You're literally about to be an actual intruder, but we invite you into our apartment, through the front door, and you'd rather not?"

Bunny said nothing, which was the wrong answer.

"What have you got planned?"

"I was going to take it easy."

"By which you mean you'll stay in that awful hotel and get drunk."

Bunny said nothing, which was all the answer she needed.

"Nope. Sorry, honey, ain't going to happen. You are coming. Diller is coming too, y'know?"

"Yeah," said Smithy, without turning around, "I'm going to drop him out to Cedarview to see his mom in the morning, and then he's coming back to our place."

Cheryl nodded. "So that settles it."

Bunny went to say something, which was also the wrong answer.

"No argument, you're coming. We're having our traditional Christmas. Smithy cooks a turkey; the turkey is undercooked. Smithy swears at the turkey and then cooks it until it is horribly overcooked. Smithy swears at it a whole lot more. We all eat three bites and then we order Chinese. Also, there's Trivial Pursuit. It's fun, you'll love it. You're family, whether you like it or not. And besides, the dog likes you."

Bunny nodded. "I appreciate what you're saying, but..."

They were interrupted by a cell phone ringing.

Smithy sighed. "Really? We're taking calls in the middle of the robbery now?"

"Shut up," said Cheryl, putting her hand into her jeans pocket and fishing it out. "It's the number."

"What num—? Oh right," said Smithy. The number was something Cheryl had come up with when she started helping Bunny with the list. They had needed a way for the women they were trying to help to get in touch with them, but they couldn't use their personal numbers, for obvious reasons. The number belonged to an unregistered disposable phone.

"It's Helena," said Cheryl.

"Shite," said Bunny. "Answer it."

Cheryl did.

"Helena, are you OK?"

Cheryl listened for a few seconds. "One second, honey," she said, before taking the phone from her ear. "She's fine. The police rang to let her know they have arrested Jonny for violating his parole, skipping bail and more – they didn't specify." She put the phone back to her ear. "That's great news, Helena, we're really pleased."

Much to Bunny's annoyance, Cheryl then held up a finger and walked a few feet away, turning her back on them. "What in the feck is she doing now?"

"I've no idea," said Smithy. "I'm kind of busy breaking into this building for you."

"Right. Yeah." Bunny lowered his voice to a whisper. "Now that she isn't here, can I ask, what does the, y'know...?"

"What?"

"The voice. What does it think of all this?"

Bunny was one of two people in the whole world who knew that, since Smithy had been the victim in a serious hit and run a few years ago, he occasionally suffered what Smithy himself considered auditory hallucinations. In simpler terms, he occasionally heard the voice of God in his head. For an atheist, this was particularly annoying. The other person who knew this secret was Diller, who was entirely convinced it was the voice of God. Bunny was still on the fence. The reason Cheryl didn't know was that Smithy didn't want the woman he enjoyed sexy time with getting distracted by wondering if

God was talking to him at that moment. She was from a family of Texan baptists and that was the kind of thing that could really blow a romantic evening horribly off course.

"I told you I wasn't going to talk about that," said Smithy.

"Right."

"But if you must know, there's been nothing."

Bunny nodded. "Is that good or bad, do you think?"

"Well, speaking as the man whose head it is, I think not hearing voices is a good thing."

"Fair point."

"Although you two have been yacking so much, I probably wouldn't have heard it anyway."

"You'd like me to shut up, wouldn't you?"

"Bunny, you can read me like a book."

Bunny shut up and Smithy went back to staring at the circuit board.

After a minute, Cheryl came back. "OK, I want you to remain calm."

"Do you mean me or him?" asked Smithy. "Because I'm trying and failing to remain focused here."

"I love you, honey, but shut up."

Smithy said nothing. Cheryl looked at Bunny. "OK, so, Helena. She didn't want to mention it before, but she once met a woman in that support group."

"Right," said Bunny.

"And she said this woman told her that a friend of hers got out of New York along with her two kids, thanks to some help from" – Cheryl looked at the name she had hastily scrawled on the back of her hand – "Father Gabriel de Marcos. Apparently he runs some kind of gang intervention thing somewhere."

"The Bronx," said Smithy, without looking up. "There was a big write-up about it in the paper recently."

"OK," said Cheryl. "Well, him."

"Right, but—" started Bunny, but he stopped when Cheryl held her finger up.

"She thinks it might be nothing, but... the woman said this priest knew a bunch of nuns who had helped get them out."

"Jesus!" said Bunny.

"Don't get your hopes up. It might not be the – what do you call 'em?"

"The Sisters of the Saint," said Bunny.

"Right."

"It's a lead though," said Bunny. "I've been here nine months – nine fecking months looking for them, and this is the first thing that's gone right!"

"Thanks," said Smithy.

"Ara shut up, y'know what I mean."

"It's good news," said Cheryl, "but don't get carried a—"

Cheryl was interrupted as Bunny swept her up into a massive bearhug. "I've got a lead!"

"OK, just..."

Bunny spun her around and was two bars into a rousing rendition of "It's Beginning to Look a lot Like Christmas" when Smithy turned around and glowered at them.

"Seriously?"

Bunny plonked Cheryl down rather unceremoniously.

"We are actually committing a crime here. Could you two stop treating it like a fun night out?"

"Sorry," said Cheryl.

"Sorry, but—" started Bunny, but Smithy silenced him with a look.

"I know. A lead. Great. Can we celebrate that after we don't get arrested?"

Bunny nodded. "Right. You're right." He turned to Cheryl. "He is. He is absolutely right."

"Shut up," said Smithy.

"Right."

Smithy nodded. "Now, Cheryl, have you got one of those silver wrappers from your gum?"

"I think so..." She found one in her back pocket. "Yes, here."

"Thank you." She handed it to him and Smithy turned back around to the circuit box. He then did something with the wrapper, after which he jammed the screwdriver into something with a considerable amount of force. There was a popping noise followed by the smell of burning.

"OK," said Smithy, "alarm is dead. We're in."

Smithy picked up his tools and walked off down the roof towards the skylight.

Cheryl looked at Bunny. "Is it weird that I'm a little turned on right now?"

I LOVE THE SMELL OF EGGNOG IN THE MORNING

Mrs Tandy took a deep breath and tried to remain calm. It had, all told, been a rather stressful week. There had been an even higher than normal level of colds and sniffles, not to mention yesterday's disastrous trip with the children into Manhattan to not see Santa. And then there were the smaller things you had to keep an eye out for, especially at this time of year. Any child living in Saint Augustine's would be painfully aware that they were different to other kids. Acting out was inevitable. Tina Lacroix had got into a fight last night with one of the older girls. Tina's auntie had said she would come from Philadelphia to take her for Christmas, but they'd returned yesterday to find a message on the home's machine saying she wasn't coming. Mrs Tandy sincerely loved her job, but there were days when it felt like having gone twelve rounds with an angry gorilla.

And then she had woken up to this – whatever this was – this morning. It had been one of her nights to sleep over and so she'd been the first one into the cafeteria at 7am, to open up for the cooks. That's when she'd seen it, although it had taken her more than a few moments to believe it. Then she had found the note and the envelope. After giving it some thought, she had phoned the police.

She knew that upstairs there were some annoyed and interested kids, and she knew Sarah was having a hard time keeping them up there.

Mrs Tandy stood with Officer Gianelli as he slurped the coffee she had made him. They had run out of small talk five minutes ago. Mrs Tandy was too nervous to chat – somehow, she knew this would go badly. It had been that kind of a week. Officer Marsden had been on the phone with the station for fifteen minutes. When she finally hung up and turned towards them, there was a palpable sense of relief shared between Mrs Tandy and Officer Gianelli, two people unburdened from the weight of failed conversation.

"OK, Mrs Tandy, here's what we know. All of these" – said Officer Marsden, waving towards the massive pile of wrapped presents that was dominating the room – "were stolen last night."

"Oh Lord," said Mrs Tandy, blessing herself furiously.

"Well, kind of," finished Officer Marsden.

"Kind of? How can something be kind of stolen?"

Officer Marsden rubbed the back of her neck. "The assistant manager from Toytopolis Toys up on Bleecker came in this morning. They had some kind of alarm fault last night. Somebody broke in and took a load of toys."

"Oh heavens…"

"But," continued Marsden, "they left a list of what they'd taken and enough money to cover it, plus repairs to the skylight they'd broken to get in."

"Is that normal?"

Marsden shook her head. "No. Burglars don't normally leave notes and they definitely don't ever leave money."

"In fact," interjected Officer Gianelli, "there was a burglary over on Hillcrest last week and that guy left…" Gianelli stopped talking when Marsden's stare penetrated his bubble of stupidity. "Never mind," he said, looking sheepish.

"So," continued Officer Marsden, turning to look at Mrs Tandy, "my boss talked to his boss, who talked to the owner of Toytopolis, and long story short – no harm, no foul. These gifts are for your kids." Marsden gave a big smile.

"And the" – Mrs Tandy lowered her voice – "money?" There had been just over seventeen thousand dollars in cash in an envelope addressed to her, and a note that said, "Dear Mrs Tandy, you seem like an honest woman. Here is a donation to Saint Augustine's so you can get that bus fixed and maybe bring all the kids to the circus or something. Merry Christmas, Santa Claus."

Office Marsden nodded. "The money is a donation, as far as we can see. All above board, bar the breaking in to leave it – which, again, is a bit unusual."

Mrs Tandy felt faint. Officer Gianelli reached out a hand to steady her. "Are you OK?"

"Sorry. Yes," she said, patting his hand. "It's just – well, this is quite a thing, isn't it?"

Marsden nodded. "A regular Christmas miracle."

"Well," said Mrs Tandy, straightening herself up, "thank you both so much for your time."

"No problem," said Marsden, who shared a look with Gianelli.

"Is that everything?" enquired Mrs Tandy.

"Well," said Marsden, "to be honest, we got Christmas Eve and Christmas Day shifts at the station because we're rookies, and it has been kind of bleak."

"I see."

"If you wouldn't mind," continued Gianelli, "it'd be cool to see the kids open their presents."

Mrs Tandy smiled. Yes, yes it would.

––––––

What followed was chaos. Joyful chaos, but chaos nonetheless. The presents had come numbered with a helpful list that explained what the content of each parcel was, so Sarah and Mrs Tandy had made sure every child got something appropriate. At the very end of the line, her face a more pronounced version of its usual mix of hope and distrust, stood Annabelle Watson.

"Annabelle," said Mrs Tandy, beckoning her over. "May I speak to you for a moment?"

Annabelle followed Mrs Tandy to the corner of the room, beside the games storage cupboard.

"Now, young lady, do you know anything about this?"

Mrs Tandy knew what the response would be by the way her face scrunched up before answering. "No. Why am I always blamed for stuff? I didn't do nothing."

"You didn't do anything."

"That's what I said."

"I'm not accusing you of... Oh, never mind. You don't have a present in the pile over there."

"Oh."

"Because you didn't get *a* present."

Annabelle just nodded.

"Because young lady, you were the only person here to get multiple presents with your name written on them."

With a smile, Mrs Tandy opened the cupboard to reveal a series of boxes. Ten minutes later, Annabelle Watson was the proud owner of a biology lab, a chemistry lab, an electronics lab and her very own laptop computer.

There had been a note.

Dear Annabelle,
You can be anything you want to be.
Merry Christmas,
SC

MEANWHILE IN DUBLIN

THIS LAST STORY WAS INSPIRED BY MY OWN RE-READING OF THE FIRST CHAPTER OF MY BOOK, *OTHER PLANS*. I REALISED THERE WOULD BE RAMIFICATIONS AND REPERCUSSIONS FOR EVERYONE BACK IN DUBLIN BECAUSE OF A REVELATION MADE WITHIN THE BOOK AND I NEEDED TO KNOW WHAT HAPPENED NEXT.

TO BE HONEST, IT SEEMED LIKE AN EXCELLENT EXCUSE TO CATCH UP WITH THE MCM CREW, WHICH WAS A DELIGHT. I'D ALSO LIKE TO CLAIM THAT THE OPENING CHAPTER WAS MY HOMAGE TO SHAKESPEARE, BUT TO BE HONEST, I'M REALLY NOT THAT CLEVER.

ALAS, POOR YORICK! I KNEW HIM, HORATIO – BIT OF A GOBSHITE, TO BE HONEST WITH YOU

"And I'll tell you something else ..."

Chuck felt his hands tighten their grip around the shovel and, for a fraction of a second, he enjoyed the image of him pulling it out of the ground, climbing out of this hole and smashing it into Money's stupid, ever-talking face.

Instead, Chuck opted to try to solve his problem with words. "No," he snapped, "you won't tell me something else. What you'll do is shut up and hold the light like you're supposed to be doing."

"What's got you in a mood?" asked Money.

This was enough to make Chuck, as keen as he was to get this over with, pause. He was aware he was considered a miserable sod; Chuck was short for Chuckles, after all, and he'd long ago resigned himself to that annoying nickname sticking. He didn't consider himself a morose person, just a realistic one. He'd been alive for forty-one years now, and had long since concluded that the world was an awful place, full of awful people doing awful things to each other, and a lot of them were also awful drivers. Admittedly, he wasn't on the moral high ground to be passing judgement on anyone else, given what he was currently up to.

"What's got me in a mood?" repeated Chuck. "Seriously? It's four in the bleedin' morning and I'm standing here in the pissing rain digging up a grave. Why don't you apply your university-educated brain to the problem and see if you can draw your own conclusion?"

Money shook his head. "The people in this organisation have a very negative attitude towards higher education."

Chuck resumed shovelling, deliberately tossing some of the dirt upwards so that it landed on Money's shoes. "No, we don't. What we have is a low tolerance for the fact you keep mentioning your bleedin' degree in English all the time. We're a criminal gang, not LinkedIn. Nobody gives a shite about your CV."

"Excuse me for trying to better myself."

"Better yourself? You know why the lads call you Money? Because it's what you come from. You've not shown any ability to generate any."

"I do alright," said Money, sounding hurt.

"No, you don't. How I know that is, it's four in the morning and you're standing in the middle of Glasnevin Cemetery holding a torch while I dig up a coffin. That is not the kind of job they give to a high-flyer."

"Yeah, well, at least I'm not the one down in the hole."

"The only reason you're not in the hole is that if I'd put you in charge of digging, the hole would only be about a foot deep by now, because you've never done a decent day's work in your life. You finished your degree in prison because not only are you work-shy, you're also a cokehead who's obsessed with greyhounds. What you should have done is given the cocaine to the dogs. That way, some of them might have actually won a race, but instead, you snorted the coke, dug yourself a metaphorical hole with the bookies and then tried to get out of it by dealing. Only you were dumb enough to deal to the granddaughter of a senior judge, who promptly blew her nostrils out while ODing on the stepped-on shite you were pedalling. Have I got any of that wrong?"

"I was unlucky."

"No," said Chuck, "you weren't. You were born lucky. You came flying out of your ma and landed on a nice soft bed of privilege. You had to make several mistakes to end up here, whereas a lad from the Fatima Mansions just has to make half of one. Believe you me, if I'd had your chances in life, I'd not be spending my Friday night digging up a coffin while a mouthy gobshite does a bad job of holding the light."

"I know what's got you in a bad mood."

Chuck paused again. Enough was enough. There was only so much a man could take. If Money so much as hinted at him being "unlucky in love", or anything within an arse's roar of that, someone was going to find this grave with an extra body in it in the morning.

It had not been a good few weeks. A couple of months ago, the big boss, Liam "Liamo" Darcy, had instructed Chuck to take Carol, Liamo's widowed mother, shopping. When Liamo asked, you did. The lad had gone a long way in a short time by being entirely devoid of restraint and dealing with those who didn't do as they were told with a terrifying ruthlessness. Chuck was glorified muscle, but he was house-trained, and able to wipe his shoes and mind his Ps and Qs well enough to be allowed indoors. Not something you could say for all of Liamo's lieutenants. And so, Chuck had done as he was told and carried Carol's bags, driven the car and dutifully followed her around the shops while she spent money like she had an infinite supply, which, seeing as her young fella was bringing half the drugs into Dublin, wasn't far off being true.

One of the shops they'd visited had been Ann Summers. Carol Darcy was in her early fifties, a gym bunny with the body to match, and he'd sat there while she'd tried on outfit after outfit, enjoying watching him squirm. Chuck was as hot-blooded as the next man, but he was aware from the get-go that he was in dangerous territory. Pissing off the boss was a great way to end up with your hot blood spread across a wide area. Being the bloke dating Liamo's ma was a high-risk venture, but then, being the dude who had rejected her advances was, arguably, an even less desirable proposition. Which is why he'd talked to Liam before "taking his ma out to dinner".

It turned out Carol had other plans and they'd not even got as far as dessert. The late Daddy Darcy had apparently been rather conservative in the bedroom area, and Carol had a list of things she wanted to try. A long list. Some items on the list had come with bibliographical references so he could read up on what was expected of him. Most of it, if Chuck was being honest, he hadn't been in to, but Liam had made a big deal about him making his beloved ma happy, so he did everything that was asked of him. He doubted Liam's instruction had been meant in that context, but still.

The affair, if you could call it that, had gone on for about six weeks, before Carol had called an end to it, much to Chuck's relief. What he was considerably less happy about was the fact that Carol had then cracked open a bottle of wine, or three, with her daughter-in-law and given her the highlights. Liam had never said anything, but the way he now looked at Chuck made it clear that the married couple had no secrets. As Daz had put it, "Nobody likes the lad who *Fifty Shades of Grey*ed his ma." Chuck was digging up somebody else's grave because he was keen to do whatever it took to make sure he didn't find himself up in the Wicklow Mountains with a gun to his head, digging his own.

For all of that, worrying about Liamo's legendary temper wasn't even the worst part. It had been the innuendos, double entendres, single entendres, and other clunky attempts at repartee made by the lads at his expense. The point when Money Martin – the useless skin-bag who couldn't even hold a torch correctly – started taking cheap shots at Chuck's expense, was the moment he decided that he'd give the world something else to remember him by. He could make the early ferry to Holyhead and then they could see how quickly they could get someone to hunt him down. They'd find him eventually, but he wouldn't make it easy for them.

"Alright," said Chuck. "Tell me, Money, what's got me in such a bad mood, then?"

Money sniffed and twirled his finger in the air. "Cemeteries. Can't help but make a man confront his own mortality."

Chuck stopped for a second, briefly considering whether Money had any idea he'd just saved his own life, and then resumed digging. "Is that right?"

"'Alas, poor Yorick! I knew him, Horatio: a fellow of infinite jest, of most excellent fancy—'"

"And you can blow that Shakespeare stuff out your arse and all," snapped Chuck as he drove the shovel into the earth.

"Excuse me?"

"No, I won't. I never understood the obsession with Shakespeare. We're standing in a country founded by poets, trade unionists and dreamers, and yet our education system shoves Shakespeare down the throats of generation after generation."

"Big fan of the Bard, are you?" asked Money, condescension dripping from his voice in a display of the poor instincts that were eventually going to get him killed.

"Fuck you. I don't need to go to university to read a book, ye know. I'm not saying the man couldn't write, but the obsession with the work of one bloke who died over four hundred years ago is ludicrous. Must drive living playwrights mad, this idea that everything stopped when old Willy popped his clogs. Like nothing before, or since, could surpass the man. Case in point, Hamlet picks up Yorick's skull and starts chatting to it, like that's a normal thing to do. Veers dangerously close to ventriloquism, if you ask me."

Chuck felt the shovel finally hit wood. *Thank God.* He was starting to wonder how deep they'd buried this thing.

"And I'll tell you something else," he continued as he redoubled his shovelling efforts, clearing the rest of the soil off the coffin now he knew its depth. "You know the reason the powers that be love carpet-bombing the youth with Shakespeare? It's because the man was a lot of things, but he was no revolutionary. He was all about currying favour with queens and cardinals. He didn't rock the boat. Hamlet can spend five acts staring at his navel, but he never contemplates why, as a prince, he should have some divine right to rule over Yorick and the rest, because that's a question those in power wouldn't like him to ask."

"Well, that's … that's …" Before Money could continue, they were interrupted by his phone ringing. The hum of Kanye West's "Gold

Digger" sounded like the loudest thing in existence as it reverberated off the surrounding gravestones.

"Turn that off," snarled Chuck.

"It's Robbie," replied Money, answering it. Robbie was one of the two lookouts that had been posted nearby in case someone wandered past and noticed what the pair were up to.

Chuck stared up at Money as he answered the call.

"What's up?" said Money, standing there listening to the voice on the end of the line.

"What's he saying?" asked Chuck, looking around nervously to see if there were any signs of someone heading towards them. The graveyard was as quiet as a, well ...

"Robbie says he's doing a McDonald's run. Wants to know if you want anything?"

"What? The fuck he is. He's supposed to be keeping watch. If he's bored, he can come and do some digging."

Rolling his eyes, Money said, "Yeah, he says ... you heard." He laughed. "Yeah, you can say that again. Alright, laters."

"What?" snapped Chuck as Money hung up the phone.

"What, what?"

"He can say what again?"

"He said you're a buzzkill."

Chuck scratched at his forehead irritably. "We're not on a night out on the sauce," he hissed. "We're here robbing a grave."

"We're not actually robbing it?"

"Yes, we are. We're digging it up," said Chuck, recommencing precisely that.

"But we're not taking anything," said Money.

"We might be."

Their primary objective was to check if the thing was empty, but if it wasn't, they were to take pictures and "a DNA sample". The way Liamo had said it, he clearly didn't know what they'd do with that when they got it either, but Chuck had been in no position to argue.

"Who even is this guy, anyway?"

Chuck shook his head but kept working away. Proof, if proof was ever needed, that Money was clueless. "Who even is this guy?" he repeated in a mocking tone. "You know nothing."

Money tsked and turned the light onto the gravestone. "Detective Sergeant Bernard 'Bunny' McGarry."

"Jesus!" said Chuck. "Don't say the name."

"Why?"

Chuck realised he couldn't express why. As if saying it out loud would summon him like Beetlejuice, the Candyman, or something. Chuck wasn't a religious man or superstitious, but still ... *this*. He'd done some bad things in his life, things he wasn't proud of, but this, if there was a heaven or a hell, this was the thing that was stamping his ticket for down south.

"He's just some copper," said Money.

"Not just some copper. The man was ..." Chuck, still clearing the last layer of earth, struggled to find the words.

He'd met Bunny twice and been arrested by him once. As these things went, Bunny had treated Chuck with respect. Some guards would've used the opportunity to put the boot in, but Bunny hadn't. He'd even allowed poor, daft Johnny Stephens, blubbing away as he had been, to ring his ma. The week before that, Chuck knew for a fact that Bunny had slammed Anto O'Reilly's head into a wall so hard it'd knocked a brick out, but then Anto had never been very good at reading the room.

"The man was what?" asked Money.

"Put it this way – you definitely don't want to be haunted by him."

Money laughed. "I'm not afraid of pigs, living or dead."

"Show some respect. Alive, this man would have gone through you like shite through a goose. Even dead, I'd fancy his chances."

"Yeah—"

"Don't," snapped Chuck, "say another word, or so help me God!"

Even Money, clueless as he was, could pick up the warning signs in Chuck's tone. He fell silent and stayed that way for the next minute or two as Chuck scraped away enough of the remaining dirt. Once accomplished, Chuck glanced down at the lid of the coffin he was standing on. He felt the urge to bless himself, but resisted. Instead, he tossed the shovel up onto the grass and held out his hand. "Give me the crowbar."

Money did as instructed.

Chuck stood there for a few seconds, holding the tool in his hands, his arms and shoulders aching from all the digging. For one mad moment he considered saying no, throwing the crowbar away, climbing out and pronouncing himself done with all this. The idea had an appeal to it. He also didn't fancy his chances of living to see another midnight.

He bent over and worked the crowbar until it found the gap between the lid and the base of the coffin. The bite that told him he had purchase. He paused for a few seconds and closed his eyes. The prayers the Christian Brothers had tried to beat into him had long been forgotten, and they'd have meant nothing to him, anyway. Still, he offered up a silent apology. Chuck had no idea why he was doing this; his only guess was that it was some form of deliberate antagonism towards the guards on the part of Liamo. If that was the idea, it struck Chuck as idiotic. You don't mess with a folk hero. This would annoy a whole lot of people who weren't in law enforcement. And all the stuff about taking a picture and getting a DNA sample? It dawned on Chuck that someone, somewhere, thought Bunny McGarry was alive. That was a whole other kind of mental. Chuck remembered the big funeral that had been held for him. More importantly, he remembered the man. In truth, a force of nature. The idea of him being dead was hard to fathom, the idea of him being somewhere quietly living incognito was even harder.

"Are you—" started Money.

"Shut up. I'm doing it."

He moved his grip on the crowbar, the metal cold and slick in his hands. There are moments. Moments when you know that you're doing the wrong thing. Beyond crime, or good or bad. Moments that you know are just plain wrong.

Then the image of Liamo Darcy staring down at him was conjured in his mind. It'd be a slow death. Nobody would be asking him questions because Chuck had no answers anyone wanted to hear. It'd be slow only because Liamo would want it to take as long as possible.

Screw it.

Chuck pulled the crowbar towards him, feeling the wood start to give.

"WHAT IN THE SHITTING HELL DO YOU THINK YOU'RE DOING, YE SCUTTERING GOBSHITE," screamed a voice that was coming both from in the coffin and beyond the grave.

The last Chuck saw of Money was him running off in the other direction, before colliding with a statue of the Virgin Mary and tumbling to the ground. Money hadn't even recognised Bunny McGarry's voice, but when a coffin starts screaming abuse at you, knowing exactly who's doing the screaming isn't that important.

Robbie rushed towards Chuck as he climbed over the fence to get out of the graveyard. "Why in the ..."

Chuck didn't even slow down as he punched Robbie square in the face and kept running. It was about four and a half miles to the ferry terminal from Glasnevin Cemetery. Chuck sprinted all the way, collapsing onto the ticket desk when he finally got there.

He would run for a long time. Years. Eventually, he ended up joining a religious cult just outside Swansea that promised salvation through fasting, prayer, and a lot of hallucinogenic drugs.

Twenty years later he would still occasionally wake up screaming, as a caustic Cork accent ripped through the still night air, calling him a scuttering gobshite.

LOOSE LIPS SINK RELATIONSHIPS

There are certain events in life that you never interrupt. The big four are, of course, births, weddings, funerals and bowel movements. Even then, that's a soft never, as circumstance can trump all other considerations. You're the acknowledged and merely tardy father of the birthee. You're already married to one of the people getting married. It's you who people think they are burying. What's more, it's also permissible to interrupt any of the big four should you wake up to find someone doing them in your back garden without permission.

Just below the big four, there is a plethora of events you really, really, *really* shouldn't interrupt, one being a wedding-dress fitting. Brigit Conroy was all too aware of this, and while she had a valid reason for her actions, she was also aware that only she would consider the situation to be a matter of utmost urgency. Nevertheless, as she shoved her head between the curtains in the fitting area of Margo's Dress Emporium, she fully expected to get it bitten off.

The five women in the room immediately turned to look at her. Brigit didn't need to be the private investigator she was to figure out who was who in the scene before her. The bride-to-be was obviously the woman standing in the middle of the room in the black-and-pink wedding dress. She looked as if she was seriously considering bursting into tears, and possibly not for the first time. There was a definite puffiness around her eyes. To her left, with a face like thunder, was the mother of the bride. Sitting beside her, the older sister of the bride, who was wearing the sort of bitter smile that never spoke well of the person wearing it, or the situation they were now doing a bad job of hiding their enjoyment of. To the other side of the bride-to-be was seated a larger lady, who was leaning forward wearing a different, if equally hard, look on her face. The fifth person was the only one Brigit actually knew – Margo, vendor of the aforementioned wedding dress.

"Hi," said Brigit. "I'm really sorry to interrupt, but, Margo, could I just have a quick word?"

Margo furrowed her brow. "I'm sorry – Brigit, isn't it?" Brigit nodded. "I'm with a client now and this is not a good time."

"I know" – she looked at the bride – "and sincerely, massive apologies. I just need the quickest of chats, and I wouldn't be asking if it wasn't urgent."

"It can't be that urgent," said Margo, plastering on one of her vast collection of fake smiles. "You've not even set a date." She turned to the rest of the room and, for some inexplicable reason, spoke in a faux whisper. "It's a complicated situation." She did that thing where she over-enunciated every syllable in the word "complicated", which made Brigit's knuckles itch.

Brigit pointed at her. "That, right there, is exactly what I need to talk to you about."

"She's busy," snapped the mother of the bride.

"I know," said Brigit. "And again, really sorry, but—"

"Actually," interrupted the bride, "seeing as you're here, we could use a fresh opinion. What do you think of this dress?" She raised her chin with the kind of brittle defiance shown by someone when things were going badly and they had just enough left in them to take one more shot.

The tension in the room ratcheted to the point at which you could cut it with a wedding-cake knife, which is exactly the same as an ordinary cake knife but would cost you twice as much. Brigit was still only a sort of bride-to-be herself, but she'd already got a handle on the sucker-squeezing industry that was the wedding-industrial complex.

Brigit glanced around at the other four faces in the room, then back at the bride. This was probably one of those situations where she should be diplomatic. She always knew when those occasions were, she just, more often than not, couldn't stop herself from charging in head-first anyway. It was one of her defining characteristics. Knowing what she was about to do and being able to stop herself were, of course, two entirely different things.

"Right," she said, "give us a twirl."

The bride duly complied, then looked at Brigit expectantly. Brigit didn't need the twirl. She just wanted to see the bride-to-be's expression after she'd completed it to confirm what she thought.

"Here's the thing," said Brigit. "And I'm sort of in the same position as you." She glanced at Margo. "Although it is, admittedly, complicated. But here's what I definitely know. It doesn't matter what I think of that dress. It doesn't matter" – she avoided looking at anyone else in the room as she said the next bit – "what anyone else thinks of that dress. It only matters what you think of that dress."

Out of the corner of her eye, Brigit could see the best friend's head pumping up and down in furious agreement, even as the other side of the room went full scowl.

"Because," she continued, "the day belongs to yourself and himself, and everyone else, whether they like it or not, are just spectators. The both of you should wear what you want, say what you want, do it where you want and do it in front of whomever you want, because, all going well, this is the one time you're doing it, and when we're all old and grey and staring out the window trying to remember if we need to go to the bathroom or if we've just been, we will, odds-on, still remember that day. And I really do know what I'm talking about here, because I used to be a nurse in a hospice. I've sat down with a lot of old folk and looked through a lot of wedding albums in my time. So, you do you. Having said that, and keeping in mind I've already explained why my opinion is worthless. I love that dress and I think you're rocking it. What's he wearing?"

The bride beamed at her. "Top hat and tails but, like, steampunk. We met at a roleplaying convention."

"That is so cool. Are you going to do something funky with the bouquet?"

She smiled and nodded at the best friend. "Ana is doing this amazing design – it's going to be made of metal."

"Oh, wow," said Brigit. "This wedding is going to be awesome!"

———

A minute later, Brigit was standing beside the counter at the front of the shop while Margo made a couple of quick apologies before coming out to speak to her. Janice, the young woman behind the counter, was looking at her nervously. She'd been the one to explain to Brigit how she couldn't disturb Margo right before Brigit had gone ahead and done precisely that. Brigit smiled at her apologetically. She really hated making things harder for someone who was just doing their job.

Margo was a brunette woman of about sixty who was renowned for running the finest dress shop in Dublin. She dressed like a woman who might need to attend a wedding at any moment, which Brigit supposed went with the job. There was always the possibility of a wedding emergency. Brigit was sort of having one of those at that moment, although not one of the normal, dress-burst-a-seam, popped-a-button type.

Margo placed one hand on the counter and lowered her voice. "I mean, you're right, but the mother has insisted on paying for the dress, and I don't know if she'll manage to wield the credit card without trying to slash her own wrists with it. Now," she continued, "as it's apparently very important, how can I help you?"

"So, I was in here a couple of weeks ago with my friend."

"I remember. The lawyer."

"Nora, that's her."

"Right. I remember everything except names. You're supposed to be getting married, only you've not told anyone as your widowed father announced he was remarrying first, and now you've to wait for them to do it as you don't want to be seen to be crowding them out. Plus, you also had to call off a wedding before, so you don't want this one to have any friction attached to it." As Margo spoke, she was half addressing Brigit and half addressing Janice behind the counter.

"That," said Brigit, slapping her hands together. "That right there is the problem."

"Which part?" asked Margo, looking excited.

"You misunderstand. All of it. Or rather, you knowing about it. You see, when we were in here, Nora and I had a couple of drinks. And I explained all of that because, well, it didn't matter. It wasn't like you knew anyone involved. And you told me about that redheaded woman who presents the weather, and how she's buying four dresses, and the couple who've bought and sold the same dress three times because she keeps calling it off. There was also the man who's marrying his secretary despite the fact he's not yet told his wife they're getting a divorce. My point being – and I would say no offence, but, well, we all know that's a pointless couple of words we throw in to soften the blow of whatever comes next – but you, Margo, are a gossip."

Margo's head drew back to display a double chin that looked odd, as she'd clearly had other work done around it, which made it stand out all the more. "Excuse me!"

"And to be clear," said Brigit, putting a hand on her own chest, "this is my fault for telling tales out of school, but I thought, doesn't matter. It's not like we know each other. It's not like you're ever going to meet anyone involved ..."

"And I am very discreet."

"Right," said Brigit. "Not to drop anyone in it – and I really am sorry for saying this, but I'm desperate – when you said that bit about being very discreet, the nice lady behind the counter just winced."

Margo's head spun round like she'd been slapped. "Janice?"

Janice gave Brigit a dirty look, then addressed her boss hesitantly.

"I mean, I wouldn't say ... I don't ... You don't mean any harm doing it, but ... you are a teeny bit of a gossip, Margo."

"Well," said Margo, stocking up on the umbrage, "naturally, I do chat to clients, but that's just part of the job." She nodded at Janice. "You're only saying that because your sister told your ex about that thing that happened at the Christmas party."

To be fair to Margo, she had the decency to slap her own hand over her mouth after the words left it. "Oh Jesus," she whispered through her fingers.

"Yeah," said Brigit. "On the upside, the first step is admitting you've a problem. And I'm sure you've got many other fine attributes as a person."

"You do," confirmed Janice. "But if I'm honest, I've stopped confiding in you about stuff."

"I ... Oh God, I am a gossip, amn't I?"

It alarmed Brigit to see that the all-business Margo looked as if she might cry. "Honestly, I didn't come in here to have a go. Actually, I really need your help. You see ..." She paused for a second, part of her brain aware that she was about to double-down on giving information to the most indiscreet woman in Dublin, but she didn't have a choice. "Remember the woman my dad is going to marry?"

"Your future stepmother," said Margo.

"We ... Let's not call her that."

"You and she don't get on great," said Margo, "and she took offence at something you said in your toast at their engagement party, and oh my God" – her eyes widened – "I just can't stop doing it, can I?"

"Look," said Brigit, "get it all out of your system now because, long story short, she wanted to come to Dublin to get a dress. I was determined to make a big deal of it so nobody could suggest I wasn't doing everything I could to be welcoming. I hired a limo. Then I realised I needed people to get in the limo and neither of my bastard sisters-in-law could make it, so I got Nora and a couple of other friends of mine" – in fact, "friend" was stretching it in one of those instances, but Brigit had been desperate – "and we're doing the whole breakfast, mimosas, wedding-dress fittings, lunch and—"

"Let me stop you there," said Margo. "I'd like to help, but I'm afraid we're fully booked for today. We did have a cancellation but—"

Brigit slapped the counter. "That's exactly the problem. Deirdre—"

"Your future stepmother?"

"Let's just go with 'father's wife-to-be'," said Brigit. "Yeah, she got the spot. She's your next appointment. I only found out this morning."

"So, you're here—" said Margo.

"Because I cannot afford to have you say anything when we rock up – today is already not going well."

"Right," said Margo. "And you're in here in …"

"About a half-hour. The girls are with Deirdre in a wine bar up on Capel Street, and I just sprinted down here to talk to you."

"Right," said Margo. "Don't worry, I'm sure it'll be fine. I've taken what you said on board."

"OK. Great. Super," said Brigit, trying to sound more reassured than she felt.

"Has she found a dress she likes yet?"

"No," said Brigit. "No, she hasn't. So far, it's been an utter disaster."

"Why?"

"I don't have time to explain now. I've been gone for fifteen minutes, and I'm supposed to be in the loo." With that, Brigit dashed out of the shop and attempted to run back to the wine bar through the throng of Saturday-morning shoppers.

Ironically, she really did need the loo now.

THE ART OF CONVERSATION

Nora shot a look at the party of women in the other corner of Lorenzo's as they roared with laughter. There was a lot of that. Too much, really. It was as if they were trying to emphasise what a great time they were having, in contrast to the group Nora was sitting with.

Lorenzo's was a wine bar on Capel Street that did a brunch menu, but Nora's group weren't there for the brunch, having had breakfast only a couple of hours ago, although it felt like longer. Time seemed to have slowed down. It was like a bad date, only there were lots of people on it and you couldn't fake a babysitting emergency and leave. To be honest, Nora was tempted to do exactly that, but she was there to support Brigit.

She looked down at the remainder of her glass of prosecco. She was definitely feeling more than a little tipsy and it was barely midday. Every time the conversation stalled, she'd been filling the gap with a drink. The problem was, the chat was grinding to a halt so frequently that if current trends continued, she'd have lost the ability to stand or speak by two o'clock. There was a popular preconception that women could talk for hours. This group was in danger of killing that stereotype for good, or, to be more precise, boring it to death. These wedding-dress shopping days were supposed to be a hoot. In fact, she and Brigit had done one only a couple of weeks ago and had a whale of a time. They'd got pissed, laughed a lot, cried a little, and Brigit had found an absolutely stunning dress. A nailed-on A-plus. They'd both cried when she'd put it on. Nora, given her own complicated romantic life, had avoided the temptation to try on a few herself. That would have been a recipe for disaster. More than a few ill-fated marriages had been forged from a woman finding a dress then needing to find a guy to marry so she could wear it.

The problem with this particular wedding-dress-acquisition adventure was that it was fundamentally a terrible mix of people. There was the currently absent Brigit – the daughter of the groom-to-be, so there was always going to be a bit of weird tension there. Then, to boost the numbers, Brigit had invited Nora, her best friend, an obvious inclusion, along with Susan Burns and Megan Wright.

Susan Burns – or, to give her full title, Detective Superintendent Susan Burns – seemed like a perfectly nice woman, albeit an obvious workaholic who had a hard time relaxing. She probably did have some funny tales about work, but she clearly didn't want to recount any of them in front of Nora, a member of the Dublin legal community. Nora had often heard Dublin described as the smallest big city in the world, and it was hard to argue with that.

Then there was Dr Megan Wright, Canadian therapist, glamour puss and speaker of truth. She and Brigit weren't even friends – as with Susan Burns, she'd only been invited in a blind panic when trying to make up the numbers.

It turned out that the presence of a therapist and a high-ranking member of law enforcement really put a dampener on the chat. When Nora had been telling stories about her beloved nightmare of a son, Megan had started asking questions in a therapisty way, which had really shut down that particular avenue of conversation. It had been bad, but it was by no means the biggest problem with having included the good doctor. The topic of men was also off limits as far as Nora was concerned, as Susan Burns was the boss of Donnacha Wilson, the man with whom she'd been in an on-again off-again relationship, and even she wasn't sure which of those two states they were currently in. World's smallest big city strikes again.

So, the combination of people didn't help, no question. However, there was a larger, more fundamental problem. The bride-to-be (the official one, as in Deirdre) appeared to be one of the worst things imaginable for an Irish person – no craic. A mousy woman in her early sixties, she was an honest-to-God librarian, and everything about her told you that. She was all of five foot four and wore thick glasses that made her eyes so big it was impossible not to look at her and be reminded of terrified woodland creatures. She barely spoke and when she did, it was so soft that you had to strain to hear her. She'd not told a single story. Worse, she didn't seem to be enjoying herself at all. She spent most of her time clutching her handbag, as if the Dublin criminal classes had smelled someone up from the country and were circling like sharks.

Apparently, she was from England originally, but having lived in Leitrim for decades now, she sounded more Leitrim than born-and-bred Brigit did. At least, she did from the few words Nora had managed to catch. She didn't appear to have a single hobby, interest, or even an opinion on anything. Nora had tried chatting to her about coming to live in Ireland, but the woman had mastered the one-word answer as a way to kill conversation stone dead. What was worse was that she, and everyone else who'd been together since breakfast at Jury's, followed by a limo trip to the first of two wedding-dress shops, clearly knew how badly this bonding session was going.

Then there was the other problem. The Megan Wright problem. Speaking of which, as Brigit's secret maid of honour for a wedding none of the rest of them knew about, Nora decided it was her job to sort that out.

"It's very nice here, isn't it?" remarked Susan Burns for the third time, looking around the bar.

They all agreed again that it was indeed nice.

Another stretch of silence followed.

"Brigit's been in the toilets an awful long time, hasn't she?" said Deirdre.

"She really has," said Megan Wright.

"It might have been the omelette at breakfast," suggested Nora, who knew for a fact that it wasn't. It was the revelation that Deirdre had scored an appointment at a certain dress shop. "I'll go and see how she's doing," she said, looking at Megan pointedly.

For the first time that day, the doctor demonstrated an ability to take a hint.

"I'll come with you."

Nora felt bad as Susan glared longingly at the departing duo like someone who had just lost out in a game of musical chairs they didn't know they were in. As the pair walked away, the crowd of women in the other corner howled with laughter again. *Alright, dial it back, ye shower of bitches.*

As soon as they were out of sight, Nora grabbed Megan by the arm and pulled her into a passageway that looked like it led into the kitchen area.

"Oh my God," whispered Megan excitedly, "have you got coke?"

"What?" snapped Nora.

"It's just, y'know, you signalled me to come with you …"

"Yeah, to leave the table where we're sitting with, I don't know if you've noticed, a high-ranking law enforcement officer. And you thought I was doing so to see if you wanted to do some cocaine snorting?"

"So," said Megan, looking slightly disappointed, "you're saying you don't have any?"

"That is very much what I'm saying. What's more, I've never had coke and I'm perfectly fine with that."

"Right. Good. To be clear, I've only had it once, maybe twice," backpedalled Megan. "I mean, it's not like I 'do coke'. It's more I have, on occasion, had some cocaine. Y'know, just to be social."

"To be social? You make it sound like karaoke."

Megan looked appalled. "I have never done karaoke."

"Whatever," said Nora. "Although, to be honest with you, I'm not sure a drug renowned for giving people an unwarranted level of confidence is a good mix with you."

"What's that supposed to mean?"

"What it means is ..." They stopped talking and each took a step back to allow a waiter holding a tray of cocktails to pass between them, before Nora glanced around and resumed. "... what the hell do you think you're doing?"

"Well, not coke, apparently," said Megan. "Which is fine. I mean, I rarely ever—"

"I was referring to what the hell was that in the dress shop?"

"I don't follow?"

"Really?" said Nora. "You don't remember saying, 'you haven't got the figure for that kind of dress', 'that colour makes you look a little washed out', and, my personal favourite, 'maybe if you lost fifteen pounds'."

"What? Deirdre said at the very start that she wanted us to be brutally honest with her."

"Of course she said that," said Nora, sounding exasperated. "People always say they want that, but nobody actually does. Honesty is like a heatwave – we all love the idea in principle, but as soon as it comes along, we're sweaty, uncomfortable and unable to sleep at night."

"So you're saying ..."

"Every dress is a triumph. She looks like a princess. Feel free to applaud if you can make it look sincere. How are you a therapist and yet have apparently not met another human being before?"

"OK," said Megan. "I'm sorry. I get it. To be honest, I don't hang out with a lot of other women. I don't have many gal pals. I don't know why."

"Aren't you in the habit of sleeping with other people's husbands?"

"That's happened, like, a couple of times at most. We're all trying to be better people, alright?"

"Fine. Good. Let's leave it there, then."

"And you definitely—"

"No, I don't have any coke."

"Good. To be clear, I didn't want any."

Nora shook her head and headed off to find the toilets.

———

Susan Burns opened her mouth. Nothing came out. Yesterday she'd led a seminar of over a hundred people from various branches of law enforcement from three different countries with the purpose of smashing a billion-dollar drug-smuggling ring and had been able to speak with confidence and authority. Today, she was really, really struggling to say anything to a perfectly nice librarian from Leitrim.

Her personal goal for this year had been, rather pathetically, "have a life". She liked being a member of the Garda Síochána. She was good at it. She also realised that she needed something more than a career. Since moving to Dublin, she'd clocked up seven, and counting, unsuccessful attempts at keeping a houseplant alive. She'd even managed to kill a cactus. She was now officially more lethal than the Mojave Desert. When Brigit had invited her to come along on this dress-shopping trip, she'd been delighted. It had sounded like fun. It said something that her phone ringing at that very moment, after her leaving strict instructions not to be disturbed, felt like being thrown a life preserver. What she'd give for a murder.

"Oh," she said to Deirdre, "I'm really sorry. I have to take this." A quick grimace. "Work."

She stood up and walked a few steps away from the table before answering. "Wilson, what's up?"

"I'm really sorry, guv. I know you said you were not to be disturbed. This is … Well, you're going to want to know. How's everything going there, by the way?"

"Let me put it this way – remember that autopsy from a couple of weeks ago, with the big, fat lad whose body had been shoved in that oil tank for three months?"

"Yeah," said Wilson, sounding confused.

"That was a lot more fun."

"Oh dear. Speaking of dead bodies—"

"Speaking of dead bodies?" repeated Susan. "Jesus, Donnacha! We're really going to have to work on your segues."

———

Brigit walked into the wine bar, trying and failing not to look out of breath. She approached the table to find Deirdre sitting alone, clutching her handbag.

"Oh," said Brigit. "Where's everybody gone?"

"Susan's taking an important phone call, and Nora and Megan went to the toilet looking for you. Did you not see them?"

Crap. "Ehm, no," said Brigit, laughing awkwardly. "I was actually off somewhere trying to sort out a little surprise for later. You caught me."

Deirdre gave a tight smile and nodded.

Great. Now Brigit was going to have to come up with a surprise too. She'd rejected out of hand Nora's idea of hiring a stripper. If she didn't come up with something else, though … Oh God, no, she was definitely going to come up with something else. She picked up the glass of prosecco she'd left, which had long since gone flat, and took a sip before putting it down again. She'd wanted to knock it back in one, but she didn't want Deirdre to think her mother had raised a drunk.

"It really is very nice here, isn't it?"

Deirdre nodded.

Brigit resisted the urge to sigh. She seriously doubted anyone was having a worse day than her.

DEAD MAN TALKING

Detective Donnacha Wilson was having the worst morning imaginable. Theoretically, making detective meant that you were done with the donkey work of policing. At least, most of it. No more crowd control. No more standing around with a dead body, waiting for the tech team or the coroner to show up. No more guard duty outside the Belgian Embassy. He'd never understood what the supposed level of threat was against the Belgians. Beyond someone having a really bad waffle, who was likely to be upset with them? Belgium was the beige of countries – nobody had a strong opinion about it either way. The only reason it had a member of the Gardaí positioned outside its embassy was because every other embassy had one. The job could be done by a waxwork in a uniform.

And yet, despite making detective, here was Wilson back guarding a body. In fact, he wasn't even really doing that, which was sort of the point. He was standing in a graveyard while Queen's *Greatest Hits* blared out of a boombox at his feet. The portable music player had been taken from Glasnevin Garda Station's canteen and the Queen CD had been in it already. Wilson had initially turned on the FM radio, but even the music stations had far too much talking for his current purposes. He was now on his second spin through the

244

CD, having had to skip a couple of the quieter moments and "Another One Bites the Dust" for obvious reasons. He had received all manner of glares, not to mention actual complaints, when people who were there to pay their respects to deceased relatives had come up and shouted at him, their volume both an indication of their depth of feeling about the inappropriateness of his current actions and the only way they could make themselves heard over the music. He had had to shout back at them to explain the situation and was starting to lose his voice, not to mention the will to live.

When he caught sight of what was now heading his way, he wanted the ground to open up and swallow him. In fact, the temptation to dive into and hide in the open grave he was standing beside was considerable. Wilson was, personally, not a religious man, but that didn't mean, as he watched the priest striding purposefully towards him, that he wasn't dreading this conversation. He was there because, whatever happened, nobody could open that coffin. Nobody, that is, until his boss DSI Susan Burns had made some phone calls and was assured that the people dealing with it would be "the right people" or, in fact, "person". Until then, it was his job to prevent anyone from trying to implement a solution to the problem. He had been hoping against hope, ever since he'd seen the funeral procession entering the far side of the cemetery, that perhaps the music wasn't carrying that far. From the beetroot-red face of the portly white-haired man of the cloth barrelling towards him, that was clearly not the case.

In an effort to fend off the worst of it, Wilson took out his Garda ID and held it up in front of him. The priest gave it the most cursory of glances before launching into the diatribe that had no doubt been building up inside him as he had stomped across the graveyard.

"What is the meaning of this sacrilegious display?"

"I'm sorry, Father," yelled Wilson over the sound of Freddie Mercury making the improbable assertion that fat-arsed girls made his world go round. "This is a police matter."

"This is a matter of respect," roared the priest in reply, spittle flecking his tight pale lips.

Wilson nodded at the open grave beside him. "I appreciate that, Father, but this grave has been interfered with and—"

"What?" bellowed the priest.

"This grave has been interfered with," repeated Wilson at the loudest volume he could manage, "and—"

The priest looked down at the open grave, the shovel still lying beside it. "That's disgraceful, but so is the music."

"I know that, Father, but—"

"I play golf with the assistant commissioner."

"The music is necessary, Father, because—"

"What?" screamed the man, while simultaneously holding his hands over his ears, which was unlikely to aid his ability to hear Wilson's explanation.

"The music is there to cover the—"

"I can't hear what you're saying."

"I appreciate that, Father, but—"

With an unexpected burst of speed, the priest nipped around Wilson and started to wallop the buttons on top of the boombox.

"Please, Father. Don't!"

As the music was turned off, what it had been masking came through loud and clear.

"... YOU'RE DOING, YE SCUTTERING GOBSHITE? I'M GOING TO RIP THE BOLLOCKS OFF YOU WHEN I GET HOLD OF YOU! YE DONKEY-BOTHERING, TINKY-WINKYED, ONE-EYED SON OF A COCK-EYED SUZIE."

The priest jumped back in shock before staring down at the coffin inside the grave as it screamed its abuse at the world. When it finally paused, he pointed a shaking finger down at the wooden casket. "Why is that man down there?"

"Because he's dead," said Wilson, a fact he knew not to be true, but which certainly wasn't public knowledge. "I mean, he's not down there. I mean, he is ... but he's dead. It's a recording, and the coffin was rigged to set it off in the event of—"

"WHAT IN THE SHITTING HELL DO YOU THINK YOU'RE DOING, YE SCUTTERING GOBSHITE? I'M GOING TO RIP THE

BOLLOCKS OFF YOU WHEN I GET HOLD OF YOU! YE DONKEY-BOTHERING, TINKY-WINKYED, ONE-EYED SON OF A COCK-EYED SUZIE."

"A recording?" echoed the priest in disbelief.

"As I was saying, it was rigged to go off if anyone tried to open the coffin."

"Why would somebody—"

"I don't know, Father. Apparently, the man in question specified it in his will."

"Well, turn it off, then."

"I wish I could, but ..." Wilson paused.

"WHAT IN THE SHITTING HELL DO YOU THINK YOU'RE DOING, YE SCUTTERING GOBSHITE? I'M GOING TO RIP THE BOLLOCKS OFF YOU WHEN I GET HOLD OF YOU! YE DONKEY-BOTHERING, TINKY-WINKYED, ONE-EYED SON OF A COCK-EYED SUZIE."

As Bunny McGarry roared his foul-mouthed admonishment at the world, the priest regarded his gravestone with a look of disgust.

When the recording once again reached the silent bit before it looped, Wilson continued, "I'm not allowed to open the coffin or interfere with it in any way, by law. I'm waiting for the coroner to get here or for the batteries to run out." *Please God*, thought Wilson for the thousandth time, *let the batteries run out*.

"But ..." The priest looked around him in desperation, then settled on, "Bury it again, then."

"I can't do that either," said Wilson. "It's a crime scene. Needs to be processed. There was a gangland murder out in Finglas last night, and the techs and coroners are over there. I'm waiting for"

"WHAT IN THE SHITTING HELL DO YOU THINK YOU'RE DOING, YE SCUTTERING GOBSHITE? I'M GOING TO RIP THE BOLLOCKS OFF YOU WHEN I GET HOLD OF YOU! YE DONKEY-BOTHERING, TINKY-WINKYED, ONE-EYED SON OF A COCK-EYED SUZIE."

"For the love of God," howled the priest, "do something!" He waved in the direction he'd come from. "We're trying to bury a ninety-eight-year-old woman over there. I can't have this savage roaring abuse throughout the service."

Wilson shrugged. "That's why I had the music on."

"Have you not got anything more appropriate?"

"I've only got the one CD and—"

"I've the greatest hits of Chris de Burgh in the car," said the priest.

"Who?"

"He's one of the greats," said the priest, looking shocked.

"Great whats?"

"WHAT IN THE SHITTING HELL ..."

The priest stormed off and Wilson turned Queen back on to drown out the sound of Bunny McGarry once again delivering a pre-recorded bollocking for the ages. A few minutes later, the priest returned and presented Wilson with a CD, which he dutifully swapped over. Seemingly satisfied with this state of affairs, the padre stomped back to his waiting funeral.

Just a few minutes later he ran back over, out of breath, but by this point "Patricia the Stripper" had almost finished. He paused to regain his breath, then shouted at Wilson some more. There was no pleasing some people.

FORE!

Badly.

If someone were to ask Paul for a one-word answer to the question of how golf was going, that would be his response. If he were granted the use of any more words, they would be of the swearing variety.

Standing in the middle of Newlands Golf Course on an overcast summer's day, Paul was learning a brutally hard life lesson. When someone asks you if you've ever played golf, if the entirety of your experience has involved playing it on a PlayStation, then the correct answer to give is *no*. Just no. Why had he not gone with no? Instead, when Brigit's older brother Donal, who always seemed intent on winding Paul up, had asked during their father's and Deirdre's engagement party, Paul had tried to give a nuanced answer, explaining how he'd experienced some of the world's finest courses virtually while being confined to their apartment when he'd broken his leg. Donal and Padraig – the marginally less annoying, youngest of Brigit's three older brothers – had then proceeded to rip the piss out of Paul for the next two hours. Sean, who was the nicest of the three brothers, was, of course, in Australia.

Paul had smiled and taken it with forced good humour while

making occasional attempts to defend the honour of virtual sports. The two brothers had responded by making beepy-boopy noises and had then taken it in turn to mime shots while asking the other one how far it had gone and was it in the hole. If nothing else, the experience had proved to Paul that perhaps being an only child wasn't as bad as he'd thought. Somehow, he'd agreed to play golf with the two brothers and their father when they were up in Dublin and Deirdre was dress shopping with Brigit. He'd fully intended to try to play some golf before it happened, but life – or, to be exact, the requirements of surveilling half a dozen builders involved in an elaborate insurance scam – had got in the way. He'd held his first golf club just last night. How hard could it be? The answer had turned out to be *really* hard. He'd broken that golf club forty minutes ago, entirely by accident. The other one he'd broken on purpose. It'd undoubtedly looked bad, but it had felt good.

They were on the twelfth hole of eighteen. They'd stopped counting Paul's shots after the fourth. Brigit's dad had tactfully suggested they call it a day after hole nine, but Paul had insisted they do the full eighteen for reasons he couldn't begin to explain to himself. It had become an exercise in trying to get to the end with even a shred of dignity left. Whether that ship had already sailed was highly debatable. If anything, he was getting worse.

On the first couple of holes, he'd at least made contact with the ball, even if the ball had shown scant interest in reaching its destination any time soon. He'd then hit a drive smack down the middle of the third fairway – unfortunately, he'd been teeing off for the fourth hole at the time. The elderly gent who'd had to be nimble to avoid Paul's wayward ball had been surprisingly understanding about it. Well, he had on that occasion. He'd been less understanding when it happened again four holes later. By that point, whatever misplaced confidence Paul possessed had long since crumbled and been buried at sea, or at least in the water feature on the ninth, along with three of Paul's golf balls.

He'd been lent a set of clubs that had belonged to the late Paddy Nellis, uncle of Paul's best mate, Phil Nellis. Phil had come along with the clubs as an unasked-for and unwanted bonus – designating himself as Paul's caddy. Still, it was nice to have the company. Paul was technically playing with the three Conroy men, but in reality was seeing them only at the tees and, eventually, the greens. The time in between they were spending on the fairway of the hole they were actually playing, which was a long way from where Paul's ball was typically ending up.

At that moment Paul was behind a big oak tree, but at least it blocked his view of the condescending smirks from the Conroys.

"Right," said Phil. "Keep your head still, look at the back of the ball, follow through."

"I did that last time."

"Well, see if you can do it better this time."

Paul sighed. "OK."

He walloped the ball with all his might.

The pair stood back to examine the result.

"What I don't get," began Phil, "is how the big divot of grass you took out of the ground went further than the ball. I mean, were ye trying to hit the ball?"

"Yes," responded Paul through gritted teeth, "I was trying to hit the ball, but I can see how the confusion could arise."

"Look at it this way," continued Phil, "last time you didn't hit the ground or the ball, so this is progress."

Paul studied his oldest friend, who was trying to smile at him encouragingly. Optimism did not look good on Phil Nellis. It just didn't suit him, much like the outfit he'd bought himself for the day. Phil being Phil, once he'd anointed himself as Paul's caddy, had wanted to dress correctly for the role. Paul didn't have the heart to mention it, but he was ninety percent sure that Phil's outfit was actually meant to be fancy dress, given that it consisted of tangerine tartan trousers, a matching hat and pink-checked sleeveless knitted vest, which if it clashed any more, would require the intervention of a UN peacekeeping force. For all that, Paul couldn't be more than ninety percent sure on the fancy-dress front because this was golf, and he'd seen quite a few people wearing outfits only marginally less ridiculous than Phil's.

"Is everything OK over there?" shouted Cormac, Brigit's father, who was notably making an effort to try to be supportive – compared to his two arsehat sons, in any case.

"Yes, thank you," Paul shouted back, trying to sound chipper. "I'm sure third time will be the charm."

"Try keeping an eye on the back of the ball."

Paul gave a thumbs-up. "Good tip. Cheers."

"I said that," said Phil.

"Everyone has said that at least twice," hissed Paul. "Including that poor auld fella I've nearly hit twice. I don't know what you all think I've been looking at."

"To be fair, on at least one occasion you had your eyes closed entirely."

"Yeah, alright."

"I'm just going to put this out there again—"

"No, Phil. While I appreciate the offer, you faking a heart attack is not a good idea."

Paul looked down at his ball in its new position and then up at the green, which was nominally about a hundred and fifty yards away, but in reality, about seventy miles. He handed the club he'd just used back to Phil.

"What do you want this time?" Phil asked.

"What was the one I had for that good shot on the last hole?"

"Ehm. Could you be more specific? Like, which one are we defining as *good*?"

Paul held out a hand. "Just ... surprise me." He thought for a second before adding, "Not by faking a heart attack." It really did pay to be as specific as possible with Phil.

Paul took the proffered club and positioned it behind the ball.

"Don't forget to bend your knees."

"If I bend my knees any more, I'll be sitting down."

"Do that thing where you put the club behind the ball, then in front of the ball, then behind it again."

"Why?" snapped Paul.

"I saw a fella doing it on a YouTube video I watched while you were up that tree."

"Well, I'm not doing it."

"OK. Try loosening your grip, then."

"Last time I did that, the club flew out of my hand and hit you."

"That's a good point. Try tightening your grip."

"I could imagine I'm throttling somebody?"

"If you think that'll help."

"Oh, I think it will."

"And try—"

"Phil, please shut up."

"I'm only trying to help."

"I know," said Paul. "And I appreciate it, but ..."

"Shut up?"

"Yeah."

"Sure. No problem."

Paul drew the club back.

"Wait!" shouted Phil.

Paul lost his balance and almost fell over before turning sharply towards Phil. "What did I just say?"

Phil flinched and Paul immediately felt bad about the threatening posture he'd fallen into with the club held over his head, mostly by accident. "There's somebody in front of you."

Paul turned around to see a golf buggy containing two men had indeed appeared on the fairway. "Oh, right, sorry. Although, seeing as they were between me and the green, they were arguably the safest people on the course."

They watched the buggy drive up to Cormac, who had a brief chat with the two men inside then pointed at Paul and Phil.

"Ah, crap," said Paul.

"Do you reckon they're the bouncers?"

"Golf courses don't have bouncers." He paused for a second. "Do they?" It hadn't come up in *Rory McIlroy's PGA Tour* on the PS4, but then Rory didn't get attacked by swans that didn't appreciate his wayward drives.

"If they mention your ball hitting that fella's golf cart, I'll swear that he drove towards it deliberately. Like one of them scammers that are always trying to cause car crashes."

Paul glanced back at Phil. "Maybe I should do the talking."

"Why are people always saying that to me?"

"We don't have the kind of time required to explain that, Phil," said Paul, as he watched the buggy draw closer. The two men did indeed have the unmistakable air of hired security about them. Both were wearing long coats and possessed the kind of physique that combined fat and muscle in a difficult-to-determine ratio, coupled with stern expressions that indicated violence was more likely than joviality. The driver was the slimmer of the two, his hair shaved close to hide its departure. The moustachioed passenger was bigger, older and looked like he'd rather be somewhere else. Paul could sympathise.

The cart stopped beside them and the older man spoke. "Are you Paul Mulchrone?" he asked in a gruff Dublin accent.

"I am," confirmed Paul.

"That'd make you Phil Nellis, then?"

"No comment," replied Phil.

The two men in the buggy looked at each other and then back at Phil.

"What?" said the driver.

"Under GDPR rules, I don't have to tell you that."

"What the fuck is—" started the driver, before his mate cut him off.

"Have it your way, sir. We're from the Gardaí and wondered if you two wouldn't mind coming with us?"

"What's this about?" asked Paul.

"I'm not at liberty to say."

"In that case," said Phil, "we are both at liberty, and that's where we'll be staying."

"What?" said the driver again. Like many people experiencing their first conversation with Phil Nellis, he was evidently finding the experience baffling.

"If you need us to answer some questions," said Paul, who, for many reasons, was less hostile towards the police than Phil, "then I'm happy to do so here, or I can drop into the station when we're done."

"Our boss wants to talk to you ASAP."

"And who would that be?" asked Paul, who was now starting to get a very bad feeling about this. "Come to that, let's see some ID. What station are you working out of?"

The driver reached his hand into his coat pocket and, after glancing around to confirm that nobody other than Paul and Phil could see them, produced a handgun.

"I told you that pretending-to-be-Gardaí bollocks wouldn't fly, Tony."

The other fella shrugged and pulled out his own gun. "It was worth a shot." He turned his focus back to Paul. "Look, the boss just wants a word and when he's done, we can drop you right back. This doesn't need to get messy."

"Who's the boss?" asked Paul.

"A man who doesn't like to be kept waiting."

Paul looked at the two men and then over behind them to where the three Conroy men were standing. The odds that these two goons were going to start shooting in the middle of a golf course were probably low, but definitely not zero.

"Who are you with?" asked the driver.

"My girlfriend's father and brothers."

"Tell them you've got to go help the Gardaí with an investigation," said the other man. "It'll make you sound dead important."

"And if I don't?"

The bigger man worked his head around his shoulders a little as he spoke. "Do you really want to get into that?"

Paul experienced a brief flash forward to the conversation where he explained to Brigit how he got her father shot. "Alright." He raised his voice. "Very sorry, lads, but Phil and I need to assist the Gardaí with a time-sensitive investigation, so we're going to have to go with these gentlemen."

The three Conroys nodded, looking suitably impressed. Once Phil had shoved their bag into the back of the golf buggy, he and Paul both climbed aboard.

"Sorry for interrupting your game," said the older man.

"To be honest," said Paul, "could really have done with you rocking up a couple of hours ago."

Paul gave the Conroys a wave as they drove off.

"Not going well, was it?"

"You could say that."

"I'll tell you how you can improve your swing—" started the driver.

"I'd rather you just shot me," said Paul, with real feeling.

SAY YES TO THE MESS

To her credit, Margo the dress-shop impresario was doing a stellar job of pretending she didn't know Brigit. Arguably, too good a job. They'd been in the shop for forty minutes now and she'd called Brigit by three different names in an effort to prove they'd never met before. She was coming off as slightly unhinged, but that was vastly preferable to the alternative. She'd also let Janice be the point woman on Deirdre's wedding-dress hunt, which seemed like a sensible option. Besides, it was hard for anyone to behave more unhinged than Megan Wright. At one point, the doctor had started waxing lyrical about the outfit Deirdre had been wearing all day. The problem was, it wasn't coming across as entirely sincere, but it was still a big improvement on her Debbie Downer performance in the first shop.

Deirdre had tried on a few options, but it was clear, despite the considerably more positive mood music coming from the group, that nothing had really caught her eye yet.

Accompanied by Janice, she headed back to the changing room just as Susan Burn's phone pinged again.

"Sorry, sorry, sorry," Susan said. "I'll turn it ..." She got lost in reading the text message. "Ehm ... Oh, actually ..." She looked at Brigit. "Any chance I could have a quick word?"

They stepped out of the curtained area then Susan motioned to Brigit that they needed to step outside the shop. From there, Susan guided Brigit into the alley beside the store and out of the Saturday-afternoon foot traffic.

"Can we make this quick?" said Brigit. "I'm worried that without us to stop her, Nora may attempt to strangle Megan with a veil." She stopped. "Oh God, you're not about to tell me you're leaving?" Brigit grabbed her arm. "Please, no. You're the only sane one."

Susan winced. "I'm afraid I am. Work thing."

"Someone better have died," said Brigit, before remembering who she was talking to. "Oh Lord, I take that back. That's a really stupid thing to say."

"Don't worry about it. Actually, nobody has, which is kind of the point."

"You've lost me."

"There's no easy way to say this," said Susan, looking around to double-check there was no possibility that anyone could overhear them. "Last night, someone attempted to dig up Bunny McGarry."

"What?" said Brigit, doing a poor job of keeping her voice down. She and Paul were the only people outside law enforcement who knew that Bunny McGarry was in fact still alive, having been smuggled out of the country while his own funeral was taking place. It had comfortably been the weirdest day of Brigit's life, and she'd had a few.

"I know," continued Susan. "It's mad. Wilson called me earlier, when you disappeared. I didn't want to say something before, as I didn't want to ruin the day."

"Have you not been paying attention, Susan? This day is going so badly, I'm not sure an actual dead body popping up could make it any worse."

"Sorry. And I'd hang around, only, well ... Wilson was trying to handle it but now someone's got the bright idea that they need to open the coffin to confirm it hasn't been interfered with."

"Hang on, someone tried to dig him up, but they were interrupted?"

"Yes, by the man himself."

Brigit rubbed her temples. "OK, I know I'm having a rough day, but I'm pretty sure you're not making any sense."

"Sorry. Do you not remember Mr McGarry's rather unusual will?"

"Will?"

"Ah," said Susan. "Now I think of it, you weren't there for that chat. The undertaker was an old friend of Bunny's. He was willing to go along with burying a coffin with no body in it, given that the deceased personally rang him to call in a favour, but he also was subsequently very particular about carrying out some unusual requests that Bunny had, for some reason, taken the time to write down in a legal document."

"Such as?"

"He had his coffin rigged so that if anyone tried to open it, it would scream abuse at them."

Brigit looked stunned for a long moment and then, much to her own surprise, burst out laughing.

"Stop it. It's not funny."

"It is," she said, wiping a tear from her eye. "It really is."

"We had to allow the undertaker to do that to get him to agree to forego the other request."

"The other request?" echoed Brigit.

"Yes, in the will there was mention of another recording Bunny wanted to have triggered by remote as his coffin was being lowered into the grave."

"Let me guess ..."

"'Going Underground' by The Jam. He sings the whole thing, apparently."

Brigit smirked again.

"Alright, it is a little funny, except now we've got a coffin screaming abuse, and it's attracting a lot of attention we don't want. I think I'm going to have to ask Dr Denise Devane to open the damned thing and re-certify Bunny McGarry as, I don't know, still dead."

"Will our state pathologist do that?"

"I'm amazed she did it the first time, but she seems to have some history with him so, hopefully."

"What's even in there?"

"I honestly don't know. That ranks a long way down my list of urgent questions. The first one would be why the hell is someone trying to dig up his coffin in the first place?"

"Jesus," said Brigit, staring down at the ground. "Any ideas?"

Susan Burns shrugged. "I mean … someone trying to antagonise the Gardaí? The man himself had no shortage of enemies. I believe that's why he wanted to boobytrap his own coffin in the first place. Apparently, some former nemesis made a very specific threat. Then, of course, let's not rule out it could just be some weirdos being weirdos, and Bunny was picked at random."

"Bit of a coincidence, though, isn't it?"

"Oh, massive," agreed the DSI. "And what I wouldn't give for it to just turn out to be some nutbar who's watched too many horror movies. What worries me is it being someone trying to draw attention to what we did and raising some really awkward questions."

"Crap," said Brigit.

"Which is why I need to get over to Glasnevin Cemetery, because Wilson's currently fending off orders from people who outrank him and it's a matter of time before someone throws their rattle out of the pram."

———

Brigit watched Susan get picked up by a Garda patrol car, and then stepped back into the shop. She'd been gone only a matter of minutes, but it appeared that may have been too long.

Megan Wright's voice carried from the other side of the curtain. "I don't care what anyone says, this dress is absolutely perfect."

"I'm not saying it isn't," responded Nora, sounding agitated.

"It's a stone cold ten out of ten. Alright, before, I was being over-the-top positive but this time, I'm one hundred percent sincere and this dress is absolutely perfect. How can you not see that?"

Brigit drew back the curtain and stepped inside. For the second time that day, she walked in on a group of five women who all turned and looked at her expectantly. Megan Wright was standing beside Deirdre to make her point. Nora and Margo were regarding Brigit with similar mortified expressions, while Janice appeared to be entirely confused by the whole thing.

Deirdre gazed at Brigit, her eyes full of hope. "What do you think, Brigit?"

Brigit paused. "Give us a twirl, Deirdre."

The bride-to-be complied. The moment she was facing away from Brigit gave Nora the opportunity to shake her head at Brigit vigorously.

Twirl completed, Deirdre looked at Brigit expectantly.

"I hate to say it," said Brigit, slapping on a wide smile she didn't feel, "but Megan is bang on. You look sensational."

Megan punched the air. "Fuck, yeah!"

Deirdre looked thrilled as Janice led her away to the changing room to assist her in getting out of the dress.

Margo moved across to Brigit and touched her arm before whispering discreetly, "I'll obviously return your deposit. I tried to ... but Janice didn't know."

"It's fine," said Brigit, determined to keep up the smile. "It's absolutely fine. There are lots of other dresses."

———

Ten minutes later the limo pulled up to the kerb outside the shop and the four remaining members of their party piled in.

"We nailed it," said Megan Wright, still on some kind of shopping high. "We absolutely nailed it."

"Yes," said Nora testily, "so you keep saying."

Back in the shop, Megan had attempted to get everyone to high five her, which had not gone over well. Only Deirdre, seeming slightly giddy for the first time, had joined in.

Today was Brigit's first time in a limo, and she was finding it a vastly overrated experience. The drinks-cabinet price list was inexplicably exorbitant. The whole vehicle smelled like liquorice, which for some reason made Brigit wonder how many people had thrown up in the back of it. And the tinted glass of the screen that divided them from the driver was oddly reflective, which meant you could see yourself all the time. Who wanted that? She looked at the three women sitting in the back with her. Alright, Megan Wright clearly did, but who else?

The only upside was that Anthony, the chauffeur, was one of those people who could happily chat away while receiving the bare minimum of responses. It had meant the least awkward parts of the day so far had been the time spent travelling from place to place.

"Where's the other lady?" asked Anthony from behind the screen.

"She's had to go," said Brigit. "Just us four hardy souls left now."

"Right so," he said, pulling out into traffic.

"Yes," said Megan, giving Nora a pointed look. "We're now out on the town without a police escort."

Nora shook her head and looked out the window.

Brigit patted her on the knee. "It's fine," she whispered.

Nora shook her head again and whispered back, "It's not. That was your dress."

Brigit raised her voice. "You must be delighted to have it sorted, Deirdre."

She smiled back at her. "I am. Thanks to all of you for the help."

"Here," said Nora, leaning forward to bang on the mirrored partition. "Anthony, we're supposed to be heading up towards Stephen's Green for lunch. You're going the wrong way."

The screen slid down to reveal Anthony wasn't alone in the front. Next to him, a blond man with a gingery beard was grinning over his shoulder at them. "I'm afraid there's been a change of plan, ladies. There's someone who wants to have a quick chat with you."

Megan gasped as the man raised his hand to reveal the gun he had trained on Anthony. An audible click followed as the central locking secured the doors.

YOU MAY BE WONDERING WHY I GATHERED YOU ALL HERE

Brigit had read enough books and seen enough movies to know that the blindfolds were a good thing. Someone not blindfolding you when they were taking you somewhere meant that they didn't care about you being able to find your way back. That opened up the possibility that you weren't ever going to leave. Still, when she and the rest of the group had been given the blindfolds, everyone in the back of the limo had panicked.

"Is this about my—" started Nora.

"Honestly," pleaded Megan, "I never knew he was—"

"Silence!" barked the blond man with the gun. "Just put on the blindfolds and everybody shut up. This won't take long if you lot behave yourselves."

Bunny, thought Brigit. *This has to be about Bunny.* Some coincidences are far too big to be actual coincidences.

She tried to do that trick where she mapped out in her head the lefts and rights the car was taking, but she lost track after a few turns. It was a lot harder than they made it look in the movies. She was also having a hard time remaining calm. Sure, she'd been in more than her fair share of sticky situations in the past, but she normally didn't bring a whole lot of innocent people along for the ride. Nora had a kid. Deirdre was marrying her father. Megan Wright … Well, she probably had something going on in her life, too. Brigit would have dearly loved to try to get some kind of message to Paul, but just before they did all the blindfold stuff, the man had got them all to pass their coats, handbags and mobile phones through the partition. He gave off the depressingly professional air of a man who had kidnapped people before.

Eventually, the limo pulled in somewhere, the thud of an up-ramp jarring its unwilling passengers, and then it came to a stop. Both rear doors opened and new voices accompanied by new hands roughly escorted the four women out of the car. They were being led somewhere. Brigit could feel concrete under her shoes and there was a tang of oil in the air.

"Put her there," said a male voice.

"Which one?" came the response.

"That one."

Brigit was shoved down onto a plastic chair and her arms were pulled back, cable ties around her wrists biting into the skin as they were drawn tight, securing her hands firmly behind her.

"Feck's sake, go easy!"

Only then was her blindfold taken off.

She was in what seemed to be some kind of garage, although no work appeared to be going on. To be fair, every time she'd dropped her car, with its plethora of ongoing problems, into a garage, not-much-happening was the default state of being. Presumably mechanics did, at some point, open bonnets et cetera and get to work, but she'd never seen it. The job seemed to consist mostly of drinking tea while confidently informing each other how professional sports teams should be run.

The blond man with the ginger beard had been joined by three other goons, a couple of whom held guns casually in their hands, not trained on anyone because their captives would be idiots to try anything.

Then there were the other prisoners.

"Hi," said Paul, sitting beside her.

"Hi," said Brigit, simultaneously both happy and unhappy to see him. "How was golf?"

"Let's not get into that now."

"Is Dad—"

"He's fine, don't worry. They think I'm helping the police with their inquiries."

She looked past Paul down the line. Phil Nellis was beside him, gagged. And down from him in the fourth chair sat Cynthia, the office manager of MCM Investigations. Which explained at least one thing. Brigit had been wondering how on earth anyone would have known where she was today. Cynthia knew everything.

"I am so sorry," said Cynthia, as if reading Brigit's mind. "They turned up at my flat and the guy had a gun and he wanted to know where you and Paul were—"

"It's alright," said Brigit calmly. "Don't worry about it, Cynthia. There's nothing you could have done."

A small part of Brigit's mind pointed out that none of them would have been there if Cynthia had actually come on the wedding-dress shopping trip, which she'd cried off, claiming she was going to be down in Limerick for the weekend visiting an aunt she'd never previously mentioned. Still, the woman was being held hostage by armed thugs, so it felt churlish to point that out.

"Why is Phil gagged?" asked Brigit.

"Because it was the only way to shut the muppet up," said one of the henchmen with conviction.

Brigit loved Phil, but even though she'd rather die than admit it out loud, she did have an idea where that assessment was coming from.

Nora, Megan and Deirdre, along with Anthony the chauffeur, were standing huddled together in the corner, confirming that they weren't the main attraction here. The blond guy unceremoniously dumped their coats and bags on the floor beside them.

"Hey," said Megan, outraged, "that coat is Fendi and you're going to get oil on it."

Nora put a hand on her and pushed her away. "Ignore the crazy lady trying to argue with the armed men. She's living proof that Canadians can actually be loud and obnoxious."

"Have you got any idea what this is about?" asked Paul in a low voice.

"Actually, I do," replied Brigit. "Susan got called away—"

"Ladies and gentlemen ..." They all looked up at the sound of a male voice. A man, who Brigit recognised, was coming down the stairs from where she assumed the garage office was. "Apologies for interrupting your weekend plans. I just needed to have a little chat with you regarding a certain matter, and I'm afraid it's time sensitive." He started to walk towards them. He was about thirty, good looking with short black hair and a muscular build. To Brigit's mind, there was something cold in those steely blue eyes, but maybe that was context influencing perception.

The man came to a halt in front of the four seated captives then glanced at the three women and Anthony standing over by the wall. "Apologies. I requested to talk to the staff of MCM Investigations. It appears the lads picked up a few extras along the way."

"Sorry, Liamo," started the blond guy, "but"

He was silenced by the raising of a single finger.

"I presume somebody thought to save me a seat?"

After an awkward moment, one of the other men ran across to a desk in the far corner of the room. He grabbed the battered leather office chair sitting there and trundled it across the floor on squeaky wheels, stopping to make an attempt at cleaning it before presenting it to his boss.

The main man pushed him away and sat down with the slightest shake of his head. Then he favoured the seated quartet with a broad smile. "Do you know who I am?"

"Yes," replied Brigit. "Liam Darcy."

"We've not crossed paths before, have we?"

"No. But you've been in the paper."

"All good, I hope?"

"Not exactly. You should ask someone to read it to you."

The fake smile cracked. Brigit's words had come out of her mouth before her brain had been afforded the chance to give a second opinion. A part of her knew that antagonising an infamous drug-dealing psychopath was not the smartest of moves, but it had already been a hell of a day and among the angst and terror, a little anger had apparently been lurking.

"You're the chatty one," said Darcy. "I can tell."

"Talk to me," interjected Paul. "Leave her out of it."

Darcy yawned. "Very noble. So, do you know what this is about?"

"No," said Paul.

He looked at Brigit. "And you?"

"I might do," said Brigit. "Fun fact for you, Liam – earlier today my friend Susan, or, as I'm guessing you know her, DSI Susan Burns, Head of the National Bureau of Criminal Investigation, was with us while we were out wedding-dress shopping."

"Now her," said Darcy, "I have definitely crossed paths with."

"Oh yeah," said Brigit. "She'll be the one to slap cuffs on you. No doubting that."

"Shame she isn't here," said Darcy, sounding testy.

"I'm sure she'll be along presently," said Brigit, who unfortunately had no reason to believe that was going to be the case, but there was no harm introducing the idea. "She had to head off because some pack of losers attempted to dig up Bunny McGarry's grave last night. God rest his soul."

She felt Paul tense in the chair beside her and Phil attempted to say something around his gag.

"Shut up," said Darcy, addressing him, "or one of the boys will shut you up."

Phil mumbled a few more incoherent words, then fell silent. Darcy turned his eyes back to Brigit. "God rest his soul? Nice touch. Cards on the table: some friends of friends of ours over in the States contacted us yesterday with the mad notion that McGarry is not only alive, but is also in America making a nuisance of himself. Now, we thought that was a load of bollocks, but these are the kind of people not even I say no to. So yes, a couple of lads went a bit route one looking for answers, which didn't pan out."

"I hear they shat themselves when the coffin started shouting at them." That same part of Brigit's brain was screaming at her now, but she seemed entirely incapable of speaking to the guy in anything less than an antagonistic manner.

Thankfully, this time, he laughed. "Yeah, I heard that too. Anyway, we quickly realised that we could get confirmation that he was still alive just by having a little chat with the man who buried the box. Took a little time, but he eventually spilled the beans. Have to admit, I thought our friends from across the pond might have been sampling a bit too much of their own merch, but it turns out they were right. They buried some sacks of sand during all that pomp and ceremony. Then, the question became who would know where he might be, and the only answer was his associates from the little detective agency he set up after he retired."

"Sorry to disappoint you, but we've no idea where Bunny is," said Paul.

"Is that right?" asked Darcy.

"Yes," said Brigit.

He nodded. "Am I right in saying you two are a couple?"

Neither of them replied.

"I'll take that as a yes." Darcy scratched at his head then leaned forward in his chair. "So, here's the problem we've got. I need to go back to these people with a lot more than a 'we don't know' because, I'll be honest with ye, they're animals. I mean, you hear some stuff in the media, but over here we've got a code. Ye know? Some basic ground rules. These people, though? These friends of friends? They'll stop at nothing, absolutely nothing, and I've got a wife and kids to think of. I mean, I'm a victim here too, you understand?"

Brigit's stomach was now a roiling pit of dread, and she could taste a warning wash of saliva in her mouth, indicating that she might be about to lose her grip on an overpriced breakfast and a couple of glasses of prosecco. "We honestly don't know anything."

"For your sake," said Darcy, "I really hope that isn't true as we're going to have to go a very long way down a very dark road before I'm willing to believe that answer. I'm going to have to hurt you in the hope that your boyfriend here will talk."

"Fuck you," said Paul, straining at his restraints. "You touch her and—"

They all looked across the room as Nora screamed, "Deirdre!"

Brigit turned her head to see her father's intended clutching her chest.

"Ah, for fuck's sake!" yelled Darcy, jumping up from his chair, more irritated than alarmed.

Deirdre staggered towards where the coats and bags lay strewn on the floor, mumbling as she flailed around with her right hand.

"What's she saying?" asked Darcy.

"Tablets," said Megan. "I think she's saying tablets."

Nora ran over to Deirdre's handbag, picked it up, and opened it. Darcy, meanwhile, pushed his chair towards her, clicking his fingers. "Jimmy, get her some water, for Christ's sake."

Nora was scrabbling in the handbag. "I can't see—"

Deirdre grabbed the bag from her, dived her hand inside and came out holding a plastic bottle of tablets. The other two women guided her onto the chair where she upended the bottle and let a couple of tablets fall into her mouth, just as the blond guy returned with a half-empty bottle of water he'd retrieved from the desk in the corner.

Deirdre gulped down the water then sat there, her eyes closed, taking slow, steady breaths.

"Are you alright there, love?" asked Darcy, prompting her to reopen her eyes.

She nodded.

"Right. Gave us all a bit of a scare, there." He turned to the blond guy. "Jimmy, what the fuck are you doing bringing an auld one with a heart problem to a fucking interrogation?"

"I didn't know, Liamo," pleaded Jimmy. "You said—"

A left uppercut to the face from Darcy sent him sprawling onto the concrete floor. He spun around to right himself, his fist clenched.

"G'wan, then," Darcy barked down at him.

Jimmy immediately relaxed his fist and held up his hands in surrender.

"Yeah, that's what I thought." He regarded Jimmy for a long second. "Toss it."

Jimmy dutifully drew his gun out of his jacket pocket and slid it away across the floor. Only then did Darcy take his eyes off him and his body language relaxed.

During the altercation, Brigit hadn't taken her own eyes off Deirdre, who seemed a lot better. Her right hand was back in her handbag, doing something. She caught Brigit's eye briefly, but then looked away.

Darcy returned his attention to her. "Alright, sweetheart. One of the lads here is going to take you back outside to the limo, and you can wait out there, OK?"

Deirdre nodded.

Darcy turned to the other two goons. "Mace, could you—"

He was cut off by the sensation of the barrel of a snub-nosed pistol being shoved into the back of his neck. If Darcy looked surprised, it was nothing to how Brigit felt.

"Alright," shouted the now remarkably sprightly Deirdre, who'd sprung up from her seated position. She spoke with a strong Scottish accent, which would have been the most surprising thing about her had she not also been holding a gun. "Any of you fuckers move and I'm blowing this bawbag's brains all over the floor."

The two goons who weren't Jimmy pointed their guns in Deirdre's direction.

Liam Darcy laughed. "Alright, love – very clever. I don't know where you got the toy gun from, but nobody here thinks you're going to actually—"

He was interrupted by the gunshot and instantaneous scream from Jimmy on the floor as Deirdre shot him in the leg.

The gun was immediately returned to its position at the nape of Liam Darcy's neck.

"Tell your men to drop their guns now, or I won't be so nice next time."

"Drop your guns," said Liam, sounding genuinely rattled.

After a second, both men complied. Jimmy, who was clutching his leg as a bloodstain bloomed across his jeans, dissolved into muffled sobs.

"Good," said Deirdre. "Nora, there's a penknife in my bag – cut the others loose. Now, Mr Darcy here and his men, all of you, hands up and move slowly towards the wall. Try something, I fucking dare ye." There was a snarl in her voice and nobody in the room believed she was messing around any more.

Paul turned to Brigit. "What in the hell is happening now?"

She shook her head, mouth agape, unable to find the words.

———

Three minutes later, having left Liam Darcy and his men – bar the wounded Jimmy – cable-tied to the body of a Ford Cortina, Brigit, the remaining members of the wedding-dress shopping trip, plus Paul, Phil and Cynthia, were back in Anthony's limousine, which was exiting a back street in what looked a lot like Phibsborough to Brigit. They'd left Jimmy with his phone so he could call for his own ambulance.

The limo was crowded, and it didn't help that everyone was talking at once.

"Who the hell were those guys?" asked Megan.

"We need to call the guards," said Nora.

"No," responded Deirdre from her place in the front seat.

"Is everybody OK?" asked Paul.

"No, I'm not OK," shouted Megan. "I've just been held at gunpoint and the bride-to-be just shot somebody."

"Alright, everybody calm down," started Brigit, before having to pause as everyone swayed dramatically to the left as the limo took a corner far too fast. "Anthony, you especially. This isn't a getaway. Nobody is after us."

"Alright. Where am I going?" shouted Anthony above the hubbub.

Brigit looked around, her mind racing. "Somewhere quiet."

———

Ten or so minutes later, they pulled over in the Phoenix Park, just a couple of hundred yards past Garda HQ, in the first parking spot they could find that wasn't taken over by someone taking the kids to the zoo. The whole thing had a surreal air to it. Megan Wright, presumably in shock, was throwing up on the four-feet-wide grass verge between the road and the footpath, while Nora, adhering to some genetically programmed sacred code, held her hair back. Paul was comforting Cynthia, who seemed to be finding it all too much as well. As was Anthony the chauffeur, standing there attempting to smoke a cigarette with shaking hands. The group was juxtaposed against a backdrop of people walking by with dogs and kids in pushchairs, all enjoying a perfectly normal Saturday afternoon. People who hadn't just been kidnapped, held at gunpoint and narrowly avoided being tortured because a librarian had shot somebody in the leg.

In fact, one of the few people who seemed calm was the aforementioned librarian. "I think we'd better have a quiet word," she said to Brigit, nodding towards the trees. Deirdre led the way and Brigit followed until they were both out of earshot.

"I'm guessing you have questions," said Deirdre.

"Yeah," said Brigit, her tone making clear the understatement inherent in that response.

"Right, well, you're not getting answers."

"Excuse me?"

Deirdre shrugged, her face expressionless. "Something in your past got us into that situation. All I can tell you is something in mine is why I carry a gun in the lining of my bag, which meant I could get us out of it."

"And that's all you're going to tell me? You shot a man, Deirdre."

"I'm aware. The choice was that or we all sit around while some psycho tortures you or Paul or whoever else he was going to get to. Would you have preferred me to just let it happen?"

"No, but …" Brigit took a breath. "Come to that, thank you."

Deirdre shrugged again. "You're welcome. All I ask is give me enough time to get out of the country before you go to the police."

"Wait, what? What are you talking about?"

Deirdre's eyes narrowed, looking at Brigit like she was being a little slow. "I shot a man, and I sure as hell can't hang about for the investigation."

"But … Dad?"

"I love your father," said Deirdre in a very simple, matter-of-fact tone. "Enough that letting his only daughter get tortured was a non-starter. Do you have any idea how much he worries about you? Proud of you too, of course. You're the apple of the man's eye, but he worries."

"I …" Brigit didn't really know what to say to that.

"I just need a little time."

"And you're running?"

"What option do I have?"

"Well … what if everyone didn't say anything?"

Deirdre looked back towards the limo. "All of them?"

"Yeah. You saved our collective bacon. We owe you."

"And you won't tell your father?"

Brigit paused. "Why don't you just tell me what you're running from?"

"No," she said simply. "Not going to happen."

Brigit threw up her hands in frustration. "Jesus, woman, you're infuriating."

"You can talk."

"And how come you were monosyllabic for the entire day?" Deirdre opened her mouth to answer, but Brigit cut her off. "No, wait

– let me guess. I brought the most highly ranked policewoman in the country wedding-dress shopping with you."

Deirdre nodded. "You weren't to know. Can I ask, though – why did you bring the Canadian?"

Brigit found herself barking a laugh. "I was short on numbers and I was trying to make an effort."

"You're not wild about me marrying your dad, are you?"

"That's a very direct question."

"It's been a day."

"It has," conceded Brigit. "And it's not you. It's me. Well, it's sort of me ... It's me working through grief in a rather unhealthy way."

"You should talk to a therapist about that. I mean, not that one – she's awful, but others are available."

This time, both women laughed.

Brigit rubbed the heel of her hand into her eye, then turned around. "Right, you stay here. I'm going to organise a conspiracy of silence."

"Before you do," said Deirdre, looking unsure for the first time, "did you really like the dress?"

"Yes," Brigit confirmed. "It's a great dress and you're going to look stunning in it."

———

Paul leaned on the car, at a loss for what he should be doing. Phil approached him. "Are you OK, Phil?" Now he thought about it, Phil had been remarkably quiet since they'd made their getaway.

He nodded. "So, is Bunny really alive?"

"Ah," said Paul, looking into his friend's eyes and seeing both the anger and the wetness there. "Yeah, he is."

"And you and Brig both knew?"

"We did but—"

Phil Nellis had been in more than his fair share of fights in his life – Paul knew that better than anyone. His win–loss record was also heavily weighted towards loss, but where they came from, you

275

couldn't back down, and Phil never had. Still, he was a gangly, awkward-looking human being who Paul had only recently seen fail to get out of a deckchair so badly that he'd ended up staggering into his daughter's paddling pool. They'd nearly had to cut him out of it. It was therefore a surprise on many levels when Phil's perfectly thrown right hook made contact with Paul's chin, sending him careening off the side of the limo and into a heap on the ground.

"What the—"

"Prick!" barked Phil, before stomping off into the early afternoon sunshine.

FREE STUFF

Hello again, lovely reader-person,

So there you go, thanks for sticking around and joining me on my *Shorts* adventures.

Bunny will be back in *Fortunate Son,* book eight of the increasingly inaccurately titled Dublin Trilogy, later in 2024.

To stay up-to-date on all things Bunny make sure you've signed up for my monthly newsletter. To sign up visit:

www.WhiteHairedIrishman.com

Oooh, and you can also listen to the Bunnycast and The Stranger Times podcasts too for more audio exclusives and short stories. They're available from all the usual places, visit my website or at thestrangertimes.co.uk.

Cheers muchly and thanks for reading,
Caimh

ALSO BY CAIMH MCDONNELL